SUZANNE JENKINS

Don't You
Forget About Me

HEART, we will forget him!
You and I, to-night!
You may forget the warmth he gave,
I will forget the light.

When you have done, pray tell me,
That I my thoughts may dim;
Haste! lest while you're lagging,
I may remember him!

—Emily Dickinson

I

When Jack Smith had a heart attack on a train bound for Long Island, he was more surprised than anyone else. It was true; he'd had a premonition that he was going to die soon. His attorney had told Jack's wife he didn't think he was going to live much longer. His lifestyle was catching up with him. A major change that might redeem a few of his past mistakes was in order. However, a heart attack would cut short his good intentions. But a heart attack would be the last thing he thought would take him down. The doctor had warned him about his cholesterol; he needed to exercise and watch his diet, and for the past year, he had been compliant. But it was too late. A rich man's lifestyle and maniacal stress, or the will of God, would do him in after all, and not his misdeeds.

In seconds after his head hit the floor, he was aware of his brother Bill taking his wallet. They had been arguing when the syncope hit him. Jack's vision was limited to exactly what was in front of his eyes. Fascinated, he thought, *Blinder vision! I'll google the phenomenon when I get home.* As he lay on the filth of the subway train, Jack saw Bill's face, red-eyed and scared to death, leaning in sideways to grope around in his brother's jacket. It was the same look he wore as a youngster when he was summoned to his father's lair. Jack wanted to yell out to him not to be afraid: *I won't let that bastard hurt you anymore!*

They were no longer children, however, and now Jack was unable to talk.

Bill stepped out of Jack's field of vision. Within seconds, another passenger found Jack and summoned help. Floating in and out of consciousness, Jack was often aware of what was happening to him as the paramedics tended to him and got him off the train and into an ambulance. It was so frustrating that he couldn't respond, and in his mind he was screaming at them. *Call Pam!* The words repeated in a loop until they became a sort of mantra that brought Jack peace and took his mind off the searing pain in his jaw and the invasive, intrusive acts of his helpers.

In the next awareness of consciousness, during a brief moment when he saw the side of a woman's face bending over him, he was able to say the words that had filled his brain for the past several hours.

"Call my wife, Pam."

The young woman, a nurse, repeated the name. "Pam?"

"My wife, Pam Smith." And he clearly spoke their telephone number at the beach. He closed his eyes and saw Pam's lovely face, but then he took his last breath and died.

Pam Smith woke up early, confused. *What day is it?* Rolling over to look at her husband Jack's side of the bed, she realized that he hadn't slept there. The sheet and blanket were pulled up tightly, with the pillows stacked and undisturbed. *Isn't it Saturday morning? He should be lying beside me.* Leaning on her elbow, she stretched over to see if he was in the bathroom. The door was open and it was dark and empty. Looking back toward the window, she saw the pink early-morning light of the sun's rays illuminating the sand, the water calm to the horizon. It would be another beautiful day at the beach. She reached for the clock. Her eyes weren't focusing this morning. This was ridiculous; she had to find her glasses to read the clock. It was only five. *Why would he be up and out already? Was he fishing today or meeting someone for an early golf game?* She got up and went into the bathroom. It was empty. Looking up at her reflection in the mirror, she remembered. Jack was dead.

He didn't come home last night because he wasn't alive. She stared at the stranger staring back at her. Her reflection shocked her; she'd been avoiding looking at herself because the physical changes were so dramatic they had to have been happening over a course of weeks and not overnight. Pain showed in her face. Jowls replaced her once tight jawline; deep marionette lines had appeared on either side of her mouth. Her neck was wrinkled. Always proud of her shapely figure, she was now as flat-chested as a ten-year-old boy. Tired of the self-examination, she left the bathroom close to tears.

She put a robe on and walked out to the kitchen. Standing in the center of the large, light-filled space, she turned to look out the windows at the Atlantic Ocean, hoping to find that special peace the house usually provided. Not today. It was a sterile, empty shell. For the first time in weeks, she began to cry. Pam's head dropped to her chest, and she allowed the tears to come. She was lonely. But it wasn't only that she missed Jack. He had hurt her so deeply by the things she had discovered about him that she was numb. Very fleeting moments of pain would magnify in enough intensity that they would penetrate the vacuum she was in. And it was only then that she would cry. It never lasted long. Just a couple of seconds, a few tears on her cheek.

As empty and meaningless as she felt right then, she would begin her day. Routine was a lifesaver. One foot literally in front of the other. A minute-by-minute surrender. *I can bathe and brush my teeth. Then I can do my hair and my makeup. Go to the kitchen and make coffee, go to the gym or not, come home and bathe again. Take a walk. Pull some weeds. Eat something.* She would make those activities stretch into a day until she could safely go to bed.

Someone might call her on the phone, her children or her sisters. Or Jack's former mistress, Sandra Benson. That would take some minutes away from the dreaded clock-watching. Life was stretching out ahead of her with no purpose, no meaning. There had to be a way she could find something to do that was worthwhile again. She went back into the lovely room she had shared with her husband for almost thirty years, and as she attempted to put aside her grief for yet another day, she stopped and said out loud, "I hate you, Jack."

I hope this guy doesn't turn out to be a jerk, Marie Fabian thought as she drove upstate to spend the weekend at Jeff Babcock's. She had met him on the beach in front of her sister Pam's house back in June. So far they had coffee together twice, lunch three times, and dinner every weekend for the past six weeks. When Jeff invited her to visit him for the weekend at his house in Rhinebeck, it seemed like a great idea to get out of the city and not go to Pam's for a change. But now, as she navigated the Taconic Parkway in weekend traffic, she wasn't so sure. Doubts floating through her mind eroded the excitement she had felt when she locked her apartment door that morning. Walking toward the garage to get her car, dragging her suitcase behind her, she caught herself whistling a little.

Now she was questioning her wisdom. *What was I thinking?* She barely knew the guy. He had lived down the beach from Pam and her late husband Jack for twenty years, and she had never seen him before. Or hadn't noticed him. Someone else was taking all her attention. Now she was faced with the possibility that Jeff would want to sleep with her that weekend. They hadn't discussed the sleeping arrangements; Marie assumed she would sleep alone. *Do I want to sleep alone?* she thought.

For a forty-five-year-old woman, Marie had little experience with dating in general and men in particular. Or, more accurately, more than one man. She was simply allowing "things" to happen with Jeff, not putting up too many boundaries, but not getting overly involved too quickly, either. She was having difficulty figuring out his intentions. Although he pursued her, once they were finally together, he wasn't acting very interested.

She turned the radio on to keep her mind thinking about something else. An old Don Henley song came on, and she belted out the chorus to "Boys of Summer":

I can tell you my love for you will still be strong
After the boys of summer have gone

It had only been weeks since Jack Smith died, and she was already going away for the weekend with another man while singing the songs Jack used to sing to her. Could it be possible that she was over Jack already? She thought back to the first time she met Jeff. She had fled the city that day, feigning illness or family emergency at work (she couldn't remember which now), getting into her car, and heading toward her sister's house in Babylon. She went over the speed limit all the way, keeping up with traffic. As soon as she got there, she put on her bathing suit, grabbed a beach chair and a paperback, and went out to sit in the sun. It was a perfect beach day, and the sand was packed with other sunbathers. The area in front of Pam's was already crowded, so she had to walk south a few yards to find an empty spot. She ended up in front of Jeff's fabulous house. The oceanfront facade and landscaping appeared in the Sunday home section of the paper just about every summer.

Most all the sunbathers followed the sun's path, moving their towels and chairs every thirty minutes or so as it traveled toward the west. But Marie liked facing the ocean. She would look up from her book periodically to stare at the water, hopefully spotting dolphins or boats, way, way out there. When Jack was alive, he always remembered to bring binoculars, and they would take turns examining the horizon for interesting finds.

Jack liked looking at people, too. He'd find lovers kissing under their umbrellas or suspicious movements underneath carefully placed towels. *He was really a pervert*, she thought to herself. *Creepy.* She relished being alone for the first time in her memory. She could nap without worrying if she drooled or snored, or mindlessly snack while she read her novel.

Jack could also be a tyrant. She remembered, on one of their beach days together when she was just twenty years old, falling asleep on a beach towel and waking up to find Jack staring at her body with his lips slightly pursed. She sat up self-consciously, hoping she hadn't farted in her sleep.

"What's wrong?" she asked him, quickly pulling her towel around her.

He was sitting next to her, scrutinizing her face and looking along the length of her.

"You're thin, but you're not in shape. You need to work out." He said, nodding his head yes at her, and turned to look out at the ocean again.

Eager to please him in every way, she agreed, saying she would start going to the fitness center at school as soon she as she got back to the city.

"Yeah right," he said sarcastically. Then more kindly, "You should ask your sister to give you some advice about a workout. Ask Pam. She's in great shape," he said with a devious smile. It was the first time Jack had ever held his wife, her sister Pam, up to Marie as an example. It would be the beginning of years of humiliation and criticism that he would pile on, playing the sisters against each other in a battle that Pam knew nothing about.

Worried that he may be plotting to end their relationship, Marie would have done anything he asked to keep him happy and near her. "Okay, I'll ask her. Maybe she'll take me to the gym with her."

But he ignored her, lying back down on the towel and closing his eyes, his forearm draped over his face, ensuring that he didn't have to see her. She held her stomach in and stood up straighter the rest of the day, regretful that she had worn a two-piece suit. That evening she would find one of the provocative underwear catalogues Pam shopped from and buy a suit with a push-up bra and tummy control panel. And that night, Jack would come to her bed, and she welcomed him, the insults at the beach already forgotten.

That day on the beach after Jack died was one of the first times that Marie felt like she was going to be all right, that she had hope for a normal future. As long as Jack was alive, she'd have been in bondage to him, even though he had stopped seeking her out. He had replaced Marie with Sandra.

She wasn't thinking about Sandra when Jeff Babcock approached her. He was walking the beach with his dog, Fred. Fred took an instant liking to Marie and would not leave her, even though Jeff called for him over and over again. Finally giving up, Jeff reluctantly walked to Marie's beach chair, collar and leash in hand.

"Sorry about this! Fred, you are bad! Bad dog!" Jeff was clearly embarrassed, but Marie was happy; she didn't really mind the dog's intrusion because his owner was so nice looking.

I wonder if he's single, she thought. He wasn't wearing a wedding band, but that didn't mean anything anymore.

He knelt down in front of Marie and started placing the collar around the Fred's neck. He held out his hand. "Jeff Babcock," he said, smiling. He had perfect white teeth. A little too tan, considering it was only June, he must go to the tanning salon. He was wearing crisp white tennis shorts and a white shirt, with the sleeves rolled up to his elbows. His hair was pure white, but he didn't look much older than Jack had been, not as fit, either. It was a relief. She let her stomach relax a little bit.

"Marie Fabian!" she said, taking his hand and shaking it. "I love dogs!" She pulled her feet in away from the licking dog.

They talked for a while, until Jeff excused himself; he had to get home to take a call.

Later that week, he asked Marie to accompany him to the retirement party of his former partner, meeting her in the city for a wonderful evening of dancing. She couldn't remember when she had had so much fun. At the end of the night, he said he had to get back to Babylon but wanted to see her the next time she was at Pam's. He didn't offer to see her home, putting her in a cab and paying the driver in advance. When they were together, it was really nothing more than companionship. He did nothing for her chemistry. Pam told her that would come in time. Men had immediate desire for someone they were attracted to; for women, it came with admiration for a man.

"I mean, a man can be attracted to a bimbo who can't construct a sentence; I'm right, don't you think? But a woman can think someone is handsome, but if he is an asshole, she won't be attracted to him no matter how good looking he is." She thought of Jack; there were exceptions to every rule.

Marie navigated the car through Albany. She was almost there. Having rarely been out of the city except for the weekly trips to Babylon, coming up here was a treat, and she was determined to enjoy herself. She thought of Jeff and his mannerisms and posture, how different he was from Jack, thankfully. Where Jack was tall and handsome, Jeff was average height and a little soft around the middle. And Jeff was soft-spoken and gentle. Jack was a larger-than-life sarcastic who didn't waste a minute or word in action or speech. Jeff was willing to sit back and allow time to pass without looking at his watch. Marie almost relaxed when she was with him. *Could it be real?* she thought. And then again, repeated *Oh, I hope he's not a jerk.*

2

Pam regrouped and began her day. She was home alone because her mother was spending a week in Connecticut with Pam's sister Susan. Nelda Fabian had moved into the apartment above the garage after Jack died and was settled in nicely at the beach. She and Pam worked out a casual routine where they could spend some time together every day without suffocating each other. They ate breakfast in the morning after Pam got home from the gym, sitting on the veranda and drinking coffee until 9:00 or so. Then Pam would continue on her own. She volunteered at the library every weekday but Wednesday, unless her children were home from college. She spent more and more time on her appearance, working out, going to the hairdresser twice a week, having manicures, pedicures, massages, and facials. She knew she was sublimating. After all, it had been less than two months since Jack had died.

Immediately after his death, crimes Jack had committed were revealed, including infidelity with her sister Marie, an affair which had its conception in her abuse at age fifteen. He was also having an affair with his research assistant, resulting in a pregnancy that was discovered after his death. Against nature, the young woman, Sandra Benson, was becoming indispensable to Pam; in a few short weeks, she was a trusted confidant, a friend. So if getting her hair done too often was the most incriminating thing that could be said about Pam Smith, so be it. She didn't know what else to do with herself yet, but in time, she was hopeful that something would materialize.

Pam was seeing another man. He was just a friend, but he was still a man. They spoke on the phone, met for coffee at each other's houses, walked the beach for exercise, and went out for dinner occasionally. She enjoyed his company for what it was—a diversion from the routine of her life without her husband. There wasn't the edge, the tension that she had with Jack.

Pam didn't feel much chemistry with Andy. But she admired him, so possibly it would come later as she had preached to Marie. In her youth, Pam remembered wanting to jump Jack. Before they got married, when they would be out together, he distracted by their friends, she would sit on the edge of the barstool with her stomach pulled in, poised, listening to his every word just in case he addressed her. When he finally turned to her, she would measure her words carefully and keep it simple. Jack laughed at her once in front of their friends when she mispronounced Alfonse D'Amato's name during a heated political discussion. She made a point of keeping her mouth shut after that. But she never stopped wanting him. The sexual tension was there until the end.

Where Andy was respectful and interested, Jack was wild and raucous. When Pam first met Jack, she remembered feeling he was sizing her up like she was a horse getting ready to be auctioned. He later told her that, when he saw her, he knew immediately that she would make a perfect wife. He needed someone who could hold her own in his aggressive family, yet who would be passive enough to not mind his domineering mother. His wife would need to be poised, attractive, and soft-spoken, but intelligent and self-confident. Pam had her awkward moments, but for the most part, she fit the bill. After they were married, and with a little help from his mother Bernice, she did just fine. He hadn't added to the list of requirements, 'someone who would look the other way and be oblivious to my dual life.'

As Saturday progressed, Pam gained some equilibrium. She poured herself a cup of coffee and remembering her sunken cheeks, got a muffin, too. She sat out on the veranda to watch the water. The dunes rose up slightly before the expanse of the beach, so if she was sitting down, she was unable to see the beach dwellers. The water stretched to the horizon, and unless there was a freighter or the miniscule sails of a boat, she saw only blue water reaching to blue sky.

When she and Jack moved to Long Island from Manhattan, the first improvement to the house was to put in the veranda. Originally, it had a small stone patio, in keeping with the white-clapboard-and-green-shutter exterior of the house. They searched for an architect willing to design a modern room with an outdoor kitchen, open to the beach. It was worth the effort.

Pam had furnished it with overstuffed canvas-covered pieces. Jack had been adamant about it being comfortable and covered in soft fabric, even if it meant having to bring the cushions in at night. "Have you ever tried to sit in one of those torture devices in my mother's garden?" he asked, referring to the wrought iron chairs that surrounded a glass table.

No matter how careful she was when she walked around the garden, Pam always managed to bash her toes against the iron legs. "I want enough seating for a crowd, too," he said. "I could never understand why Bernice insisted on that little table and four chairs when she had six people plus kids every Sunday."

So, for dining, Jack bought a huge round table with twelve chairs and a smaller square table that sat four. The entire veranda was covered with transparent bug netting and had a motorized roof that was handy during summer rains. Entire seasons passed by when the living and dining rooms inside the house would go unused. The veranda had worked its magic.

Now that Jack was gone, she continued to enjoy the beauty of the view. The years that he and Pam lived apart—he in the city during the week while she stayed at the beach alone—couldn't prepare her for this time. Every Friday night he would come home. The week was spent in preparation for it: perfect house, perfect food prepared, perfect children waiting, perfect wife. As the hour of his arrival grew close, her heart would start beating faster and harder. The sound of his voice over the telephone or a glimpse of him driving up the driveway continued to thrill her in spite of the years they had been together. She would stand in the door that led from the garage to the house, watching as the automatic door slowly opened, and handsome Jack would pull in his car, a big smile for his wife on his face. He was getting better looking with age, his jaw still chiseled and firm. He was slightly gray at the temples, but you didn't notice it because his head of hair was so thick and wavy, always perfectly cut and combed.

Pam couldn't remember Jack ever needing a haircut, even in his youth when the boys in their group allowed their hair to grow long. They were the perfect couple, perfectly groomed and perfectly matched. He'd stretch his long legs out of the car and reach in the backseat for his laundry bag. He always brought his dirty clothes home on the train from Manhattan, like a college kid. She insisted on it.

"What will you need me for if you start sending your clothes out?" She'd take his clothes and briefcase from him, he'd bend down to kiss her on the lips, and they would walk into the house together. There was always a drink waiting for him on the kitchen counter and he would pick that up first and walk to the large windows that overlooked the water. In the winter the view, often moonlit, was the first thing he would look at. They would sit on the window seat, looking out at the black water while a fire burned in the fireplace. But in the summer, they went outdoors. Pam took a plate of hors d'oeuvres out of the refrigerator, walking toward the veranda.

"Let's sit out here," she'd say. It was their routine. Jack would take his jacket off and throw it over the chair. They'd sit facing the beach, and he'd have his drink and snack. They would talk, getting caught up in spite of having spoken on the phone three and four times a day. After he finished his drink, Jack retreated into their bedroom to shower while Pam got dinner ready. They'd eat on the veranda as long as the weather held out, often staying out there until after midnight. Jack would make the first move to go in, Pam holding on to every second she could with him.

"What'd you say, wife? Time to hit the hay?" Said with a gleam in his eye, he'd reach out for her hand to pull her out of her chair, and the two of them would take their dishes into the kitchen. He'd grab her hand again and lead her to their bedroom. They had a comfortable routine, and he was the first to admit that it brought him pleasure, not boredom, although after he died, Pam would wonder. They'd make love, and when they were finished, like a script, Jack grabbed the remote and turned the Weather Channel on so he could plan his weekend. And then he'd floss his teeth. Pam often buried her head in her pillow so he wouldn't know she was laughing at him, although she wasn't fooling anyone. At Jack's funeral, his high school friend Ben said that Jack had the nicest teeth because he had flossed daily since he was a child. It was yet another obsession of his.

Pam loved her life with Jack, even though he was gone all week and never took a break once he got home. He packed every minute with activities; golfing, tennis, and swimming in the summer, and during the cold-weather months, he played games nonstop with his children or took them on adventures that Pam wasn't interested in, often skiing or snowboarding. He'd leave Monday morning for the city, and it was always difficult for her. Finally, Jack asked her not to get up with him; he couldn't stand leaving her when she was so sad. The last Monday he left for Manhattan before he died, he didn't even wake her to say good-bye. For months, she knew that something was wrong because he didn't initiate making love to her. Making excuses for him, hoping it was nothing serious, Pam figured he was just tired. Once she discovered he had been having an affair with Sandra, she understood why he had changed. But it scared her now. *If Jack had lived, would he have been preparing to leave me for Sandra?* She would never know. It had occurred to her to ask Sandra, but their relationship was already strained, and Pam didn't want that extra burden on it. Confirming it may have been the final travesty, one that Pam couldn't overlook. Wouldn't it be a matter of time before her anger at Sandra and Marie had to be faced?

Pam didn't feel there was anything to look forward to anymore. When the children had come home for the July Fourth holiday, Pam's fervor for living had returned. There was something to do every day. Lisa, just twenty years old, demanded her mother's attention, and Pam bestowed it upon her. She was cooked for, pampered with foot rubs and manicures, and taken on shopping trips. Brent, almost twenty-two, was more inclined to vegetate when he was home and this time he was dejected, missing the companionship of his father, desiring to golf or play tennis, but his favorite partner was gone. Marie did okay as a stand-in. *Better than no one*, Brent silently thought. He was barely able to tolerate her insipid demeanor, mistaking her full-blown clinical depression for lack of personality. The two of them banged the ball around with violence, whether tennis or golf made no difference. And at the end of each game, they agreed it was just what they had needed. And then came the shocker; both children were going back to school, after all, and not staying in Babylon for the rest of the summer as Pam had hoped.

Every visit home after that first homecoming would be just as painful as the day they came home for his funeral.

"You are here all the time. Every day, you wake up and he is gone, and little by little, you are adapting," Lisa explained to her mother. "We come home, and it's a shock that Dad isn't here. We have to get used to it all over again. Is it always going to be like this?"

Pam reached out and hugged her son and daughter, wishing their pain away. But it would be their own process to undertake, grieving for their beloved father. They didn't know the whole truth yet; she would delay it as long as possible, having threatened their aunt and grandmother with death and dismemberment if they squealed. When the truth about Sandra and the baby came out, that they would be having a sibling soon, she didn't know what to expect. Would they be devastated when they heard the news, the betrayal of their father more than they could handle? Or would they embrace Sandra and the coming baby as she had? Accept that their father had feet of clay and was as vulnerable to failure as any other? Only time would tell.

The holiday was over, and the time for both children to return to their respective colleges had come and gone. Once again, Pam was despondent. She knew the day would come when they wouldn't be coming home during breaks and holidays. What would she do with her time then?

She drank her coffee in silence, listening to the sounds of summer: gulls calling, laughter from a group of teens throwing a Frisbee back and forth, the waves hitting the sand. She got up and switched on the radio behind her.

She remembered, in her youth, going to the beach at Coney Island with her sisters Susan and Sharon and listening to neighboring radios blasting out the latest songs. The girls would sing along, hysterically laughing at the out-of-tune harmony. Some of her fondest memories were of lying on the beach covered in baby oil, listening to the radio. They would spend the entire day there, roasting in the sun. There was a snack bar on the boardwalk above the beach, and the memory of the smell of frying onions and hamburgers and vinegar-doused French fries made her appetite return. The order came packaged in white butcher paper in a flimsy cardboard box. They always got heavy glass mugs of root beer to drink. Pam never worried about her weight; she was naturally thin. Her sisters would conspire to fatten her up, but it didn't work. "I hate you," Susan would complain. But jealousy of her sister didn't prevent her from buying the biggest burger on the menu and getting one for Pam, too. When Pam was finished after a bite or two, her sisters gobbled up the leftovers.

Pam finished her coffee and left the radio on, grabbing her sun hat and a folded-up beach chair. She walked the wooden path that lead to the beach, wanting to sit there for a while by chance some inspiration, some epiphany, would cross her. In the weeks prior to Jack's death, she felt restless and a foreboding that she had never experienced before. *It's your age*, the still, small voice said. *Be patient.* And sure enough, before she had even gained admittance to his deathbed, Pam saw the other woman as she left Jack's final room. Sandra Benson had seen Jack's body before Pam did.

As she sat on the beach, a silent observer of those bodies lying around her, the unforgettable memory of knowing the second she laid eyes on Sandra that Jack had *loved* her drifted through her mind. The sudden knowledge had taken her by such surprise that she teetered on her feet and had to be supported by the nurse in charge of Jack's body. Thinking the wife was swooning due to grief, the nurse was prepared to care for her as she had for the husband. Tenderly guiding her into the room where Jack's body lay, and where Sandra had just exited, the scent of her shampoo on still wet hair lingered, filling Pam's olfactory with an overwhelming connection to her husband. She had smelled that scent on him before.

Thankfully, the odor of coconut-based suntan lotion wafted toward Pam as these unwelcome thoughts pestered her, banishing the remembered scent for the time being. In the proceeding weeks, she had grown to know that scent and to love its source. Sandra was the only other person who knew Jack as she knew him—the fake Jack, to be sure, but the one who persisted through the past thirty-five years of marriage. He was the Jack who gave gifts, who was reliable, who had a smile on his face almost all of the time. That Jack was the Jack the children knew, the father who worshiped his children but was ignorant of the pain he would be causing them in the days to come. Odors, colors, activities, the very house she lived in were monuments to the life she had lived with him, the life that had turned out to be a smoke screen, a sham, a house built on sand.

Jack was a liar of the most adroit kind. He had years of experience in secrets and lies after his childhood of abuse.

Pam was almost able to forgive him when she thought of what his life in that house must have been like.

"Poor Jack," she said out loud. The beach was starting to lose its allure, so she got up, folded up her chair, and turned back to the house. She could hear the phone ringing and, once she got on the wooden pathway, ran to get it. It was Detective Andrews. Andy. She was happy to feel a little thrill when she saw his number on caller ID.

"Well, hello, Detective Andrews," she said. "How are you today?" she asked.

"Hello, Mrs. Smith," he answered. "I am parked outside of your house, as a matter of fact."

"Well, come on in! I just came in from the beach." They hung up, and seconds later, he was walking through the door, Pam holding it open for him. She decided weeks ago that she would keep their relationship on the formal side for as long as possible.

He knew how lucky he was to find a decent, intelligent woman who was single, had no financial problems, and carried little baggage outside of having two college-aged kids and being a widowed mother. There were a lot of single, middle-aged women on Long Island, and he felt like a magnet for them. He would be as patient as she required.

Marie pulled off Route 9 into Rhinebeck. Jeff's house was in the center of town he told her, near the Village Inn. She drove slowly, looking for addresses on mailboxes, when she spotted him standing on a patch of lawn in front of the smallest house she had ever seen. There was a driveway next to his house, and he was pointing to it, so she turned in and stopped the car. He was right at her door with happiness all over his face as he greeted her.

"Wow! You made wonderful time! I'm so happy to see you." He offered her his hand as she pulled her legs out of the car, stretching as she stood up.

"What a cute little town!" she said, going from a stretch to putting her arms around his neck as they embraced. "It's so good to see you!"

He kissed her on the cheek. "Thanks for driving up here," he said as they moved apart.

She went to unlock her trunk and get her bag out. They walked hand in hand, she telling him about the traffic and how beautiful the mountains and woods were after the concrete of the city. All of her worries, her concerns about his intentions and character, dissipated. He wasn't a jerk, after all, just a really nice guy.

He took her bag, and they held hands again, walking up the path to his house. Traffic was heavy on the street; the village was a historic spot and a place known for its ambience. Weekend tourists were as thick here as they were at the beach. She found herself wondering how he happened to have two vacation properties.

His house was built by Dutch settlers and was in perfect condition, thanks to his painstaking restoration. When Marie entered the house through the front door, she had the sensation that she should duck down, as the ceilings were so low. They were standing in the living room. Jeff hung back and let Marie take her time looking around. He was so proud of himself! It was an oddly furnished room, stuffed with oversized pieces that left little room to navigate. There was hardly enough room for anything but the utilitarian, yet Jeff had managed to cram a complete library of winemaking books into the space, along with collections of bric-a-brac and several baskets of folded laundry. Shocked, Marie wondered what his place in Babylon was like on the inside. A narrow, curved staircase was along the wall on the right, and Jeff started going up, ducking his head to avoid bashing himself. She followed him.

"Watch your step here," he warned as they came to a turn in the staircase, the steps wide near the wall and tapering to a point on the room side. She could imagine having to navigate this booby trap after a glass of wine. "I thought you would be comfortable here," he said, entering a lovely, albeit small, bedroom. It had a narrow twin four-poster canopy bed against the inside wall, with a wing chair at a low desk by the window. Fortunately, the clutter on the lower level had not found its way up here. It would be a room where she might be comfortable for the rest of her life if she had to. Opposite the bed was a flat-screen television.

"Oh! I didn't expect this!" she said as she saw a doorway on the other side of the TV that led to a small, but complete bathroom. It was new and spotless.

"It's surprising where you can stick those things," he said. "This tiny place actually has four bathrooms! Wait until you see the basement." He chuckled, excited to show her his pièce de résistance—the wine cellar and tasting room. The Hudson Valley was known for its vineyards, and he was an avid supporter of local vintners.

He took her on a tour of the house. The wine cellar was world class; it got her curiosity going. *Who is this guy?* He was becoming more and more attractive to her the longer they were together. The impulse was to pull back, to avoid any dangerous liaisons. But where caution used to guide her, interest now took over. Here was a man who had not one, but two fun places to live, was semiretired from a lucrative law practice, and was amicably divorced with grown children who didn't seem to be too needy. Maybe she should count her blessings.

3

The young and beautiful Sandra Benson was debating what to do with herself for the weekend. The prospects of staying home, puttering around her apartment, and not answering the phone were very appealing. Last night, however, after she got home from work, Bernice Smith, Jack's mother, had called her and invited her to spend the weekend at her mansion, five blocks away from Sandra's apartment. The story of the mansion's ownership was rather convoluted; Jack had mortgaged it for the family when their business fell on hard times, and then Pam loaned more money to Bernice now that Jack was dead and no longer giving her an allowance.

"What's keeping you from foreclosing?" Sandra had asked Pam. "You have every right to, especially after the shitty way your mother-in-law has treated you. I'm not as forgiving as you are." Sandra could feel the heat spreading through her body after she made that faux pas.

"What do I want with that moldering place?" Pam had retorted, ignoring the other remark. "I could never live there year round, and it certainly wouldn't sell in this real estate market. No, I don't think so." She often fantasized about what would have happened if Bernice had died first. *Jack would have insisted we move into the mansion—or would he have?* "I don't want to talk about that place anymore today, okay?"

Sandra was ready to change the subject, too. But it would be another topic that Pam was beginning to find irritating.

"Did you think any more about telling the kids about the baby?" Sandra was not about to let this issue get swept under the rug.

"I did, actually. I decided that I am going to wait until you are further along. You'll be showing, and they won't have long to stew about it." Why Sandra thought it was necessary to make her announcement so soon after Jack's death continued to puzzle Pam. Was she trying to stake her claim in his life while everyone was an emotional wreck?

Pam tried to not examine the situation too closely because she wanted to keep peace. Plus, she needed Sandra. She would do what was necessary to keep Sandra in her life—for now.

This weekend, Sandra decided she was not going to Long Island or to the Smith Mansion. She planned on cleaning her apartment, reading trashy novels, and watching TV. She had missed Jack all week, waking up crying twice, unable to find joy in any of the things that used to bring her happiness. She had an appointment with her obstetrician and blurted out the story of the baby's father dying before he knew she was pregnant. Did the doctor look at her with skepticism? *Oh, so what*, she thought to herself. The doctor was being paid to take care of her health, not question her moral standing in the community.

The shocker was that she was a full four weeks further along in her pregnancy than she had thought originally. Jack might have known about the baby if she were more in touch with her body. The knowledge may have changed the entire outcome of their lives together; he would have told Pam, they would have separated, Sandra and Jack would have moved into his apartment on Madison Avenue together. He wouldn't have taken that final train ride and would still be alive. It would be a daydream repeated from time to time when the pain of his absence grew to be too much for her. It was easier to fantasize a different ending than to accept that she was having his child alone, to raise by herself over the years to come. Having Pam as a friend and supporter was lovely. But she was no replacement for Jack. *Face it,* she thought to herself, *sometimes you just have to press a little flesh.*

William Harold Smith was finding it difficult to relax in his jail cell. His restlessness could stem from either the prospect of being set free for the first time in two months or from a deep desire to kill his sister-in-law Pam. Each night, two scenes alternately ran through his mind. He couldn't get the vision out of his head of his mother crying as the police dragged him from the hospital, his arm in a cast after surgery to repair a shattered elbow. They were taking him to a black van with the words "Prisoner Transport" decaled on the side to haul him to jail. The second was the scene of Pam standing over him after she had aimed her gun, Jack's gun, at him and fired, hitting his arm.

He hadn't intended on hurting her stupid mother, Nelda. It was ridiculous that anyone would think he was capable of cutting a human being's throat, even with the knife pressed up against her skin. He was just trying to scare her, trying to elicit sympathy from Pam so she would hand over some money. He realized now that it was a contradiction. He was frantic, not thinking straight. You should either scare the hell out of someone or make them feel sorry for you, not try for both. It won't work.

Pam was so angry with him she pressed charges against him, too. His attorney said it wasn't over with yet; there was a trial coming up regarding some credit card charges—and worse. Because Pam had identified him as the person who had stolen Jack's wallet after he collapsed on the train, Bill was being charged with theft and assault.

He had been so confused and wasn't making the right decisions about anything. His financial status had him in a vice grip. He had been desperate. He knew Jack was still in the city because they had fought over the phone Friday night. Bill threatened Jack with driving to Long Island to get money from him, and Jack told him he was staying in the city that night. They arranged for Bill to meet Jack on the train at Grand Central at 10:00 on Saturday morning. He'd be waiting for Bill in the second car, and Jack would give him a check at that time. He said that it was going to be the final one, that if Bill couldn't find a way to make his business solvent, he better get another job. Jack had called Bill's cell phone Saturday morning.

"Okay, Buddy-boy, I'm stepping on the train right now. Meet me at Grand Central. I'm not getting off the train, so this better be fast." He could hear Bill breathing into the phone, but so far, he had said nothing after his hello. "I know you're there. You better answer, Buddy, or I'm hanging up and the deal is off."

"I'm here, Jack! Why are you rushing me? And stop calling me Buddy! Can't we be reasonable about this?" Bill was feeling wild; he had to get Jack to understand how dire things had gotten, to get him to feel the same hysteria Bill was feeling. "Dad destroyed the business; he drove it into the ground. There is nothing left. We are ruined. I need more than a loan. I need a job!" Bill was wailing now. But Jack was not moved.

"I know all this, Buddy-boy. It's not my problem. I said I would help you out, and I have. Meet me on the train or forget it." He hung up.

Bill ran out of his house in the Village without saying good-bye to his wife, Anne. She was used to his theatrics by now, but was worried because she wasn't sure if she was going to be blamed for whatever was happening.

Bill just made it onto the platform, having paid a fare that wouldn't be used. Jack was where he said he would be, but he didn't have a check ready as he had said.

"I decided that you aren't going to bully me anymore," Jack said. "Here's a restraining order; if you come near me or my family, I'll press charges, do you understand me?" The bell whistled, indicating the train was about to leave the station. Jack was reaching into his jacket to grab the envelope containing the restraining order when he fell over. No indication that anything was wrong had been given, no grabbing of the chest or contortion of the face; he silently fell.

Bill reached into Jack's jacket and grabbed the envelope, and his fingers touched the wallet; he didn't plan to take it, but it was right there, waiting. At the last moment, he was able to leap to freedom before the train doors closed. Just seconds had passed, less than a minute for the entire scenario to run through. He didn't think Jack would die! He loved his brother! At the very worst, he thought he may have simply fainted. *But a fatal heart attack? No fucking way!*

Their mutual friends and relatives always said Bill looked up to Jack with reverence. "My brother, Jack," Bill would say when he was introducing him to friends. He'd have a big smile on his face and a hand outstretched worshipfully in Jack's direction. No other words were necessary; it was clear what Bill thought of his older brother. Bill was bigger than Jack, but only in physical stature. Jack eventually escaped their nightmare of a childhood. He left Bill behind, but not before threatening Harold with death. He did it the day he left home to move in with Pam.

"If you touch Bill again, I will kill you," he had said to the old man. "I'll make sure that your clients, your staff, and my mother knows the truth." And he was serious. It worked, because Harold never came near his son again, unless it was in the presence of other people. He avoided being alone with Bill because the temptation to abuse his own flesh and blood was strong. His compulsion was magnified by habit. The boys were always there and available to him, so whatever his impulse, be it to beat and cause physical pain or to force himself sexually on his sons, once they were no longer available to him, the habit of it was the toughest to overcome.

His wife, Bernice, was overjoyed to be the recipient of so much attention from her husband. They hadn't had sex for years. Suddenly, after having left her bed to sleep in his study for the past decade, he was coming to her night after night and making love to her with such passion and physical aggression she was afraid he might have a heart attack.

Sixty-four days, twelve hours, and sixteen minutes after he was incarcerated, Bill was released from Rikers Island Prison into the custody of his angry wife, Anne. He smelled bad and looked thin, haggard, and contrite. She was livid. Anne hated driving in the city, and this was the worst time of day to do so. Traffic into Queens had been horrendous, and by the time she got to the prison parking lot, her hands were shaking so badly she couldn't get the keys out of the ignition.

They walked out of the prison's main building side by side, Anne not having made eye contact or directly speaking to him once. Now there didn't seem to be a way she could avoid it. Opening the trunk, she pointed to its interior before walking around to the driver's side to open the door.

"Put your stuff in there," she growled. "None of that crap is coming into the house without being fumigated."

He did as he was told, closing the trunk with a thud. Having been pushed around and told what to do every second of every day for the past two months, he hadn't noticed yet that his wife had crossed that imaginary line drawn on their wedding day fifteen years ago: *Never, ever talk disrespectfully to Bill Smith, or suffer the consequences.*

At that moment, she cared less if he were to haul off and smack her across the face. She would gouge his eyes out if he dared to get smart with her. She bristled at the memory of him standing in a bright-orange jumpsuit with his head bowed, listening to the judge read off the charges against him and then, three days later, his sentencing. Now that they were alone, the torrent of words she had practiced throwing at him didn't come. The only thing she could muster up was disgust. If their marriage could survive this, if there was a marriage left at all, he would have to make restitution to his sister-in-law. Anne tolerated her, and she loved Pam's children, Lisa and Brent. Would they ever be able to forgive Bill for what he had done?

They put their seat belts on, and Anne went to put the key in the ignition, when Bill reached over and put his hand over hers.

"Not just yet, okay, Anne? Can we take a minute and talk before we head for home?"

They didn't move. She pitched forward slightly to reach the steering column; he turned toward her, holding on to her hand. She started to pull away, and he released his grip.

"Look, let me try to explain." He was beseeching her, trying to get her to look at him by hanging on to the steering wheel. "I won't make excuses, but I do have an explanation."

Anne was incredulous. She turned to look at him with wide eyes. Finally, she spoke up. "I don't think I want to hear what you have to say. I know we're broke. Why I had to find out from the police is beyond me. I am not sure you can explain that away." She turned from him, giving up. *It's hopeless*, she thought to herself. *He's going to try to weasel his way out as he always does.* And she would be paralyzed and unable to leave him.

"I'm so sorry about it! I was too embarrassed to admit it to you. And then when that happened on the train, there didn't seem to be anything to say because he was going to save us. I never dreamed he was going to die! I thought he had just fainted! He promised me that he would help me. And then to go and die without having settled anything? Well, it just took me by surprise. I loved Jack! He was my big brother!" And for the first time since he had been shot by Pam, shot with a gun right in the elbow with a force that knocked him to the ground, he started to cry.

It had the opposite effect on Anne, however. "Stop it, Bill! Crying is not going to help, and it will only make things worse for me. I'm pissed!" she yelled. "You are such a goddamned liar! Pam said you went to this Sandra girl's apartment. Jack's girlfriend. Why the hell would you do that? Why would you harass Pam when she had just lost her husband? Who are you, anyway? Jesus Christ! A butcher knife against her mother's throat? You are so lucky you didn't get an attempted murder charge! The only reason you didn't is because Pam's dating one of the detectives and he asked for leniency."

This news blew Bill Smith away. *My brother has only been dead for a few weeks, and she's dating already?* Now it was his turn to be livid. "What the hell are you talking about?" he yelled at his wife. "She is an idiot! Goddamned Pam, dating a cop? Jack deserves better than that! I tell you he would kill her if he could!"

Anne looked over at her husband like he had two heads. *Who the hell is he kidding?*

"Do I have to remind you that that snake of a brother of yours was having an affair with someone half his age and that she is pregnant? She is practically living with your mother, I better tell you!" Anne had waited to use that little juicy bit of gossip for just the right moment. Possibly, her timing was off. Bill was staring at her with bugged eyes, sweating, and mouth hanging open. Anne had to look away; she was afraid she would start laughing at the vision.

"What the hell are you talking about?" he repeated, screaming. "Why would my mother let her in the house?"

Anne may have misjudged her timing. She looked at him, concerned he was going to go crazy right in the car. It was too late to defuse the situation; he had taken her bait.

"What is with the people in this family being taken in by that woman? First, Jack, then Pam, now my mother?" Bill put his head in his hands.

Anne could see that he was on the edge, but she thought of something that might cool it down. "I think Sandra might be helping out with some of the bills." Anne had no idea if it was true, but it sounded good. Hopefully, it would calm him down and give her time to get them home safely. Then if and when he found out that it was a lie, she would deal with it. The conversation was over, that much was clear.

"Can we go home now?" Bill whined.

Anne put the key back in the ignition and started the engine. They didn't say another word to each other as Anne aimed the car toward the Triboro Bridge.

4

Rhinebeck, New York, is home to the Culinary Institute of American. Jeff Babcock, retired attorney and recent graduate of the CIA, was an accomplished chef. By Sunday, eating disorder–sufferer Marie Fabian discovered that life with Jeff meant three home-cooked meals, homemade desserts, and the best American wines available. They spent part of Saturday and Sunday shopping for food, going into Hyde Park for groceries, and then returning to Rhinebeck for early varieties of vegetables at the farmers' market. Marie fought the urge to look at her watch. Jeff chose early peas, beans, and tricolor carrots with care; he would wash them one at a time and tenderly steam them with a delicate shallot butter sauce.

The kitchen in his Rhinebeck house was a cook's delight, with high-end professional appliances, gleaming marble pastry countertops, and ample seating for guests, all designed to fit a ten-foot-by-ten-foot space. Marie decided she wouldn't invite him to her apartment, after all; she used her oven to store shoes. While Jeff cooked, she sat on a stool at the counter, sipping a glass of wine, nibbling the vegetables he had prepared for her, bored to tears. There was plenty of time for him to find out the truth about Marie and her relationship with food.

"This wine is amazing," Marie slurred. "These carrots are wonderful, too." She pushed the image of Jack Smith grilling steaks on the veranda, along with that of her last meal of SpaghettiOs the other night, out of her mind. She willed this new picture of a handsome gentleman wearing a red-and-white-striped apron that his daughter sewed for him, standing at the stove, cooking just for her. She wasn't having much success.

"Thank the weather for both," he said. "Our growing season has been phenomenal in spite of the heavy snow last spring." Marie stifled a yawn. He turned from the stove, pan in hand, and dished a small crab cake onto a saucer, topping it with a creamy béarnaise sauce. "Here, try this," he said. "Those crabs we got this morning? And the eggs from the farmers' market? You won't get anything fresher than this."

Marie picked up a fork to take a bite of the crab cake. She heard a *snap* where the thin, browned crust broke, exposing the tender interior. "Oh my God," she moaned as she tasted how delicious the crab cake was. "This is better than sex." She closed her eyes and chewed. Realizing what she had just said, the food turned to dust in her mouth. *Oops.*

Jeff was smiling at her. He obviously didn't think the comment was inappropriate, nor did he pick up on it and say anything in return. He began eating one as well. The late afternoon was spent eating and talking and drinking a generous amount of Jeff's wine collection. By 7:00, reality hit. She had an hour drive home and was feeling more than a little woozy.

"I better make some coffee," Jeff said. "You can have dessert and then think about leaving."

Marie didn't want to go back home, though. She didn't want to go to work on Monday or pretend she liked her apartment anymore. The contrast of this kind man with his homey place and her lonely, dead neighborhood and office full of unfriendly, uninterested people made Marie recognize that she needed to make some changes in her life. Everything about the way she lived spoke of Jack; it was arranged to make it convenient for him to get to her. With Jack dead and gone, there was no reason on earth she should stay there. But where would she go? Babylon? She could never afford it. The thought of moving from her apartment was exhausting. Maybe she would wait a little longer. She heard that, after a spouse dies, widows should wait one year before doing anything drastic like moving. Maybe it applied to sisters-in-law, too. Could she wait that long? Would she be able to tolerate being miserable for another year?

They finished eating and then came the inevitable. Jeff looked at his watch.

"Maybe you better think about getting on the road," he said. She felt a little put off that he wasn't asking her to stay another night, encouraging her to leave for the city in the morning. He went up the stairs with her, standing in the doorway as she gathered up her belongings and stuffed things into her suitcase.

"Well, thanks for coming up!" he said. "We will have to do it again. Next month is the big Food Fest; if you liked this weekend, you'll love Food Fest weekend."

The phone in his hallway started ringing. Looking at it sideways, he gave up and went to answer it. Whispering, he hung up, his anxiety palpable. He picked up her suitcase and followed her down the stairs and out the front door, carrying it to her car. He stowed her case in the trunk and then turned to hug her good-bye.

"Drive safely," he said as he held the car door opened for her as she got in.

She smiled up at him, tired but okay to drive. She could hear more telephone-ringing coming from the house; he began fidgeting and glancing back at the house as she fumbled buckling her seat belt.

"Thanks again," she said. "Talk to you later?"

He nodded yes, and as she backed out of the driveway, yawning, it occurred to her that he hadn't kissed her. Jeff was running back to his house. She didn't wait until she was out of Rhinebeck to pull over to the side of the road and stick her finger down her throat.

5

There is only so much cleaning that can be done to a small apartment, so by Saturday afternoon, Sandra was getting restless and decided to take Bernice Smith up on her offer. She showered and dressed in jeans and a T-shirt, and then picked up the phone to call her. Her maid answered the phone, but within seconds, Bernice was there, animated, hopeful.

"My dear! I am so glad you called! What can I do for you?" Sandra was always a little confused by the jubilance that her calls elicited, but let it go. *What does Bernice expect of me?*

"Hi, Bernice, I was hoping to take you up on your offer for a visit. Is it okay if I come by now?"

Bernice hesitated just a second. "Why, of course! I'll send Ben. Stay right where you are!"

The weather was hot and muggy, so Sandra took the offer of the limousine. It was better than having to find a cab on a Saturday afternoon. "Thank you, I'll accept the ride this time!" She said good-bye and went to gather up her purse and put her shoes on. She had a pleasant emptiness in her head; going to Bernice's meant a wonderful meal, total comfort, and relaxation, truly the best of the good life. Sandra knew it was at Pam's expense. Bernice rang the bell for Mildred as soon as she hung up from talking with Sandra. Mildred came right away.

"Yes, madam," she said. It was the fifth time that morning that the bell had summoned her; she was having a time of it with pain in her back bad enough to keep her up all night. And now Bernice was acting like she did in the old days, keeping the staff running for no apparent reason. Mildred decided she may have to say something if this was another call just so Bernice would know she wasn't alone.

"Sandra Benson, Jack's young woman, is coming. Will you let Ben know? He has her address. And I'll want luncheon served as soon as she gets here. Please tell Cook."

Mildred turned to leave, rolling her eyes. When she got back to the kitchen, she relayed the messages to Ben and Alice.

Alice was pouring coffee for them. "How I am supposed to fix a luncheon with no food? Someone needs to tell her so she can wake up from her fairytale." She went to a desk where her menus and recipe books were arranged neatly. "I'll have to do something with bread; that I can make from scratch. Today we need to tell her, the three of us."

"What are we supposed to say?" Ben said. Then he laughed. "Good luck with that! She won't care if there is no money! 'Just do it!' will be her answer." Her three devoted house staff were all thinking the same thing, but no one was saying it out loud: *Our days here are numbered.*

Alice decided on a simple lunch of puff pastry stuffed with chicken salad. She could make enough of that for two women with the leftovers from last night's dinner. They would last another day.

Ben left to get Sandra, when the phone rang. Mildred picked it up. She put the caller on hold, whispering to

Alice as she left the kitchen to get Bernice to take the call, "The prodigal son."

Alice shook her head with raised eyebrows. "Oh boy!"

Mildred came back a few minutes later. "Three for luncheon."

Bernice was excited! She knew Bill might be released from prison early, but a whole month! It was just testimony to his innocence that he was out already and to his love for her as his mother that he just arrived home and wanted to come to see her. It didn't occur to her that he might have bad news. She went up to her bedroom to prepare for her guests. The idea that she would have both her beloved son and the unborn baby of her late son in the house at the same time thrilled her. She had forgotten the screaming scene when she told Bill about the baby. Bernice had a tendency to idealize even the most distorted encounter.

She freshened her makeup and dabbed perfume behind her ears. Her sons were proud of their mother's exquisite grooming and appearance. She didn't want to let Bill down. Her failing eyesight hid the food stains on the front of her shirt from her view, and she couldn't remember the last time she showered. It would not be missed by her child.

She heard the car pull around; Sandra must have arrived. She left the seclusion of her bedroom and slowly walked down the stairs, aware that she had grown frail this summer. She no longer went to the gym; the membership was too expensive to continue. She didn't walk much. At her age, decline happened rapidly if you didn't watch it.

Sandra was standing in the entryway, waiting for Bernice to descend. They waved to each other.

"Hi! Thank you for having me!" Sandra said, doing her best to hide her shock at Bernice's appearance. She met her at the bottom stair, and they embraced. "How are you?" she asked, trying to keep the concern from her voice. She had lost weight, and the most worrisome was the condition of her clothes and hair. Always pristine, she was almost slovenly today.

"I'm doing well! But what about you?" she asked, looking down at Sandra's still flat belly. *She's entering her second trimester; shouldn't she be showing at least a little bit?*

"Oh, we're just fine, with the emphasis on *we*," she laughed.

Bernice took Sandra's arm, and they walked together toward the den. Sandra would have to speak to Pam about Bernice's appearance.

"By the way, Bill is coming over for lunch, too. You'll get to meet him under better circumstances." Bernice looked at Sandra to gauge her reaction to this news. It wasn't good.

"Well, I better leave, then." She shook off Bernice's arm and headed for the door.

"Wait! Please, Sandra. I didn't set this up; he just called, truly. Not five minutes ago. Won't you see him? Give him a chance to apologize to you."

Sandra thought, *Yeah, like that is going to happen.* But she did slow down. *Why didn't I just stay home today?*

"Bill has no reason to apologize to me, but that doesn't mean I approve of what he did. He left Jack to die on the train and then tried to kill Pam's mother. He should tell you and Pam he's sorry, not me." Sandra could feel her voice getting shrill, but it was too late. They would have it out now, something she had wanted to avoid at all costs.

"But Jack didn't die on the train. Pam told me. He died at the hospital." Bernice was acting confused, like she was hearing something she hadn't heard before. Then, "Why does everyone say he dropped dead on the train? I loathe that visual!" Bernice sat down on the closest chair and, with face covered, started to weep.

It was at this inopportune time that Bill decided to bust through the front door like a linebacker. "Mother!" he yelled for her. "I'm home!" The cheerfulness stopped as soon as he saw Bernice slumped over in a chair up against the entryway wall. "Mother! What in God's name! What the hell is wrong with her?" he yelled, seeing Sandra for the first time. "What'd you say to her?"

"Calm down, Bill," Bernice said, trying to pull herself together. "We were just having a moment, Sandra and I." She sat up straight and started to dig through her pockets for a tissue.

It was then that Bill noticed his mother had changed in the past sixty days. The toll his incarceration had taken on her surpassed what the death of both her husband and son did. "Mother, for God's sake, what happened to you?" he said without restraint.

Sandra bowed her head and turned away, embarrassed for both of them. She wished she could disappear, but something told her that her presence might be useful to the family now, that she owed something to Jack to stay here and finish what she had started.

"Why haven't you been getting your hair done?" He was making reference to the yellowed gray of her shaggy hair, recently cut in a youthful pixie style as soon as Jack's funeral was over, after having been worn in a gleaming silver French twist for thirty years. Then he leaned forward and gently, with his hand under her chin, lifted her head slightly to look into her eyes. "Why haven't you changed your clothes? Mom, what is going on here?" Bill was suddenly frightened. He wasn't ready for Bernice to die and leave him alone. He didn't want to be grown up, the head of a family. He went to her side and helped her stand up.

"I'm very well able to stand on my own, if you don't mind. Insulting me in my own home and then insinuating that I am unable to function." Her old pride had returned.

Bill stifled a sigh of relief. He looked at Sandra and tried to smile. She could almost read his mind. She was being given an opening here to take and bond as part of the family or to remain an outsider.

"Bernice, I don't think that is what Bill means at all, do you, Bill?" She came to Bernice's other side and took her hand. "Let's go back into the den, okay? I'm sorry I raised my voice, Bernice," Sandra said to her.

Bernice looked confused for a moment. "What were we fighting about, anyway?" She laughed then. "Oh, right! You, Bill, we were fighting about you."

It was his turn to look confused. "What did I do? I haven't even been around for two months."

They took their seats in the den around the game table.

Bernice rang for Mildred. "Let's eat, okay? I'm about ready to faint."

Mildred brought the lunch tray in and decided there on the spot that she was going to speak to Mr. Bill about the money situation. Newly home from jail or not, now was the time. No one was prepared to work forever without pay.

"Sir, may I speak to you privately?" Mildred said to Bill under her breath.

Thinking she wanted to talk about the condition of his mother, he stood up, making the excuse to go to the bathroom to wash his hands, and whispered, "Yes," back to Mildred.

They met in the hallway leading to the kitchen.

"Sir," Mildred began, "we in the kitchen think you should know that finances here have reached a critical point. We haven't been paid in over a month, and there is no money for food or to pay the bills we normally take care of, for the gardener, or for gas for the car." She stopped, looking him right in the eye.

"I thought my sister-in-law was taking care of money while I was gone," he said. Then he remembered, just that morning, Anne saying Sandra was giving Bernice money. He could feel his face turning red, his blood pressure going up rapidly. "This is news to me." He was looking off into space. *What the hell am I going to do now? I don't have a penny. That goddamned Pam!*

Mildred was waiting patiently, but wasn't going to budge until he gave her some answers.

"Let me look into it, okay? Can you and the others hold on for a few more days?" He knew that he needed some finesse right now, a commodity not normally used in a prison cell. Did he even remember how to charm?

"Thank you so much for not jumping ship, Mildred! I appreciate it so very much! I'll get back to you, okay?" He took her hand and patted it.

She immediately went into the bathroom and washed it off.

Bill stood in the hallway for a few minutes, collecting himself. He was at a total loss for what the next move should be. He knew that anger wasn't going to get him anywhere; it was too late for that. He had to be honest with his mother, and he supposed Sandra as well. Something had to be done, right that afternoon, probably asking Sandra or Pam for money. They didn't need to keep the staff on, but he wasn't going to do anything rash. He was beginning to think he made a mistake getting out of jail early.

Walking back to the den, he could hear pleasant conversation between his mother and Sandra. It was totally against everything he knew to bring up any unpleasantness during a meal. He would have to take a stand and be strong for once. And he had to control his temper. It had landed him in hot water with his brother and look where that lead. Both women looked up when he walked into the room. He decided to just say it.

"Mother, the staff hasn't been paid in over a month." He sat down with a thud.

Bernice's hand was poised over the serving spoon, ready to scoop up a puffed pastry shell full of chicken and place one on each plate. Her hand hovered over the spoon. "That's nonsense. I paid them myself, I am sure of it. What a thing to bring up during lunch, in front of our guest!" She reached for the spoon, ignoring Bill.

"Mother, listen to me. Put the spoon down and listen. We are broke. We don't have the money to pay your staff, or to pay for food, or to buy gas for the limousine." He waited, and Bernice continued to dish up lunch. Bill reached over his mother and gently took the spoon out of her hand. "You are going to face this right now," he said firmly. The dialogue was giving Sandra a glimpse into why people lost their temper with Bernice. She could be obstinate. "We have a choice. We can ask Pam," and then he turned to look at Sandra, "or we can ask you," he said, directing his comment to her. "You benefited by my brother's death." He raised his hand when she began to protest. "Not intentionally, but you did. Let's face the facts here. My brother was pissed off at me because I failed to live up to his work ethic."

Sandra had to admit that was probably true. Bill wasn't dynamic. He was weak. But that may not have been entirely his fault.

"We were desperate for his help and he gave it to us. He gave Mother a generous stipend for the year after my father died. You knew that. He promised me that he would field clients my way. And now you haven't honored his intentions." Bill sat down at the table, across from Sandra. He fought back tears. "When I learned that he willed his *business* to you, I knew we were in trouble. By not giving it to his wife, keeping it in the family, it would make it that much harder for us to benefit in any way."

Bernice knew why Jack had been so angry, but she wasn't going to bring it up in front of Sandra. She prayed silently that Bill wouldn't, either. *It would be the final dev-*

astation. Now this lovely young lady knows we're broke. Can I keep a little of my pride?

"I'm not sure what I have to do with this," Sandra said. "Your mother invited me here for lunch. I'm didn't come here to argue with you." She thought, *It'll be over my dead body that he gets one percent of the business Jack left to me.* He had left it to her to protect Pam; Sandra could see that now. The date of the restraining order and the day Jack changed his will, giving his business interest to her, were close.

She was so pleased with herself! She couldn't wait to tell Pam! This sudden epiphany made so much sense. Jack knew that the money issues here were escalating and Bill was going to be trouble. Jack hinted that he felt like he might be dying soon. She wasn't the only person who noticed; even his own lawyer told Pam he felt that. He knew that Pam was too kind to deny Bill; if she had the controlling interest in the business, he would hound her to death. Sandra was tougher. Bill would not be able to harass her like he could Pam. Sandra felt vindicated. Jack hadn't left the business to her because it would benefit her, after all. It had been to protect Pam.

Lunch was ruined. Bernice was numb. *What does Bill expect of me?* She didn't know what to do. She looked beseechingly at Sandra. "Is there any way you can help us?" she asked.

Sandra stood up and walked toward the French doors that lead to a beautiful walled courtyard. It was August, and the flowers were still abundant, no sign of dog days out here. It was evident that the gardener was coming frequently, that one of the unpaid bills would be from the greenhouse. "Well, let me ask you first. Is there any way you can help yourself?" She looked from Bill to Bernice and waited.

Neither said a word.

"Okay, let me word it differently. If I were to give you money right now, how would it change anything? You would still be broke tomorrow, correct? There wouldn't be any income coming into this house or yours either, correct, Bill?" *After all, the guy was just sprung from jail. What income was he going to have?* She waited. "The way I see things, you are living above your means here. You both want to have expensive lifestyles, yet there is no money to support it. Can I ask what is going on with your office?" She could tell that she had hit a nerve; Bill was bright red in the face. But to his credit, he was keeping it together.

"It's closed. The business is closed." He was embarrassed to say it in front of his mother, even though she had to know it was his father, her late husband, who had driven the business into the ground, keeping it going by selling off investments and allowing his family to believe everything was okay when it was really over. Bill would have been forced to face reality and look for another job if he had known how bad things were. But would he have? He floundered for a full year after Harold died, trying to stay afloat with no business. Sandra just didn't understand it. Maybe he was daft.

She looked him in the eye. "I have to think about this. But you do, too. I am going to talk to Pam to see if she can come up with anything."

Bernice started to protest, and Sandra put up her hand to shut her up.

"I'm not keeping this from her, if that is what you are going to suggest. She is in this, too. I can't risk what is, in all actuality, her money. I want you both to think about how you can help. If it's putting your houses up for sale, your office, too, so be it. Someone has to go to work. The way I am seeing it, I am the only one working here, and I don't like it." She reached for her purse. This was not the way she wanted to spend her Saturday afternoon. "I am going home. Don't get up." She bent to kiss Bernice on her cheek, patted her hand, looked at Bill, and left the house.

6

Sandra moved quickly to get out of the house before Bill, or worse, Bernice called after her. She needn't have worried. They sat there, numb. What Sandra had said was true, but something they didn't want to face. They needed to sell the houses. They didn't even have the money to rent a cheap apartment. At the same time, as though choreographed, they said, "Maybe Pam would let us live in the Madison Avenue apartment." They looked at each other but didn't laugh. It was too gruesome to laugh about.

Bill looked around the room. *Just the artwork hanging in here is worth a small fortune. Why hadn't we done something sooner, like auction some of this art?* "You know, Mom, maybe we should think about having an auction. We can cull the flock, so to speak. There are boxes of things in the attic and even more in the office." Bill knew he was grasping at straws. But the truth was that the house had been in the family since it was built over a hundred years ago. There could be priceless artifacts hidden away. He knew for a fact that the painting over the fireplace in the dining room was by a famous Dutch painter. He got up to find a pen and piece of paper. "Come with me. I'm going to start listing stuff we can sell." He turned to look at his mother, who was looking at him like he had two heads. "Mother, come on! You can sell some of this crap or lose your house. What would be more embarrassing to you?"

Bernice got up then, not without difficulty. She felt like she was a hundred years old. "I need to get back to the gym," she said as she joined Bill.

"You need to get to the beauty salon," he replied, Bernice giving him a dirty look in return.

As soon as she was far enough from the house that Bill wasn't a threat, Sandra called Pam on her cell. Taking care as she crossed a car-filled Broadway, she prayed silently that Pam would be home to answer the phone. The machine picked up with the nondescript voice answering.

"Pam, I am walking down Broadway after leaving the mansion. Give me a call when you get in. I am afraid I may have started World War Three today." She ended the call and put her cell away. Remembering she hadn't eaten lunch, she decided to stop in Zabar's on her way home; it would save her from having to go out again. She took her time in the store, walking up and down the aisles, putting whatever was appetizing into her basket. She still hadn't gained any weight yet with the pregnancy and, at over five months, was just starting to show. Her doctor told her that because she was tall, the baby had a lot of room to grow before he would push outward. They encouraged her to increase her calories. Sandra added a ready-made sandwich and a half-gallon of gourmet ice cream to the imported cheeses and freshly baked bread in her basket. She paid for her groceries and left the store, walking fast so her ice cream wouldn't melt in the heat. Then her phone rang. It was Pam.

"What happened?" she asked, without saying hello.

Sandra told her everything.

"It sounds worse when I repeat it," she said. "I just couldn't let them go on thinking that we would give them money and they would do nothing to get themselves out of this mess."

"I have been giving them money," Pam said when Sandra was finished. "I continued giving Bernice two thousand dollars a week. I gave it in a check, however, because I want a record, and I sent it to Anne." *Oh, oh*, Pam thought. "Maybe that wasn't such a smart move. Let me check my bank statement, okay? I'll call you right back."

They hung up, and Sandra started walking faster, the condensation from the ice cream making a puddle in the bottom of the plastic grocery bag. She turned right on her street and saw him standing in front of her apartment building before he saw her. She backed up quickly, going around the corner. She was not going to allow Bill to come into her apartment today after he pulled a knife on Nelda. And she was angry. He made her feel unsafe, and she didn't like being scared. She slipped into the bagel place on the corner of her street. If she stretched on tiptoe and looked out the end of the window, she could still see him in front of her building. She ordered a bagel so she could stay in the store until Bill left.

The woman behind the counter gave Sandra her bagel and a glass of water. Nodding toward Sandra's tummy, she said, "You better drink in this heat." Sandra thanked her. *I guess I'm not that flat, after all,* she thought.

Pam called back.

"My checks were cashed. That is so unlike Anne! I guess I should have contacted her, but we never stayed in touch. Maybe pressing charges against her husband didn't go over well. She must have been forging Bernice's name."

"Pam, Bill is standing right in front of my apartment. I'm hiding in the bagel place on Broadway." Sandra was craning her neck to look down the street again. He was still there. "What should I do?" She was getting angry. She couldn't hide all afternoon, and she didn't want to have an argument on the street.

"Oh no!" Pam exclaimed. "He is such a pain in the ass! Call the police, Sandra!"

Sandra thought for a minute and then asked Pam if she had Bill's cell phone number. "I can call him and tell him I know he is there," Sandra said.

Pam dug through some papers and came up with what she thought was his number. And then she thought of something else. "Sandra, Andy is here, and he wants me to call the police anyway. Anne has taken checks meant for Bernice and forged her name. If we tell Bill this, only God knows what he will do. He might even harm her. You better call the police, too. Oh, this is getting to be too much!" *Why did he get out of jail so early?* Pam thought. Sandra wrote the number down as Pam read it off. "What are you going to say to him?" Pam asked.

"I think I will say that I want him to leave or I am going to call the police." *I just want to get home!* Sandra thought. "I'll call you when I'm finished talking to him." They said their good-byes, Pam asking her to be careful. Sandra keyed in the number Pam had given her and then craned her neck again to see if he was still there. She watched him get his phone from his pocket and answer it.

"Hello, Sandra. Why aren't you answering your door? I'm standing outside of your building."

"If you don't leave, I'm calling the police. You just got out of prison today; you must be on parole or something. Am I correct?"

"Jesus Christ! Please don't call them! I am not going to do anything to you! I just need to tell you about an idea we had right after you left. The house is full of art we can sell. We were hoping you would think it was proactive enough to base a loan on."

Sandra thought that sounded reasonable. But regardless, she didn't want him hanging around her apartment. "Bill that is a great idea. I definitely will consider loaning you money based on the value of the art. But you should be there now at the mansion, listing it and estimating its worth. You should be able to get an idea of its value right online." She watched him pace back and forth in front of her building. *Why isn't he walking away?* "Are you leaving my building?" she asked.

"I'm leaving now," he said.

But she could see him there. *How can I get him to leave without revealing my position?*

"Okay, call me when you have your list ready." And she hung up.

She then keyed in 911. There was a police car in the neighborhood. She watched it speed up Broadway and then turn onto Eighty-second Street. Bill saw it as it rounded the corner, coming toward him. She watched him looking around, trying to figure out where she was. She could see one of the officers talking to him from their car. Then the doors opened and they got out. One of them was talking on his phone. Sandra imagined him talking to Pam, getting the scoop on the whole ugly story. Sandra's heart sunk as they put handcuffs on Bill, leading him to the car. He got into the backseat with their help. The officers got in and sped off again. It wasn't what she wanted to happen, but he wouldn't listen to her.

She threw her bagel plate and water cup in the trash can, along with her bag of melted ice cream. She walked as fast as she could to her building, fearful that the police would find out it was all a mistake and bring Bill back. She ran up the walkway to the building, got the door opened, and locked behind her. She hurried to her apartment, making sure the chain was on the door, and wedged a kitchen chair under the handle once she was safely inside.

The apartment had two floors, and the lower floor had a rear-access door. She ran down the stairs to make sure the door and windows were locked, reinforcing the door with another chair. The windows were a concern. She had never felt so insecure before, and Bill was responsible for it. She would call a carpenter on Monday and get a shutter made to fit over the lower-level window. In the meantime, she struggled with a large dresser, pushing it across the carpeting to rest in front of the window. It would have to do for now. She went from room to room, closing shades, making sure everything was secure.

Her phone rang; it was the police. They were going to send someone around to take a statement from her. It was such a mess already, and he had only been out of jail for a few hours.

7

Fortunately for Pam and Sandra, Andy Andrews was spending the day at the beach when Sandra called to tell her about the mansion confrontation. He was never happier than when his knowledge could be put to use by his friends. When Sandra called the first time, they were taking a walk and didn't hear the phone. It was obvious to him that the police would have to be called; this Bill guy was a walking time bomb, and unless his shenanigans were documented, if and when he really threatened Sandra, they would have no history to back up their story. Pam felt awful for her late husband's family. They were disintegrating at record speed. That Anne had gotten herself involved was so sad because it meant she might have to do jail time for theft.

Anne Smith was folding laundry when the police came to her door. She was taken by such surprise; it never even occurred to her that she didn't have to let them in her house. The checks were the farthest thing from her mind. They didn't have a warrant yet, but simply wanted to question her. She led them to the dining area of their small brownstone. She had always hated living in the Village like a student. Bill loved it since his college days, forced to go to school in the city and live at home by his domineering father. Anne didn't know the whole truth. Once he was

going to get married, he wanted to live down here, hoping
to recapture some of the glamour of living downtown in
a historic atmosphere. It fell flat. He didn't have a group
of friends who lived here anymore. Anne didn't like their
house; it was too dark, the only light coming from north-
facing windows. She felt like she was living in gloom all
the time. The eating area was the worst; it was placed in
the center of the structure and had no natural light at all.
To use it meant turning on the light above the table, a hid-
eous glass-and-brass concoction that Bill's dad had given
them and was therefore sacrosanct. It cast huge shadows
across the table and was barely good for illuminating their
plates and little else.

Even the police officers seemed a little confused
by the interior of the house. Was she going to pray with
them? It was like the alcove of a church; the only things
missing were candles and the scent of incense.

"Would you like a cup of coffee? I was just going to
pour one for myself." She pulled out two chairs, waiting
for their answer.

"Coffee would be great—black, please. I'm Tom, and
this is Jim," the younger man said.

The older officer smiled and said, "No thanks." She
went to the kitchen and returned shortly with two mugs
of black coffee.

"Do you know why we are here?" he asked. Anne
thought it was because of Bill's release that morning from
prison and said so. They officers rifled through a stack of
papers they brought and looked at each other, shrugging
their shoulders. It was news to them. "Tell us about why he
was in prison." Anne related the minimal details she knew,

including the gruesome story of the knife against Pam's mother's throat. It sounds so awful. *Why had I waited for him?* She repeated it out loud to the men.

"I'm not sure why I am still here, why I didn't leave him. But I am sure you don't want to hear about that." She held her mug of coffee, looking down into it as though it contained the answers to life. "I have never said this out loud, but I am afraid of my husband. Why I am telling you two is a mystery; I know there is nothing you can do about it."

"The reason we are here is because a woman has filed a complaint, charging you with forgery and theft. Do you know of any reason why she would do that?" Anne sat back in her chair. *So that's what this is all about.* She had almost forgotten about it. There was no earthly reason to lie.

"The woman, Pam, correct? She's my sister-in-law. She was helping us out each month. Her husband was giving us two thousand a week before he died because my husband's business tanked. When my husband went to jail, she started sending the checks here, but they were made out to my mother-in-law. She is old and having a hard time with the death of her son, so rather than bother her, I just forged her name, as I do on almost all the correspondence and banking of hers. I certainly wasn't stealing it."

"Well, actually, you were. If someone writes a name on a check and you copy it without that person's consent, it is stealing," Tom said. "I think we may have a simple misunderstanding here." They pushed their chairs back and stood up, very synchronized and professional. "We'll take your statement back to headquarters and see if we can straighten this out." Tom extended his hand to Anne.

She walked them to the front door and saw them out. She closed the door behind her, locking it, just in case.

It was time to pick her boys up from preschool. She was sorry Bill had rushed off like the ass that he was, to "surprise" his mother, leaving her alone on their first day back together in over two months. There didn't seem any point in telling the boys he was home. Yet one more hurtful experience regarding their father to add to the many others, such as forgotten birthdays and cruel spankings for no reason. She wondered why she had mentioned to the officers that she was afraid of Bill. *What good did it do?* They didn't acknowledge her comment. She cleaned up the coffee mugs and grabbed her purse, heading for the door. She would walk to pick up her sons and maybe find something entertaining for the three of them to do for the afternoon. It made no sense to hang around, waiting for Bill to show up when guilt or his mother pushed him home.

8

As difficult as it was, Bill managed not to break down crying during the ride downtown in the back of the police car. He was totally spent. It hadn't occurred to him that Sandra would call the cops. Once again, he had underestimated her. They must have been waiting around the corner, because just as she hung up with him, they were there. He was pretty sure that, once he explained why he was at Sandra's, they would release him. When they were at the mansion together, he had never come near her in a threatening way. He didn't understand why she had reacted so strongly.

The squad car pulled into a parking garage under the station. One of the officers opened the door for Bill. He struggled to get out with his hands shackled. The urge to sprint away was strong; the officer must have sensed he was ready to bolt because he took him gently but firmly by the upper arm and led him into the building. No one spoke as they rode the elevator together. Once they got to the office, the man let go of his arm.

"Come with me," Jim said. He was getting sick and tired of rich people making more work for him. He led Bill to a small room.

Interrogation popped into Bill's mind when he saw the table and two chairs. He hesitated before walking through the door, frightened at the confined space.

Jim explained, "Someone is using my desk right now. We'll be more comfortable in here." A lunatic was screaming in the background. "Don't mind the noise. He's here once a week. Have a seat." He pulled out one of the chairs for Bill to sit in. "Do you want something to drink?" Bill shook his head no. Jim left the room, closing the door behind him.

Bill was so nervous. *What if they take me back to jail?* For the first time since he had arrived home, he thought of Anne and the boys. He hadn't seen his sons yet. It was obvious his wife was furious with him. Maybe he shouldn't have rushed off to see his mother like he did.

The officer returned with two cups of coffee and a notepad. It looked like Bill would get coffee whether he wanted it or not.

"So tell me what happened today." He looked at Bill and smiled. Bill had nothing to hide. There was no reason to withhold anything.

"I got out of jail this morning," Bill said. Jim put his pen down and looked at him. *How did I miss this news when I did the background check on this guy?*

"What were the charges?" the officer asked. Bill looked at him, confused.

"Why were you incarcerated?" he clarified. *So this is one of those guys who just looks smart.*

"I put a knife to my sister-in-law's mother's throat."

Where have I heard that story before, just today? Jim put his pen down and excused himself. "I'll be right back," he said.

Bill sat there, bored, thinking about his kids, his mother, his life. *What would I have done differently?* He hated business. He would have liked to have been a nurse. He loved his mandatory biology class freshman year. But when he approached his father about it, the old man had a fit.

"Go to medical school, for Christ's sake! No son of mine is going to be a nurse." Bill knew he wasn't smart enough to go to either medical or nursing school. He barely got through college. He just didn't have the confidence needed to do much with his life outside of what fell into his lap. That included finding his wife.

Anne was his roommate's sister, attractive but shy. She followed him around, and since he wasn't aggressive enough to make a pass at her, they hung out together and nothing more. Eventually, they had been together long enough that it was expected they would get married. He went to his brother, Jack, for advice.

"How'd you know that Pam was the one?" he had asked innocently.

Jack felt sorry for his brother; he was still an idealist, no matter what his life had been like. "She fit in with the family. That was the only criteria." Jack admitted that he was attracted to her as well. But it was more important that a wife would be there by his side through thick and thin. Pam was devoted, if nothing else.

Anne certainly fit the mold. However, where Pam was carefree and accepting, Anne was suspicious and unsatisfied. She hated Bernice's intrusion into their home life from the beginning. She and Bill fought passionately about it.

It was during one these confrontations that Bill found out how much he liked hitting his wife. There was nothing better than to haul off and smack her across her smug face. If she wasn't expecting it, his open hand could send her flying across the room. He rationalized that as long as he didn't punch her, it was okay. He knew that if he started punching her, he would be unable to stop. He'd end up beating her to death.

Soon even their sex life included violence. He couldn't get an erection without first hitting her hard; the sound of his hand against her flesh made blood surge into his penis. By the time his father died, he couldn't ejaculate without hitting her. Foreplay for Anne was getting smacked by her husband. His incarceration was the first time in years when she wasn't hit on a daily basis. Of course, the hitting would have to resume as soon as they spent any real time together. In spite of their history, Anne was still pissed off at Bill for not wanting to spend time with her. *Maybe she was a masochist*, Bill thought.

Jim returned to the interrogation room with a thick wad of printed paper. There was a wealth of information about this defendant. He had a long history of run-ins with the law, starting with public intoxication during his college years to domestic violence when neighbors called police during a fight the Smiths had late one night. Although the wife refused to press charges, police had documented that handprints were visible on both sides of her face. He had a lawsuit pending in Manhattan for credit card theft. The term he had just finished serving was for attempted murder on Long Island. He had gotten off with a light sentence because his sister-in-law had asked for mercy. Bill was lucky he hadn't been tried in the city. He'd be in Rikers for much longer.

"Okay, so you tried to kill your sister's mother, correct?"

Rather than correct him, Bill let it go. He was getting tired. What difference did it make? He'd already been tried on that count; they couldn't try him again.

"It says here you are getting ready to be tried on credit card theft. Do you want to tell me about that?"

Bill was slumped forward in his chair. *How'd I get to this point?* "There's really nothing to tell. I was having a meeting with my brother and he collapsed. I took his wallet, and after he died, I used his credit cards. I was desperate."

Jim thought, *A man would have to be to stoop that low.* "What lead to your desperation?" Jim wanted to know on a human basis why someone with every advantage would end up with unpaid bills, stalking a woman young enough to be his daughter.

"My father drove the family business into the ground, and I didn't find out how much trouble we were in until after he died, last year. We are totally broke. I mean, if it hadn't been for my brother giving my mother and I money, we would have lost our houses."

There was a knock on the door.

Jim got up to open it, and someone outside handed him a sheet of paper. He sat down to read it. *So this is where I heard this story today.* When he was finished, he looked up at Bill. "Your wife is going to be charged with theft as well. She forged some checks your late brother's wife sent to your mother. Do you know anything about that?"

That was the final straw. Bill would either explode there in police custody or start crying. It was safer to cry.

9

Pam was so grateful that Andy had helped Sandra out with Bill that she decided she would break down and actually cook for him. It had been a while since she spent any time in the kitchen. What was once a delight for her, cooking for her husband and family, had become drudgery. Her mother gladly took over the task and spent a large portion of every day planning and cooking meals for she and Pam.

"Now, I don't want you to get used to it, but I thought I might cook dinner for us," she said to him. They were, once again, sitting on the veranda, reading and drinking iced tea, looking out over the ocean.

Andy laughed. "You don't have to cook. Let's go out," he said.

She shook her head. Later, she would remember that he had tried to change her mind. "No, not tonight. You helped me, and now I want to do something nice for you. I do need to run out, though. Want to come with me?" She was thinking steak on the grill, a salad, and some fresh veggies, if she could find anything in season. "What's your favorite accompaniment with steak?"

He thought for a few minutes. "Spaghetti with oil and garlic," he answered.

She tried not to make a face. "A lotta carbs. Where'd that come from?" She had never heard of it before.

"My real name is Andretti. Italian through and through."

"Why'd you change it?" she asked.

"My dad got tired of people asking him if we were related to the race car driver," he replied.

"Were you?" she asked, interested.

"Yes."

They both started laughing.

"Well, Detective Andretti, you are having steak and spaghetti tonight. I'm intrigued now. We are both Italian...But my people have been here so long we don't even eat pasta."

"Right," Andy said, "Fabian. It never sunk in. Any relation?" He asked, smiling.

"No!"

They laughed again. The best part of her relationship with him was the laughter. They just enjoyed being together.

"Two Italians. I have no Italian traditions at all. Does your family?" Pam asked.

"Oh God, yes. We used to have the meal with seven fishes on Christmas Eve, Mass every Sunday without fail, and macaroni with gravy for Sunday dinner. My wife was very old school; we had the same thing every single day of the week. I looked forward to meals each night because I knew what she was going to cook. She would change the old recipes occasionally, so we never got tired of it."

"I guess I'm surprised that she was so old fashioned because of the makeup being delivered to the house," Pam replied. Andy confessed that he didn't cancel the delivery of makeup she had ordered after her death. Every month for two years, a package was delivered. Pam was really interested in hearing about Andy's wife.

"Right, she was a stickler about her appearance." He looked at Pam and smiled. "Like you. You are very attractive, do you know that?"

"Yes, well. Move on. You're making me nervous."

"She loved to cook authentic Italian. It was more a hobby for her than a chore. She went to classes, had every book written on it. She made her own pasta, everything always from scratch. But she didn't do breakfast or lunch. Just dinner. 'Eat up!' she would say each night. 'This is all three meals!' My girls were whizzes at fixing their own breakfast from the time they were four. They made themselves peanut butter and jelly sandwiches for school. I'd help them when I was home, reminding them to eat fruit, drink milk. 'No one in this house is starving,' she would say if I criticized her. Now, of course, we miss dinner. None of my girls are interested in cooking. We give the pizza joint down the road a good business."

"I'd like to meet your children someday. Do they know you are seeing someone?" *What if they hated that he was dating?*

"They are thrilled! 'Dad!' they would say to me. 'Get out and see people!' But you have to understand that there is not a big choice of women out there. When I met you, I thought, 'You better go for it. She is a once-in-a-lifetime woman!'"

Pam got up and went to his chair, grabbing his hand. "Come on, you are making me nervous again! Let's go to the grocery store." She pulled him up from his chair, and they left the house. They were making their own traditions. She and Jack had never gone to the grocery store together.

By dinnertime, Sandra was starting to recover after her frightening encounter. She ate her sandwich from Zabar's. But she felt like a prisoner. She had needed to get out of the house and connect with another human being and because of asshole Bill, was unable to. Now that the fear had abated, she found herself wondering what Bernice was doing, if she had heard the news about the police picking up her son again. Wisdom told Sandra to do nothing; someone would contact Bill's mother soon enough with news.

A new, harder to define emotion was what she was feeling for Pam, who had seemed to move on with her life at precision speed and was spending a glorious day at the beach with Detective Andy. When no invitation had been issued for the beach that weekend, Sandra had mixed feelings. On one hand, she needed to take care of business at her apartment. Being away every weekend like she had been doing since Jack died meant playing catch-up all week. She was always one step behind, not having grocery shopping done, or dry cleaning picked up, or her apartment cleaned, all the things that women who worked long hours struggled with. But when she was there alone, those tasks didn't seem so earth shattering. She could pick up a few things from Zabar's or put a load of laundry in each night. It didn't all have to be done at once, did it? How had she become so dependent on Pam? It was ridiculous, really. They had nothing in common but Jack, and he was dead. If he were still alive, they would be archenemies.

She went down to the lower level and picked up the remote, switching the TV on. It was then that she noticed something different, something out of place. Looking up at the exit door to the backyard, she saw the safety chain still in place. The dresser was still in front of the window, and the arrangement of glass bottles she had put on the top of it in case someone tried to get in were undisturbed. It was a smell. The smell of a man, clean, but his sweat musky and just this side of unpleasant. She reached for the light switch and turned the overhead lights on.

"Hello?" She could barely get it out. She walked to the bathroom door and reached in for the light, switching it on. Empty. The staircase to the upstairs elongated exponentially. She ran for it, which was ridiculous because there was no one there. When she got to the top of the stairs, she hesitated. *What if someone had been in my bedroom the whole time?* Her heart was beating wildly in her chest. She repeated the same procedure in each room, reaching in, feeling for the light switch, turning the light on, and searching, under her bed, in her bathroom and closet. There was no sign that anyone had been there. But the smell lingered. She peeked out the curtain to the back in case someone with BO was in her yard. It was empty.

That fucker has succeeded into making me paranoid and frightened. At that moment, her buzzer went off. She nearly jumped into the ceiling. The intercom was in the front hallway, so she ran out to it, pushing the buzzer and speaking a frightened hello. If it was Bill again, she was definitely buying a gun on Monday. As it turned out, gratefully, wonderfully, the police had come to take her statement. She had completely forgotten about it. She didn't say anything more, just pushed the unlock button. Seconds later, there was a knock on her door. She peered out the peephole, and there were two men in plainclothes standing at her door.

"Can I see some ID?" she asked. Without hesitation, both men put their picture IDs up for her to see. She unlocked her door, taking the chain off and opening up for the police. "Sorry, come in," she said.

"It's good to cautious," the older of the two said. Sandra thought it was strange that policemen always traveled in pairs of differing ages. As they walked by her into the apartment, she sniffed them. Just in case. The smell in her downstairs wasn't them. The younger man caught the sniff and looked at her in a strange way.

"I noticed the smell of a man in my basement a few minutes ago, and it has scared the heck out of me."

"I'm Tom, and this is Jim," said the younger man. "So was it us?" he asked.

"No. Here, have a seat." She pointed to the round table off her galley kitchen. It was at a window that overlooked a blind alleyway. There were several birdfeeders hanging in a tree of heaven. She had made her own view.

Tom glanced at her, taking in that view as well. She was so pretty. "Do you want us to take a look around first?" Tom asked.

"Would you mind? I don't need to tell you that I was nervous about that jerk coming to my apartment and then to notice that someone was here..." She shuddered, remembering the hair rising up on the back of her neck.

Jim put his arm out in a "show me the way" movement. They went down the lower level and searched under the bed, behind the couch, in the bathroom again, and nothing. They went out the back door and searched around the concrete patio and the blind alley, but saw nothing suspicious. In spite of the negative search, Sandra could not relax. She felt certain someone had been in her house, either while she was upstairs or before she got home, and in the hurriedness of locking herself in, she hadn't noticed the odor. The men followed her back upstairs, Tom keeping his eyes averted so he wasn't overtly staring at the young woman's ass.

She automatically went into the galley kitchen and put the teapot on, gathering mugs for three people. They asked her about the neighborhood, how long she had lived there, chatty questions, safe conversation that slowly helped put Sandra at ease. Soon they would begin questioning her about the creep who was waiting for her to come home.

Carrying a tray with the tea things in, Sandra was happy for the company and proceeded to put mugs in front of each man. They were watching her, enjoying the view. Even the older man, Jim, seemed oblivious to anything but Sandra moving around her kitchen. It brought a smile to his face. His wife would say, "Keep dreaming, buster."

"Coffee or tea?" she asked, breaking the revelry. "It's instant, if that is okay." Jim took the coffee; Tom asked for tea. She went back to the kitchen and brought out a box of Krispy Kremes. "Didn't expect this, did you?" she said, responding to the shocked look on their faces. She put little plates in front of each man and got one for herself.

"What happened today?" Tom asked her. He reached into the box of donuts and took a glazed one for himself, which would amount to an extra thirty minutes on the elliptical machine.

Sandra told them about the confrontation at Bernice's and then how Bill must have followed her home, missing that she went into Zabar's. She could tell that both men were curious about her relationship with the Smiths. She decided to let them ask questions, and she would give them what they needed and no more. She wasn't about to appeal to their curiosity.

"So do you have a history with Bill Smith?" Jim asked. "It's only relevant as far as him stalking you."

Sandra debated whether or not to tell them about Jack. She decided it was important because of the way he had died, but then remembered that if Bill were in custody, they would probably follow the trail of charges and see that he had one for assault. "I am a friend of the family." She decided that any more information than that was irrelevant. "As far as a relationship with just Bill goes, no."

"Was he interested in having a romantic relationship with you? I'm just trying to establish why he would come here," Tom said. He was also interested in finding this out for his own personal knowledge.

"He's trying to borrow money from me." Then she thought that the business thing might be important. "I am part owner of a business that used to belong to his brother. He was hoping we would field clients his way. That is not going to happen, and I think he is holding a grudge."

Tom was writing down this information.

"You may have to consider filing a restraining order against this man," Jim said. "He sounds pretty desperate. The truth is he might be going back to jail because of his high jinx today. In that case, you will be safe. But if he gets out, we need to think of your safety, and I think a restraining order with a unit assigned here might be a good idea." He looked at Tom for confirmation. He'd be willing to spend the night if necessary, but kept that to himself.

"Absolutely. If you would like, you could come downtown with us. We can walk you through the process," Tom agreed.

"The sooner you take care of it, the better. The event just happened today and filing right away shows the impact Bill Smith has on your well-being. Feeling unsafe is very subjective; no one can refute it." He was fighting with himself not to take another donut, and lost. He reached into the box and took one more. "Okay, I think we are about done here. If we stay much longer, this box will be empty." He tried not to lick his fingers.

They stood up, the men taking their mugs to the kitchen. Sandra was glad she had straightened up her apartment. She noticed the one named Tom looking around, admiring the place. They waited while she got her purse and keys.

Jim motioned down the stairs with his finger. "Want me to take another look? I'll check the locks again."

Sandra nodded yes, smiling.

Upon return, he validated her concern. "I smelled a smell down there, too," he said. *Great*, she thought. *What the hell could it be?*

10

Pam and Andy spent a full hour in the grocery store, discussing like and dislikes, comparing brands, arguing about the benefits of buying organic, local, in season. He had picked up a bunch of tomatoes from Chile.

"I don't think so!" she exclaimed. "Let's buy hydroponics, grown ten miles from here."

"They cost four dollars a pound!" he said.

"Too bad. You are putting that garbage in your body. Do you think it has one nutrient left after it's been on a freight train for ten days? No way!" She took him by the arm and dragged him to the other side of the veggie case. "All of these greens were harvested right here this weekend. We'll make a salad with a few peas and some yummy early peppers thrown in. It's too early for tomatoes in the mid-Atlantic."

He laughed, surprised at her passion for food. "Did you shop like this when Jack was alive?" he asked, honestly interested.

"About four times a week," she said. "I was at the farmers' market every day during the weekend. Now that my mother is cooking, I never think about it. It has left a void because it was something I enjoyed. Not baking or fancy things. Meat and potatoes. Fish and salad. Boring stuff."

"Those are my kind of meals," Andy said. "Replace the potato with macaroni."

They pushed the cart together over to the fresh pasta aisle.

"I probably won't make it from scratch. Is this okay?"

He nodded yes.

"The truth is I like the old-fashioned dry kind, too." She put several packages in the basket.

He thought that was a good sign. She was stocking up for him.

They finished their shopping and drove back to Pam's house. She was starting to feel a little weary. Would she ever again want to be around someone twenty-four/seven? She wondered if he expected her to spend the evening with him after they ate, even though they had spent the day together. They got to the beach and unloaded the groceries. It was nearing 6:00, not too early to eat. She would grill steaks out on the veranda.

"Can you boil water?" she asked Andy.

"Barely. Do you want me to do the pasta?"

"Do you mind? We can fire up the stove out there."

They gathered up all the things they would need to cook outside.

The beach crowd was starting to thin out as dinnertime approached. Pam had loved this time of the evening when Jack was alive. He would come in from his day of whatever activity he had been involved in and, after he showered, join her to keep her company while she prepared their meal. Knowing that he had spent the day with her sister and probably had sex with her, too, didn't diminish the impact the time they spent together had on her. Feeling like a deflated balloon, she plunked down in a chair. Andy could see that something had distressed her.

"What just happened?" he asked her. They had decided early on that, no matter how painful, honesty had to be the best policy. He sat down beside her, looking out over the ocean. Gulls were crying, and the waves were hitting the beach with force today.

"I guess I'm thinking of someone who I used to do these things with, someone who I thought was a certain type of person and who turned out to be a much different man." She had never divulged any of the gruesome details of her marriage; just him knowing her financial status was quite enough for starters.

Andy didn't know if he should say anything in response to her statement. If she wanted to elaborate, she could. He was tempted to offer to leave, but thinking that may be what she wanted, he hesitated. "How so?" he finally asked.

She looked at him. "Do you really want to know? I'm not sure you should. It will change your opinion of me, that's inevitable. I can almost hear you thinking, 'How could she be so stupid?' And I don't know that I am ready to 'out' Jack with you yet. We don't know each other well enough." She felt a strong loyalty to her late husband, no matter how horrible a reprobate he may have been. She didn't think she could bear being put into a position of having to defend him, especially to an almost stranger.

"I think I know what you mean. There are things about my wife that explain a lot about the man that I am, but it wouldn't be loyal of me to expose her frailties to you yet."

She was looking at him thinking, *You have no idea.*

"And I promise you, no matter what were to happen between us, I will never toss anything Jack did up to you."

It was the first time he had used Jack's name. It lingered in the air above their heads for a few seconds, vibrating. Jack.

"Okay, well, suffice it to say that he was not the man I thought he was. That's about all I can get out right now. He was...unfaithful. That is a mild word for what he was to our marriage." She sat back, certain now that she was not cooking dinner for them. "Look, Andy, I am in a state. Thank you for not trying to talk me out of it. I think it is just part of the grieving process. Would you mind very much if we called it a night?" She looked at him imploringly.

"No, I understand. I won't pretend I'm not disappointed because I really wanted to see you tonight." He stood up then, thinking they needed to say good-bye and not drag it out, for her sake. He reached out for her and pulled her to him gently, as a friend would. They weren't lovers yet. He kept his arm around her shoulders as they walked to the front door. He opened it, and they smiled and said good-bye. She didn't watch him walk to his car as she had in the past, but shut the door and locked it. She needed to put her pj's on, fix something inappropriate to eat, and eat it in front of the television while sitting in bed. Just thinking about it made her feel better. She gathered up the stuff they had hauled out to the veranda and stashed it away. She looked in the pantry and pulled out a box of the kid's Cocoa Krispies. It was probably stale, but she didn't care. She got a big mixing bowl out and poured at least half the box in it and then poured milk over that. She got a spoon and took the bowl into her bedroom. It was another Saturday night in Babylon.

II

Columbus Circle in the Upper West Side of Manhattan was an enclave of wealth and prestige. Slowly, inevitably homogenized business was taking over, and the predictable generic retail stores were opening up, while the small, independent places were closing. The wonderful little coffee shop that Bernice and Jack went to for their weekly lunch finally succumbed and closed their doors. It was such a slap in her face; she took it personally. They should have warned her so she could visit one last time. She had walked there alone Saturday morning to have breakfast. The shock of it not being open was bad enough, but when she realized it had gone out of business, she came close to falling over on the sidewalk. Barely making it home, she struggled to get up the stairs and into her room.

"Oh Jack, our place is closed for good," she said to his ghost. She closed her eyes, remembering the times they went there together before he found out the truth about his father and didn't speak to her again. Bowing her head, she started to weep. It was so infrequent that she allowed herself to feel, to grieve. Her daughter-in-law had asked her how she did it. How did she suffer such loss and go on as though nothing had changed?

"It takes too long to recover if I allow myself to feel too much," she had replied. A good analogy, she thought, was having a lazy day, one in which you didn't bother to put makeup on, or brush your teeth, or even get dressed. You could do that in your youth and get up the next day, preparing to face the world again. When you aged, that slight lapse would make it almost impossible to recover from. At her age, she had to stay on her toes, stay vigilant. She understood, for the first time, those women in rest homes who didn't even bother to comb their hair. It was enough that they managed to brush their teeth. Taking care of her physical body was getting harder and harder; remembering if she had washed her face was even a chore. *What is happening to me?* Now she was struggling to get out of bed. She hadn't showered in days. Bill had noticed right away, and she was embarrassed.

She heard the buzzer on the front door. *Who would bother me on a Sunday morning without calling first?* She hoped it was the paperboy. She wasn't ready to entertain her grandchildren today; small children would be intolerable. There was a knock on her bedroom door. Bernice said to come in. It was Mildred, but Pam was behind her. *Oh God. No.*

"It's you," Bernice said. She started to weep again. "Who told you to come here?" Pam was the last person she needed to see right at that moment.

Pam walked over to the chair where her mother-in-law was sitting and knelt down in front of her. She gathered her in her arms and starting gently rubbing her back. "I'm so sorry. I should have called you. Please forgive me." Pam held her while she cried, patiently waiting for the moment to pass. She took one arm off of her and leaned over to get a tissue from her dressing table. She put it up to Bernice's face and gently wiped the skin under her eyes.

Bernice wondered how Pam always managed to have breath like fresh flowers. She didn't want to admit there was anything about Pam that was likable.

"Please forgive me," Pam repeated. "I should have never let so much time pass between visits." She didn't know if Bernice knew what had transpired yesterday; Mildred wasn't able to tell her much. Pam felt she had to stay loyal to Anne, but the truth had to come out. Sandra was on her way over, and they would tell Bernice together. She stood up and took Bernice's hands to help her up. "How about a nice shower?"

Bernice allowed herself to be lead to the bathroom. Mildred stood with her head bowed, ashamed in some way for not being more observant to what was happening with her employer. Pam helped her mother-in-law get into the shower stall. She was shocked at how thin Bernice had gotten this summer, little more than a skeleton with skin over the bones. She remembered her own frail frame. Mildred got fresh clothes out. Pam washed her hair, and when she was finished, the two of them primped and powdered Bernice. She looked like her old self when they got done. Pam suspected that she was suffering from depression. She would take her to the doctor on Monday. The attention made Bernice feel better. Pam opened the makeup drawer and pulled out powder and lipstick for her to apply. Not wanting to undermine her self-respect was important. Pam understood how fragile Bernice had become. Pam had moments of it herself.

Through the previous night, Pam had gone over again and again what had happened to her husband's family. The financial failure was grave enough, but then to have Anne and Bill pull their crap? It was just too much. The best thing that could happen would be to have him go back to jail for a long time. She didn't know yet if he had been released or if he was on his way back to Rikers. She wasn't sure what was going to happen to Anne. Pam didn't want her to go jail for what she had done because it would mean the boys being without both parents. Bill certainly wasn't in any shape to care for two young children. Pam would do what she could to see that justice was done, but the family's needs were met as well.

"Thank you, Pam. Thank you," Bernice said to her. She knew she had been hard on her daughter-in-law over the years, even cruel. Now she was the only one who seemed to care about her.

"Would you like luncheon served, madam?" Mildred asked, keeping the formality alive for the sake of the old lady, whose days in this lavish setting may be numbered.

"Yes, please, Mildred. Thank you," Bernice said.

The three women went down the stairs together, talking about how Bernice had started her weekend, with the discovery that the coffee shop where she and Jack went to eat every week for years had finally closed its doors for good. She was still upset about it.

"Maybe you shouldn't walk that far from the house, Bernice. Why didn't Ben take you?" *She was paying for a full-time driver. What the hell was she walking around New York for?*

"To tell you the truth, I forgot about him. I know, I am losing it." At least she was smiling.

"No, I think you have clinical depression, and we are going to go to the doctor tomorrow to find out if there isn't anything he can give you. Memory loss like that can be from something as simple as depression. Let's just check it out." She was glad she wasn't getting an argument. As long as she was the only one with money, she was fairly sure she would be getting her way all the time.

As soon as she could, Pam gave the staff their back pay, apologizing to them for the inconvenience. She didn't go into details with them. Cash for groceries and gasoline for the limousine was also handed over to Mildred, with the instructions to save receipts. She asked her for bills for the gardener, too. The expenses for this old house would be looked at carefully; if Bernice could stay here, she may have to be put on a budget. It would be something that would be discussed. She was certain of one important point, and that was that the contents of this house would be going to an auction house before the summer was over.

Sandra finally arrived just as Mildred was serving lunch in the den. She bent over and kissed Bernice on the cheek. "Hello, again!"

She and Pam embraced and gave each other a peck on the cheek.

Bernice was confused, looking from woman to woman and back. "Did I forget something? I feel like I planned a party and then didn't invite myself."

They laughed and sat down across from Bernice.

"No, dear, you didn't forget anything," Sandra answered. "We invited ourselves here because we have some news. We thought it would be better if we were both here with you. I almost don't know where to start." Sandra looked at Pam for help. Maybe they should have planned this better.

"Well, let's start with money. That seems to be what is foremost on everyone's mind. When Sandra was here yesterday, you and Bill asked her for money. Do you remember that?" Pam asked.

Bernice nodded her head yes.

"Okay, good! Well, we found out through a circuitous way that Anne had been intercepting the checks I have been sending for you each week. I sent the same amount Jack did, since that seemed to be enough to keep the house running smoothly. Two thousand dollars a week. Do you both follow me?"

Sandra said, "Yes," while Bernice, in shock, nodded her head.

"Did you ask Anne about it?" Bernice asked.

Here goes, thought Pam. "Actually, Bernice, I called the police instead."

"Why'd you do that?" Bernice snapped. "Why not just confront her? Why'd you have to involve the police?" Her voice had gotten loud enough to alert Mildred, who came to the den and shut the doors leading to the main hallway. "What possible good did it do to get the police involved? What did Anne do?"

Bernice was clearly upset, so Pam decided to keep it simple. They probably would not be telling her about Sandra's encounter with Bill, either.

"Bernice, Anne forged your name on checks meant for you. It was my money. Your staff has gone without pay for over a month. Did you know that? No bills have been paid. Mildred was buying food with her own money." She gave Bernice a chance to catch up.

Instead, she rang for Mildred. The door to the den opened.

"Mildred, come in. Please tell my daughter-in-law that I have been paying you."

Mildred took another step into the room. "No, madam, we haven't been paid. Miss Pam paid us this morning for the past seven weeks."

Bernice looked like she had been slapped. "Are you telling me no one has been paid?"

She was looking at Pam, so Pam answered her.

"That's what she is telling you. The gardener hasn't been paid, and Ben has been buying gas out of his pocket as well. Did you think you were paying them?" Pam thought, *Maybe it is more than depression, after all.*

"I'm not sure what I thought now. My God! What the heck have I been doing all summer? Millie, why didn't you tell me you hadn't been paid? I feel horrible!"

"You just lost your son, madam. We could wait. We were sure that once Mr. Bill got out of...um...jail that he would take care of it."

He sure did, Pam thought. No one said anything for a moment. And then for the second time that day, Bernice bowed her head and started to weep. Pam got up and put her hand on Mildred's arm.

"You can go now, Mildred. Thank you."

She left the room, softly closing the door behind her.

"Oh my God, what is happening to me? Of course I don't have any money! What was I thinking that I could

88

stay in this house, week after week?" She looked up at
Pam. "What am I going to do?"

Pam was going to grab the opportunity. "Bernice,
Bill mentioned to Sandra yesterday that you had agreed to
sell off the art in the house and in storage. Is that correct?"

Bernice slowly shook her head yes. "I thought it was
a bad dream. This collection is beyond price; it was in
Harold's family forever. He will never forgive me."

"I think he would want you to keep living here as long
as you could, and if that meant selling something that you
aren't looking at, then he would agree. Don't sell what you
really love, like the portrait in your bedroom. But all the
pieces in storage and upstairs that no one sees, let someone else who really wants it enjoy it every day." *Oh Jesus,
I sound like a broken record.* "Look at it this way, Bernice.
Once us elders die, the kids will have to get rid of all of this
stuff and the stuff in my house and in Bill's, so why wait for
them to do it? It will make life so much easier for them."

"But it's their inheritance!" she whined.

"If you are living in a crappy apartment somewhere,
what is their inheritance going to be? Jack left me comfortable, but I'm not Trump, for God's sake. We have to be
realistic about this. Artwork that is boxed up and possibly
getting ruined is worth nothing."

"She's right, Bernice," said Sandra. "We talked about
you living in the Madison Avenue apartment, but after
this place, you would be miserable there." She walked over
to the courtyard. "You would miss this, for one thing."

They looked out the window at the colorful display
and the fountain.

"All right. It makes sense. And I would get to stay in the house. But what if the collection doesn't bring in enough money? What then?" It seemed as though the fog were clearing and Bernice was finally getting the point.

"We will cross that bridge when we come to it, okay? Besides, just what is in this room alone would support you for years." Pam had had enough. She wondered if Sandra could tie things up. She wanted to get out of that house. She would have to come back the next day to take Bernice to the doctor.

"I'll let you think about it for a while, okay? I have to get back home; my mother is returning from Connecticut this afternoon." She gathered up her purse and gloves. "Can you believe I drove into Manhattan on a Sunday? I ought to have my head examined."

They said their good-byes, and Pam left.

She had parked her car in the back, by the garage, so she would have to walk around the house from the front door. She saw a police car out in front. *What the heck is going on?* She walked back through the hall.

"Sandra, could I see you out here?" she called into the den.

Sandra came right out. "What's up?" she asked.

"There's a cop car out in front! Do you suppose they are looking for Bill?"

"No, I meant to tell you about it, but I haven't had time. I filed a restraining order against Bill, and they also have a detail follow me around. It's a guy named Tom..." Sandra smiled, and the implication was clear.

"Only you could have your own personal policeman at the expense of the NYPD." Pam laughed. "Okay, well, as long as they're outside, you'll be safe, I guess. Do we even know what has happened to Bill and Anne?"

Sandra took her hand and led her to the door. "Let's go find out. Wait one minute." She ran back to the den to tell Bernice she would be back.

When she returned, they walked out to the police car together.

"This is my sister-in-law, Pam," Sandra said to Tom Adams.

They exchanged pleasantries.

Then Pam whispered, "Sister-in-law?"

Sandra didn't get it right away. "Oh my God! It just slipped out! I'm sorry. I hope it doesn't seem disrespectful."

Pam thought for a moment. "No. I like it. Call me later!" They hugged, and Pam said good-bye to the young detective. She smelled a romance brewing. She wondered if he knew about the baby. Jack's baby. A pang of heartache made a brief appearance. She thought about both of them being involved with cops. That would be a real coincidence. *Oh well, he was just keeping an eye on her, not asking her to get married.* "Wait! We forgot to ask about Anne and Bill!" Pam walked back to the car.

"Do you have any news about Bonnie and Clyde?" Sandra asked Tom.

"He's still in city jail, and she's home with their kids. We are waiting for hallowed Monday."

The women nodded to each other, and Pam went to her car, leaving Sandra to go back in with Bernice. She was going to say good-bye to her and go back home with Detective Adams.

Pam drove the car out of the mansion drive and headed toward the Fifty-ninth Street Bridge. Traffic was horrible coming into the city, against her, so the drive home should be okay. She wondered why she had lied about her mother coming home. Nelda wasn't due home until next Friday. She felt it her obligation to make sure her mother-in-law was okay, but to stay there any longer, even with Sandra there, felt intolerable. So much water under the bridge. Mildly nauseated and headachy, she couldn't shake the despair she began having when Andy was with her last night. She had a feeling she couldn't rationalize that something more was going to happen. The horror of the Smiths hadn't stopped with Jack's death.

12

Marie couldn't wait to get home. Although the weekend was very relaxing, with great accommodations and delicious food and wine, there was something not gelling about Jeff Babcock. She couldn't put her finger on it. But she felt like she was wasting her time. For one thing, he wasn't very protective of her. She was a little put off that he didn't stop serving her wine sooner. Like coffee was going to keep her from getting a DUI. Yes, she was an adult, but he was pushing it on her and then telling her she needed to get on the road. *What was his hurry?* A real gentleman would have insisted she spend the night and leave for work early Monday morning. She thought of his phone ringing, the eagerness he had to get back in the house to answer. *Was he double dating?*

Finally, the lights of the city appeared below her. Merging on the Henry Hudson, she thought how lucky she was to have such a great apartment. Then she reminded herself that she was being schizophrenic. She hated her apartment! Anyway, she would love it tonight because it wasn't upstate. What she really hated was anything old and moldering, like that "new condo wannabe" Jeff lived in, with its fancy plumbing fixtures attached to ancient old plumbing. He had said to her at least fifty times, "Don't flush more than six sheets of toilet paper down at a time." *Huh? You've got to be kidding me!*

Face it, kiddo, she thought to herself, *no one is going to be able to replace Jack.* She wondered how Pam did it. Sure, Andy was nice looking, and he was obviously head over heels in love with Pam. But he was no Jack. Jack was so smooth. He was larger than life. Jeff Babcock was a nobody. He had two nice vacation homes, but they weren't that nice. And he was a fabulous cook. However, it wasn't the greatest selling point for an anorexic. She wondered if they would be together long enough for that lovely fact about her to be revealed. She pulled into her parking garage and parked the car. It felt so good to be home.

Dragging her suitcase into the elevator, she pushed the button to her floor. When she stepped into the hallway, a fleeting sense of gratitude overcame her. She unlocked her door, and the lighted vista of New Jersey was the first thing to greet her. It was so beautiful. The sun had just set, the lights from Weehawken were starting to come on, and the red reflection on the Palisades...Well, it was breathtaking. She could afford to be grateful, just for a second. "Thank you, God. Forgive me for being miserable," she said to the ceiling.

Anne Smith was in trouble. *What the hell am I going to do?* She never thought she would get caught cashing Pam's checks. The truth was she didn't see anything wrong with it, so what was there to get caught? She stuck to her story that she thought the money was for her use while Bill was incarcerated. So they could take her to court, and she would prettily cry her way out of trouble. It was that absolute asshole of a husband of hers who was to blame, and she was going to make sure he paid.

Around lunchtime on Sunday, Tom Adams came into the precinct to finish up some work. On top of a pile of papers on his desk was a copy of a refusal to hear William Smith due to lack of evidence.

"Fuck," Tom said out loud. This meant Bill would be released today. It had been almost twenty-four hours since they brought him in. Now time was up, and the judge was refusing to hear the evidence that he broke parole by causing a disturbance. It had been a slim chance to get him back to Rikers, but they wanted to take it, mainly to keep him from harassing Sandra Benson.

Well, he had exactly twenty-four hours, and Tom would wait until thirty seconds before the time was up to unlock the cell door. Smith's attorney hadn't tried to have him released earlier; there was no sign that he had even called his attorney. Tom guessed there was a money issue, but in that case, a public defender would have been provided, and it looked like he refused. Either Bill Smith had given up or was avoiding going home.

For the second time in two days, Anne Smith received a phone call from prison, telling her she could come pick up her husband. The previous night, when he didn't come home from his mother's, she didn't even bother to call there. She didn't care. Her boys had a wonderful Saturday with their mother, and she didn't see any reason in hell to disrupt that. So when the call came Sunday to come pick Bill up downtown, she simply told the caller to "drop dead" and hung up. He could get his own fucking ride home.

She fixed lunch for her boys and then asked a neighbor who had babysat for them yesterday to watch them again. She wasn't going to hide what was going on or pretend that everything was okay. "Bill spent the night in jail again and is coming home today. I don't want him upsetting the boys."

Her neighbor was more than happy to help out if it would keep her son's playmates safe. The screaming and sounds of flesh slapping flesh had reverberated through the neighborhood before. *It has been so peaceful this summer while that prick was in jail.*

"Feel free to call 911 if you hear anything suspicious," Anne whispered as she walked out the door, waving goodbye to her sons.

Around 1:00, Anne heard a cab pull up in front of their brownstone. She didn't have to look to know who it was. She wondered how he was going to manage to twist this around to be her fault. *Did he know about the check thing yet?* He didn't have a key, but she decided to let him knock to get in. She wasn't going to greet him at the door.

He knocked. She opened the door, trying as hard as she could to keep her face expressionless. *At least he has the decency to be contrite*, she thought as she stepped aside to let him pass. He was trying to keep the expression on his face neutral, too. She imagined them going at each other, beating with their fists and rolling on the floor. Or if she had a gun, putting the barrel right up to his nose and pulling the trigger.

Bill threw his belongings down on the chair and went right to the dining room table, pulling out a chair. "What's for lunch? I'm starving."

So typical of him, she thought. *No hello, no attempt at hugging. How have I stayed with him all these years?* She went into the kitchen and dished up the leftovers from her sons' lunch. She placed the plate in front of him.

"Yum! What's this? Boxed macaroni and cheese! Hot dogs! I'm home!" he yelled to the air sarcastically.

Anne wanted to pick the plate up and smash his face with it, but instead, she said, "Yes, it's what the boys had. I'd have prepared a gourmet meal for you if I had known you were going to visit your family today." She tried to keep the sarcasm out of her voice; it would hold up better in court that way.

"Well, this is just delicious, thank you so much!" He ate the food without any further comment.

Anne stood in the kitchen doorway, arms folded across the front of her body. *Bill looks like hell. But that was his doing*, she thought.

"Where are my sons?" he finally asked.

"Next door. We need to talk, and they are scared enough of you not to expose them to any more fights." She knew she had, once again, crossed that invisible boundary with him.

"The only reason my sons are afraid of me is because of the garbage you fed their heads while I was gone."

"Whatever, Bill. I'm not fighting with you. Tell me what we are going to do next. I understand that we are ruined. It was lovely of you to go away for the summer and leave me with sixty dollars in the bank."

"Right! Let's talk about that. So you were forging my mother's checks? Did I hear that correctly?"

"You did. But that isn't anything for you to worry about. You will do time for your own fun and games. By the way, what took you to jail yesterday? I can't wait to find out."

"Actually, I scared the shit out of my late brother's girlfriend." He smiled up at Anne, knowing that would piss her off.

"I figured as much. Well, Bill, it's obvious we can't stay together. You are going to have to kill me before I let you near the boys, unless someone else is here to referee. The neighbors are ready to call the cops if they hear anything over here, even a knock on the floor. So don't get any ideas. The only reason I let you in today is so you can get your clothes. Go to your mother's." Anne went to the back of the house, where there was a small office. She closed and locked the door behind her. She had her cell phone all ready with 911 on speed dial. She wasn't taking any chances.

She heard Bill get up, the legs of the chair scraping on the wooden floor. He walked across the room, and then there was the sound of cutlery and china being placed in the sink. It amazed her, once again, that his wrath rarely came out against inanimate objects. He didn't throw things. She remembered he may have thrown his keys at her once; she had a small cut under her left eye that had required stitches, but she wasn't sure if it was the keys or his hand that had done the damage. Although she had never come right out and called the police on him, the neighbors had intervened enough times and the police had seen enough handprints on her flesh to know that she was being victimized. At least her hope was that they did.

From where he stood at the end of the hallway, Bill saw the closed door of the office. He examined his choices at that point. He could give in to what he wanted to do, which was to fly down the hall, bash the door down, take Anne by her scrawny throat, and squeeze the life out of her, or go upstairs to their room and pack a bag to take to his mother's. If he gave in to his first choice, he would end up in jail again. He thought of his father, which he didn't do very often. He didn't have to; Harold's acts were emblazoned upon his brain. But, at this moment, he thought specifically of the devastation the man left in his wake. *Do I want that same legacy for my boys?* Walking into their living room and sitting down on the world's most uncomfortable chair, Bill leaned over to pick up a portrait of his children. It was over a year old, and they had grown from babyhood to preschool in that time. He traced the lines of their faces with his finger. They were so innocent. Both of them were a perfect combination of he and Anne. Had his father ever looked at his sons the same way? Or had he planned on brutalizing them from the beginning?

He wished Jack were still alive. Then he could finally talk to him about their childhood. He knew Jack had tried to protect him, that he had threatened Harold. The only time the two of them ever talked about what they experienced was when Jack got that lawyer to write up a false document charging Harold with sodomy and child rape. He only did it to threaten the old man. There were no legal grounds to charge him; the acts had taken place forty years before. Harold dropped dead of a heart attack shortly after receiving the document; Jack didn't even have the luxury of seeing the man squirm. At the time, Bill was in such denial that he was angry with Jack, accusing him of trying to humiliate the whole family, to ruin the business. Of course, it was already ruined.

His father did not love him; it was impossible. A man cannot rape his son and love him at the same time. Bill had been able to separate what was happening to him, the reality of the act, the pain, from his conscious mind. He often had the sensation that he was leaving the room where his father was raping him. When he was thirteen, he had braces put on his teeth. His father held his hand across the boy's mouth to keep him from screaming. The first time Harold raped Bill after the braces were put on, the entire interior of his mouth was lacerated, blood pouring from him like a faucet. He had no awareness of it. When Harold was finished with him, he threw a towel at him and told him to clean his mouth off. He went into his bathroom and turned the light on. When he saw himself, saw the blood all over his face and the stream of blood coming from his lip, he gave an ear-splitting scream. But then something awful happened. He continued to scream and was either unable to stop or had no awareness that he could. What was supposed to be one burst of fear turned into a long, pulsating yodel of screaming that could be heard throughout the house, out into the courtyard, and down to Columbus Circle.

Bernice was in a drunken stupor in her room, and Jack was in the courtyard with friends of his, waiting for Harold to coach their soccer practice. The horrible screaming reached Jack's ears, and he knew what it was. He dismissed his friends, telling them to leave and that practice would be canceled. Then, shooting his father a look of death, he ran up to his brother's room. He grabbed the boy and cradled him, whispering to him that he would be okay, that he would be fine, that nothing like that would happen to him again as long as he was able to protect him. Of course, that turned out to be impossible, until Jack realized he could expose his father's deeds to the world. The only thing that kept him from doing so up till then was pride, but he no longer had pride or hope. Harold would continue to attempt to harm his boys in this way, but would not succeed. After this particular incident, he could only beat them. The rape and sodomy was over.

Bill, now in the present, lowered his head and began to sob for the third time that weekend. Everything about his life had been one big lie.

13

Puttering around her apartment, unpacking from her trip to Jeff's, and getting ready for work the next day, Marie Fabian thought about her life. She had wanted to write as a young person. But Jack, in his infinite wisdom, told her that she wouldn't be able to support herself if she wrote the way she thought of writing.

"You can always be a technical writer," he said to her. "That way you can write and make a living." Now that she thought about it, he may have been trying to prevent her from writing about him. In all the years of their relationship, from her early abuse by him until their adult relationship came to an end when he started seeing Sandra, Marie kept a diary. Nowadays they call it journaling. But back in her youth, she kept her private thoughts under lock and key. Her sister Sharon had given her the first diary—a vinyl-covered book with a cartoon of Annette Funicello as a Mouseketeer on the cover. It had a small lead lock with a key on a string. The innocent icon of her childhood held a volume of adult sexual knowledge. She hid the diary in the basement of her family home in Brooklyn and wore the key around her neck. She wrote copiously about her life with Jack and Pam before they had children. Once the babies came, she filled a book a month.

After the first sexual encounter with Jack, she came home and was up all night, writing page after page of incriminating narrative. She still had them, stacks and stacks of notebooks. In her forty-five-year lifetime, she had had two abortions—Jack's babies—and two serious bouts of anorexia that required hospitalization. She had a lot to say about surviving abuse. The sad fact was that she listened to Jack and didn't become a writer. But she wasn't dead yet.

She would go to her job as a technical editor and do what she had to do to pay her mortgage, but starting Monday, she would begin to write her story. Jack may have thought that not leaving any money to her in his will would force her to work to support herself, but it didn't occur to him that, if he died, she would suddenly have every single night of the rest of her life without him, long stretches of time, just made for writing. If that was, in fact, his plan, it had backfired on him.

She was stuffing sheets into her washing machine when the thought came over her: *There might be life without Jack.* Allowing the sheets to fall to the floor, she once again that evening felt the power of the universe and its plan for her life. Slowly dropping to her knees, she bowed her head and started to weep. It was possible that what had been a wasted life may end up having some relevance, after all.

After a productive ride from the city, Pam returned home with a list of things she wanted to accomplish running through her head. In spite of not feeling well, she made some decisions. First of all, she wanted to spruce up the veranda. Autumn at the beach was a lovely time of year. They had a heater out there for chilly days and nights, so even though it was nearing the end of summer, she figured there was at least two more months of veranda weather. She was going to get new furniture and do some landscaping. She wanted less of Jack, more of her, out there.

Secondly, she wanted to connect with Anne today. Something Bernice had said resonated with her. *Had she asked Anne about the checks?* Pam did what Andy had told her to do once the discovery that the checks had been cashed was made. She should have called Anne immediately and given her an opportunity to tell her side of the story. It wasn't too late; Monday was still a long way off.

And third, she wanted to call her sister Marie. They had been avoiding serious conversation, and she felt awful about it. She held no ill will toward her regarding her relationship with Jack. She understood what had happened and took responsibility for her part in it. Why she chose to ignore warning signs that her sister was having an affair with her husband was something that she was going to have to investigate when she felt up to it. They were practically begging her to intervene. She remembered an episode years before when Marie and Jack had a screaming fight on the beach one evening that could be heard in the house, through closed doors and windows. Pam got the children occupied in the den by turning the television up louder. When it was over, Marie came into the house and went straight to her room, closing the door. Jack came into the kitchen, where Pam was preparing Saturday-night dinner. He was chuckling to himself.

"What was that all about?" Pam asked him. "The kids and I could hear you yelling at each other, but I couldn't make out the words you were saying."

Jack laughed out loud. "She is pissed off about last weekend. She actually said she was going to report me."

"I'm afraid to ask for what," Pam replied, trying to remember what they had done a week before. She vaguely remembered that they had a tennis match, which often provoked an argument between the two of them.

"Ask her," Jack said in his cocky way, sure that Marie wouldn't do or say anything that would jeopardize her relationship with him.

So the next morning, after her sister's anger had defused and she was feeling protective of Jack again, Pam cornered her. "Jack said you told him you were going to report him. Who were you going to report him to?"

Marie was clearly uncomfortable, looking a little surprised that Jack would reveal that information to his wife. "To anybody who would listen," Marie answered. If she had been asked the night before, she would have said, "Child Protective Services." But this morning, she had already forgiven him; he had visited her in the night for makeup sex and was in Marie's good graces once again.

Examining why she failed to protect her sister would be done at another time. Right now, all she wanted to do was heal from the trauma of losing her husband and find out what she could about his other life.

She made a conscious decision every morning to change her source of thinking from an angry perspective to one of forgiveness and love. She understood that since Jack was dead, the only one she would be hurting was herself and, ultimately, her children if she dwelled on his misdeeds. She dealt with each new revelation as it came to her, getting angry, finding a rationalization for it that satisfied her for the time being, and then putting it out of her head. Even seeing Marie and Sandra every weekend had taken a toll; the two of them had issues that they wanted to hash out, and it was becoming too much for Pam. She decided a little space was called for.

But right now she missed her sister. She put her purse and gloves away and changed her Sunday city clothes for comfortable jeans and picked up the phone to call Marie, who was in Rhinebeck. She was grocery shopping upstate for the third time that weekend.

"What's going on? Is he having a party?" Pam asked.

"Not that I know of," Marie whispered. "It's all we have done—go to the grocery store in Hyde Park, drive back here, go to the farmers' market, drive back up to another grocery store. I'm losing my appetite just repeating it."

"You won't believe this, but I had a date at a grocery store last night, too," Pam admitted.

"How was it?" Marie asked.

"Okay while we were there, but not so good once we got back here. I started thinking about you know who."

"Oh, Pam," Marie said. "I keep comparing this poor man to Jack," she whispered again.

"How's he measuring up?" Pam wanted to know.

"He lost," Marie said and started laughing. "No one will win that contest."

Pam smiled. "Oh Lord, I guess it's hopeless."

The two women said good-bye to each other, with promises they would talk when Marie got back to the city that evening.

While she was still in a talking mode, Pam looked for Anne's phone number and dialed it.

She answered on the first ring.

"Anne, it's Pam," she said.

There was silence.

I'm not saying anything, Pam thought. *Maybe she will hang up.*

Finally, though, Anne spoke. "I was wondering when you were going to call me." She had a tone to her voice that Pam found disconcerting.

Is Anne going to blame me for something? "Why is that?" she asked, deciding to play dumb.

"Well, since you shot him, since you shot Bill, and your accusations put my husband in jail for two months, it would seem like the decent thing to do would be to at least find out how we are doing," Anne said.

"How *are* you doing, Anne? It's not that I didn't want to know or didn't think of you. There were other things on my mind this summer, that's all. It was nothing personal," Pam explained, thinking, *Why am I even going there?*

"I think you have a lot of nerve calling me. Did you ever once think that we might be in trouble here with Bill gone? You knew about the mess we were in financially, in large part because of Jack."

"I am sorry. I did know about the mess you were in, which is why I continued sending money to Bernice. My understanding was that she shared that money with you and Bill." Pam decided to ignore the comment about Jack.

"It never occurred to you that my boys would love to spend a day on the beach or that I would like to get out of the city?" Anne said.

"Actually, no, I never thought of it. Why didn't you call me and ask? Or just come over? This house has been open to anyone who chose to use it all the years we have lived here. My feeling has always been that it was too far from the resorts, that it wasn't a real vacation spot." And then Pam remembered Bill's insulting comment to Jack. "Bill even told Jack one time when he refused our offer to have you here for the weekend that, if we wanted company, we should have bought in the Hamptons."

"That's an outright lie! I was in on that conversation! Why would we want to come there and have you flaunt your perfect life in front of us? I knew Jack had taken more than his share from the business so you could have that house! It was Jack's fault that we were in trouble!"

"Anne, you have to believe me when I tell you that my life is far from perfect, and if you feel we flaunted that in front of you, I am truly sorry. Truly. And as far as Jack taking more than his share from the business, he only worked for Harold for a short time. He went out on his own before we were even married. He started his business when he was still in graduate school."

"I know for a fact that Harold financed Jack's business and the start-up was all from him; Bill sacrificed so Jack would have clients." Anne was out of breath. Pam thought *Anne might be repeating lies Bill told her to keep her from being angry with him.*

"Bill was still in high school when Jack went out on his own! Anne, I can prove what I am telling you. No one wanted to ruin Harold or see him ruin his business. You just have to trust me." And then, suddenly, Pam wasn't so sure. *What if Jack had lied about the business the same way he*

lied about everything else, completely and without conscience?
She didn't want to talk to Anne anymore, not now or the
next day or the day after that. Anne could hire attorneys
to figure out who stole what from whom, if need be, but
Pam wasn't going there. She hung up without saying good-
bye.

Stunned, Pam sat down on a stool next to the phone.
She let the phone drop from her hands. *What in the hell
was that?* She started laughing. She roared with laughter
a good ten minutes, tears rolling down her cheeks. She
slid to the cold stone floor and rocked with laughter. *Oh
my God! I have lost my mind!* And then she started to weep.
Still crying, she pulled herself up and went to the front
door and locked it, then moved to the sliders out to the
veranda and locked those as well. She wanted to be left
alone, she wanted to miss her husband, and she wanted to
grieve. Hopefully, Anne hadn't recorded their conversation. But Pam knew one thing for sure: She was pressing
charges against her sister-in-law, making Anne a target for
her broken heart. She was finished being a doormat. Pam
had shot Anne's husband, Bill, and if she had to, she would
do it over again to protect her loved ones. Exhausted, she
went to her room, pulled back the bedding, and got into
bed for a long summer's sleep.

Bill left his house in Greenwich Village and got a
cab headed uptown. He was forty-seven years old, and he
was going to live with his mother. Well, at least he would
spend the night there that night. He was taking it one
day at a time. He didn't call ahead; Bernice would ask too

many questions of him. It was easier to just arrive there unannounced.

Bernice was sitting in the courtyard, thumbing through a magazine. She didn't hear Mildred open the door for Bill. She would bring him out to Bernice, overnight bag in hand.

"What's this?" she asked, looking down at his carryall.

He swung it up onto an empty chair. Waiting until Mildred had left, he answered, "Okay with you if I stay a couple of days? Anne's on the rag."

"Oh God, don't be so disgusting," Bernice answered, but she laughed. "You're welcome to stay here as long as you want, but you should be with your family." She didn't like enabling her boys to mistreat their wives. She was afraid it might backfire. "Pam was here earlier," she added, with just a slight twist to her lips.

"What the hell did she want?" Bill asked. "Hasn't she caused enough trouble around here?" He dropped in a chair. "Buzz for Mildred, will you, Mother? I'm starving."

"She paid the staff and gave me some money for food and incidentals. We should be nicer to her." Bernice was still smirking.

"Did she give you money for the beauty salon? You sure look a lot better." He looked at the paper, reaching over to choose a section.

Bernice remembered the gentle way Pam bathed her and did her hair for her. "No. And don't be rude."

"She called the cops on my wife," Bill added.

Bernice nodded her head yes. "She told me. I guess it was her right. What did your wife keep that money for, anyway? The checks were made out to me," she said smugly.

"I don't know. We never got around to talking about it." Bill thought of his wife locking herself in the back room of their house. She was protecting herself from him, frightened he would beat her. She was right; he wanted to. He felt aroused just yelling at her through the door. Before he left to go to his mother's, he jacked-off in their bathroom, making sure to leave the evidence for that bitch to see. He knew he was slipping into a place of insanity where, if he weren't careful, he would not be able to come back from. Then he thought of Sandra. "So did anyone else show up today?" he asked his mother.

Bernice thought a moment. He could see her struggling to remember what she did five minutes ago.

"Sandra. Sandra came, too. They talked me into selling Harold's art collection. It's for the best. Pam said she thought just what was in this room alone was probably worth over one million dollars. I'm ready to find out. What about you? It's your inheritance." Bernice looked at him. It would ultimately be up to him.

"I don't want an inheritance. I want to live now. I can't even afford to feed my boys." He remembered that he hadn't seen his sons yet. Tomorrow couldn't come soon enough. Anne might go to jail. He would bring his sons here to live and sell the house in the Village. It had been a huge mistake buying it.

"How are they?" his mother asked, looking intently at him. "Have you even seen them yet?"

He shook his head no.

"Ha! I didn't think so." She looked down at her magazine.

"Mother, what the hell does that mean?" He was challenging his own mother. This had never happened before in his recollection. Falsely, she had been held in highest esteem by both of her sons, the misdeeds of her parenting buried along with the ugly secrets her husband kept. "You weren't exactly Mother Superior," he said, not sure if the reference was appropriate, but not caring at that point. Like Anne yelling at Bill, Bill had just crossed a line with his mother that had been drawn many years before.

"My children were always fed, and there was always a parent available to them here in this house." She blanched slightly, hoping that her son would not go there. But she had started it.

Bill leaned over, close to his mother, and all of the tenderness he had felt for her yesterday dissolved. His wrath for his father may be unleashed full force on his mother if he didn't do something to control it.

"Mildred fed us, Mother dear. Mildred, not you. And do you remember why our maid had to feed us?" He forced his mother to look at him by standing up and leaning across the table so he was face to face with her. "Answer me, Mother." He had managed to keep his voice low, but it was more intimidating that way. Bernice pulled away from him, scared of him and what he was about to say to her.

"Yes, I remember why!" She didn't say *because I was drunk* out loud, but she thought it. And looking him in the eye, she repeated, "I remember."

"So you don't want to go there now, do you?"

She shook her head no.

"I didn't think so," Bill said. "Hurry up and ring for Mildred. I want to eat and then get started making our list. We need to call an auction house tomorrow. They will be thrilled to get this house, I can tell you that much." He sat down, throwing his mother a kiss. "Love you, Mom!"

14

Tom Adams was known as a good guy around the precinct. He was young, just twenty-nine, the son and grandson of policemen, and he was neither Italian nor Irish, so he managed to avoid any in-house altercations. His counterparts in the force, young men who took advantage of their status as officers of the NYPD and had reputations as scoundrels with the women, were in awe of Tom.

"So you are an urban legend," Sandra told him.

Tom laughed. He was the guy who older cops were trying to fix their daughters up with for a date. "No, I don't think so. I'm just a nice guy." He smiled at her as they sat in the unmarked car in front of her apartment. After they left Bernice, he took her to his favorite place in the neighborhood for lunch. Time flew when he was with her. "You could say I'm trustworthy."

Sandra looked at him. *Oh my God, that smile.* He was so terrifically handsome; even his teeth were perfect. But it wasn't in a smug, self-satisfied way as Jack had been. *Too gorgeous for his own good* was the silent thought of the other women in the office about Jack.

"Can you come in?" she blurted out without thinking. "Oh, of course you can't; you're on duty."

He looked at his wristwatch. "I'm finished in ten minutes. Let's go in." They got out of the car, leaving it on the street. Being a policeman had some advantages. He followed close behind her as she walked up to her door.

Down the street, from approximately the same place where Sandra had watched him talking on his cell phone to her the day before, Bill Smith observed the attractive couple as Sandra attempted to unlock the door to her apartment. Bill watched as she struggled with the key, and the handsome man placed his hand over hers to assist her. Sandra turned around and looked up at the man as he looked down at her face. Bill could see her smiling, all the way down the street. He was seething.

He'd dropped off his suitcase at his mother's house, and while she talked nonstop about Sandra, they made a list of the art that hung on the street level of the house. He was determined to go to Sandra's as soon as he could slip away. Now he had to wait for this pencil-neck to leave her apartment. Not that he had anything to hide! He simply didn't want to share his time with her while another man was around. *Who is this guy, anyway?* Bill hadn't noticed the unmarked car parked on the street, blocking eastbound traffic on Eighty-second Street.

Sandra led the way down the dark hallway to her apartment door. She could feel Tom behind her, and she liked it. She would not resist this relationship. There was no reason to; he was single, employed, and seemed to like her. She would reveal the only fly in the ointment—Jack's unborn baby. But, so far, Tom had given her no reason to think that what was happening here was anything more than a police detective watching over his charge. He hadn't said one thing that could even be misconstrued as flirtatious or romantic. And until he did, her secret would remain just that. She was barely showing, so he probably wouldn't guess it—yet.

"I'm going to fix a cup of tea. Would you like one?" she asked. She put her purse down and walked into the kitchen, Tom following behind her. She turned to see if he was nodding an answer, and then he made a move that gave her the reason she sought.

He put his hands on her shoulders, pulled her to him, and kissed her smack on the mouth. She didn't resist, but sort of fell against him and put her hands up on his shoulders, too. They finally made their way around his head.

She ended the kiss and put her head on his chest, snickering. "Was that a yes or a no?"

He held her gently but firmly and then laughed a full, deep, hearty laugh. "A yes," he answered, looking down into her eyes. "Wow, I'm not sure what just happened, but I guess a thank-you is in order."

She backed up a little from him. "You don't know what happened? You kissed me full on the lips, and I kissed you back!" She laughed, needing so badly to keep things real, not to read anything into what he had done. *Let it be real.*

She allowed him to pull her to him again, but this time, it was just for a hug. If this moment could last, she would do what she could to facilitate it. Only pulling away when she felt the time was right, she went back to fixing their tea. She took the teakettle from the stove, filled it with water, and placed it back on the stove, and all the while, Tom was right behind her, with his hands on her shoulders, offering her companionship and not willing to break the mood, the physical connection. Sandra decided then she had to tell him about the baby. He would accept it or not. They barely knew each other, but she felt the instant attraction, and it was obvious he did, too.

"Here, let me take this to the table," she said, lifting the tray with the tea things on it. "Come sit with me. I have something to say to you."

He followed her obediently to the table and sat down. He was thinking, *I'm in trouble for stealing a kiss.* She put a mug down in front of each chair and took the tea things off the tray. He sat in the same chair he sat in yesterday, and she took the tray back to the kitchen. Tom watched her and smiled. *Boy oh boy, I didn't expect feeling this!* he thought. He'd never lived with a woman or been engaged or even wanted to "go steady" with someone. Sandra came back from the kitchen with the teakettle and poured hot water into each mug. She was graceful for being so tall. Poised and willowy. She sensed him smiling at her and smiled back, although she didn't look up at him. She didn't want to lose her nerve.

"So sit down and talk to me. I'm moving too fast, is that right? You want me to slow down. I stole a kiss and am proud of it!"

They laughed together.

"No, that's not it," she replied. She cupped the tea-cup with her hands to warm them, even though it was ninety degrees outside, and looked into the cup. "I wasn't going to tell you what I am about to tell you because it wasn't relevant. But since the kiss—and now tell me if I am wrong." She looked right up into eyes. "But we have something here, am I right?"

He nodded yes without hesitation and said, "We definitely have something."

"Well then, I have to tell you—I'm pregnant."

He looked into her eyes, the smile still on his face. He pushed the chair back and stood up, all six feet three of him, and walked around to her side, bending over her and looking down at her belly. "May I?" he asked.

She nodded yes.

He placed one hand on the back of her chair and the other over her belly. No one else had felt the baby move yet, or really even acknowledged it yet, outside of Pam. Her heart soared. She had just laid eyes on this man one day ago. Was she daft?

"The father of the baby is dead," she told him. "Bill's brother, Jack. It's another reason that Bill is so angry with me. Jack was married," she added. "But his wife, Pam—the woman I introduced you to this morning—and I have become the best of friends."

The sensation Tom had, he would later tell Sandra, was of being on a small boat with her, out in the middle of the ocean. They had no paddles or motor, but the wind was blowing them to all the right places. He pulled up a chair so he could keep his hand on Sandra's belly.

"How far along are you?" he asked her.

"Almost five months," she answered. "Jack didn't know about the baby. We would have probably broken up if he hadn't died," she lied. "He loved his wife; our relationship had run its course." She didn't add that if he had known about the baby, she was almost certain he would have left Pam and they would have gotten married. She would never repeat that; it was possible she had it all wrong.

"The baby doesn't change the way I *think* I could feel about you," he said. "I mean, I am trying to be as truthful as I can, and I have never, ever felt this way about anyone before after twenty-four hours." He chuckled. "You're probably thinking, 'What a schmuck.' Go ahead, say it." He was laughing, though. She liked him more and more. "Thank you for telling me, though. I'm not scared off or anything." *Not yet, anyway.* He picked up his mug and sipped hot tea, thinking to himself, *Tea, babies...Oh my God, if my mother could see me now,* while another voice said a little louder, *Run, Tom, run.*

15

On Monday morning, the company Marie worked for merged with a larger firm, one whose employees were going to move into the Midtown offices that Marie loathed so completely. When she arrived at work that day, the receptionist whispered that a bevy of cute men from across town had just arrived with boxes of files—their new coworkers. Marie's ears perked up. She was ready for some cute men. *Hopefully, they weren't all married*, she thought. *Married or gay.*

"Meeting in the conference room in fifteen," her boss yelled to her from down the hall. Marie frowned; he was such a jerk. She went to her office, head down and eyes averted. Strangers were standing around, talking, staring at her, smiling, and trying for friendliness. She wasn't biting. She had been ignored by the staff for all the years she worked there, and there was no reason to change the system now. Closing the door quickly behind her, she was happy that she had her own office, and there wasn't any chance that someone new would be sharing it. It was hardly big enough for one person.

She turned on her computer and went to the window to look out while it started up. She could see the top of the Empire State Building if she looked between buildings. Off to the right was the UPS terminal. She loved watching the trucks zoom in and out, picturing them empty going in and ready to explode they were so full going out. The men who worked there were potential dates, but she never looked, never gave them a minute of her time, because she had a permanent date with Jack. Maybe she should give those men a second chance. Later, she would go to the deli on the corner for lunch and, this time, not be oblivious to the conversation swirling around her. So many years had passed, and she was no longer young.

Her phone ringing brought her back to reality.

"Fabian," she said, loving the sound of it and its pretentiousness.

"Hey, Fabian, it's Babcock here. How you doin' this beautiful morning?" Jeff asked.

"Hi, Jeff, I'm good. What about you?" Marie asked in return, crestfallen. For a moment there, she had forgotten that someone else was dead.

"I'm good, too. Whatcha doin' for lunch today? I have to be in town around one, and I thought we could meet."

"I will know in an hour or so, okay? We have new staff starting today, and there is a big meeting at nine-thirty. My boss may be expecting us for lunch." Marie missed lunching with someone; most of her days for the past twenty years were spent eating hot dogs from a vending cart with Jack. Or going with him to Ali Baba's for the best Middle Eastern food each Friday, although she was sure it was for the belly dancers. A list of wonderful restaurants filed through her head, and then she remembered there was someone else waiting on the line for her, someone who was alive and not married. "Can I let you know?" she asked.

"That would be fine. I'll call you around eleven-thirty, okay? I hope you can go. My brother and his wife are in town, and I'd like them to meet you," he added.

Her heart beat a little faster. "Okay, fine, talk to you later." And she hung up. She put the phone back in its cradle and sat down at her computer. He wanted to introduce her to his family. She moved the mouse, and the screen saver popped on—a big picture of Jack, handsome in a white tennis sweater, his arm around a younger, smiling Marie. She stuck her tongue out at him and said to the image, "You are replaced."

The staff meeting was interesting because an announcement was made that, unbeknownst to Marie, the new writers were to report to her for assignments. Even after working there for over twenty years, she didn't know much about her colleagues, nor was she interested, and they returned the sentiment. By 11:00 that morning, she knew that she would be able to meet Jeff for a quick cup of coffee, but not lunch. He was fine with that; he really just wanted to introduce his brother to Marie. They made arrangements to meet at the TGI Friday's by Madison Square Garden; his brother would be getting on a train at Penn Station when they were finished, and she would have a short cab ride. She thought that was an odd place for a gourmand to choose in a city teeming with fabulous restaurants.

She arrived right on time; Jeff and his brother and sister-in-law were waiting for her outside of the restaurant. Jeff made a big show of greeting her, hugging her and kissing her on the mouth. She was suspicious right off the bat.

The brother, John, and his wife, Betty, seemed absolutely thrilled to meet Marie. Over coffee, they went into great detail about how they had been praying that Jeff would meet the perfect woman and then listed all the attributes they wanted that woman to have.

You've got to be kidding me, Marie thought. Among the many qualities Jeff's girlfriend needed to have, "being saved" topped the list.

"Do you know Jesus as your savior?" Betty asked.

"I went to Catholic school as a kid. Does that count?" Marie asked, knowing full well that she was about to get a lengthy lecture on being "born again." She needed to get back to the office, though, so standing up, she put out her hand. "It was so nice meeting you, but I have to get back to my office. We have an entire company that merged with us today, and unfortunately, I am in charge of their work assignments."

Everyone stood up and shook her hand, including Jeff, whose excitement since her arrival seemed to have diminished. She would be walking out of the restaurant alone.

For the first time in her distant memory, Marie was excited about going back to the office after lunch. It was a combination of the eager faces awaiting her and getting away from Jeff and his boring brother. Work might not be so horrible, after all; there would be other human beings who wanted to talk to her, who were interested in her. She herded everyone back into the conference room, where she would divide up projects among the new players. She sized up each one as they passed by her, smiling and shaking their hands. The requisite beautiful blonde—*why in the hell was there one in every group?*—was followed by the faction of entry-level journalism majors who couldn't get jobs at the *Times* or AP. Then there was the lone middle-aged woman, possibly longing for retirement and tired of working and juggling family and husband. Marie would go easy on her. And finally came the squadron of men, from ages thirty to sixty, probably all married, but a few gay men thrown in, who were angry that they had to work in this new environment, but even angrier that they had to work for her.

One guy in particular stood out as they filed past her—older, at least sixty, built, and graying, but not totally gray. He was as tall as Jack, so Marie, who was tall for a woman, had to look up.

He smiled at her and said hi.

"Welcome!" she said to him with her biggest smile. And then to the group at large, "Welcome to you all. Have a seat, and we'll get started."

There was chatter and the shuffling of chairs on carpeting. When everyone appeared settled, she started.

"We have so much work right now that if the assignment I give you today is not to your liking, I'm sure I can do better for you next time," she said. "As you heard earlier, my name is Marie Fabian. I've been here for a long time, and it seems like just yesterday—or forever, depending on the way the day is going. Your presence here is a tremendous boon for us; we have been short of staff for the past five years. I won't take up any more of your time so we can get down to work. The way we decided to distribute the work is to divide you up into four groups. I'll call out four names, and you may choose whose team you want to be on. Try to divide yourself so that there are five people on each team. We're adults; this should work, right?"

There was laughter all around.

She called out the four team leaders' names and then gave the green light for the group to choose who they wanted to work with. Except for the middle-aged woman, everyone joined a team. She'd make six to one team. Marie looked at her list and called out the woman's name.

"Carolyn?"

The woman nodded yes.

"I need some help with a special project." The others looked her way as she walked forward. Marie was glad; she hoped it stirred up some jealousy. "I am going to pass out file folders of work to the team leaders," Marie continued to the group. "It is your responsibility to see that everything I give you today is addressed by Thursday at our weekly staff meeting. Okay?" There was a general murmur of agreement. Before lunch, everyone had been given their office or cubical.

"You can stay in here to talk about how the work will be divided up and then you may go to your own space or stay here in the conference room. There's a Starbucks down on Thirty-third that we often go to to work when we can't stand the office anymore. Make sure you have your cell phone and that your team leader approves of you working off-site. That's about it. You know where to get me if you need any further direction." She motioned to Carolyn. "Come with me. I think you'll like what I have for you."

One of the last surveys Jack's company was commissioned to do before he died was to find out exactly how the youngest of the baby boomers who lived in Manhattan were planning on spending their retirement. The research filled an entire file cabinet. It needed to be collated, graphs developed, reports written. It specified a development on the west side of the city, close to everything a retiree might need. It would be a project that would keep one lucky writer busy for at least a month. Marie presented the work to Carolyn as though it were the holy grail of technical writing jobs. It really was; Marie was supposed to have worked on it herself. But now she could safely pass it on to someone else and not feel possessive or controlling about it. Carolyn had come with good recommendations.

"Come into my office," Marie said. She could not remember the last time someone besides herself had crossed her threshold. "I use the term 'office' loosely. 'Closet' is more appropriate." The two women walked in, and Marie shut the door. She had taken the explanatory files out to show to whoever drew the lucky straw. "Have a seat," she said, pointing to a folding chair set up to hold overflow from the desk. "The project I am going to ask you do is dear to my heart. I was waiting for someone who I could trust to take over. Your references are flawless. I think that I am a pretty good judge of character and that you could be trusted with this." *What the hell does that mean?* she thought. *I'm a terrible judge!* "Would you like to give it a try?"

Carolyn was smiling and looked pleased. "I'd like to give it a try," she responded, taking the file from Marie and opening it up. She leafed through the first ten or so pages.

"Take a look at this one file and then you can dig into the other two hundred," Marie said. They laughed. Marie stuck her hand out. "Thank you, Carolyn. I'll have one of the janitors wheel the file cabinet into your office later today. Let's talk before we leave tonight, okay?"

They agreed to meet at 6:00, and Carolyn left Marie's office, closing the door behind her. It wasn't really a "close the door" office; in the past, there wasn't enough staff to make it necessary to close doors. Now, however, people were walking down the hall all day long.

Marie, at last, turned her attention to her computer. She worked nonstop for the next four hours and, finally, at 6:00, turned everything off and went to meet Carolyn in her office. On the way there, it occurred to her that, for a good part of the day, Jack Smith's name or face didn't enter her mind—as a matter of fact, not since she had first turned on her computer that morning and saw the picture of them together.

Ha-ha, Jack, you didn't wreck my day, you didn't wreck my day, she sang to herself. *Jerk.*

16

Carolyn Fitzsimmons closed the door of her tiny, airless office, throwing the thick file of paper onto her new desk. She wasn't complaining about the work or the office; she had never had her own space like this before. She wondered if it was mandatory to knock or if people would open her door and just come in. If that were the case, she would be careful about falling asleep sitting up, as she had so ably taught herself to do this year. Menopause had opened the door to so many new experiences. Exhaustion and insomnia were her constant companions. She had watched her body morph from an average-sized, moderately fit woman to a saggy, haggard, misshapen crone. *What the hell had happened to the woman I used to be?* Her husband road her constantly about the need to exercise and watch her diet. He could easily spend the entire weekend on the golf course, but by the time she got done cleaning the house, running errands, doing the laundry, and watching three soccer games in a row, the last thing she wanted to do was get on the treadmill. She tried to explain to him that change of life was responsible for most of what he saw her going through.

"Don't give me that horseshit," he replied unsympathetically. "We're the same age, and I have never been in better shape."

"The only reason you're still alive is because I took Paxil when you had your mid-life crisis," she yelled back to him.

He just laughed at her. "I know I gave you a rough way to go there for a while. Forgive me?" He asked, kissing her on her forehead.

It was true that he was a miserable prick just a few years ago, mean to her, more critical than he had ever been. And now the reward she got was to see him looking so handsome and fit that she hardly recognized him at times, and she never more miserable.

"I guess so," she replied. "It's pretty tough to stay mad at such a good-looking guy."

"Stop acting like such a dimwit and figure out a way to fit the exercise in with your responsibilities here." He waited for her response, sure he had hit a nerve.

"You didn't think I was a dimwit when I was sucking your penis last night, now did you?" The words slipped out of her mouth, surprising both of them. He was a good man, just a jerk at times. She had taken him by surprise, and he grabbed her and held her in a passionate embrace, dipping her over. "Yeah, now you want me to kiss you!" she said. They had been married all of their life, and although they didn't always show the respect to each other that they should, they had never been unfaithful.

The icing on the cake was finding out that the company she was vested in, where she had spent twenty-five years giving everything she had, was going to be sold. She was the oldest woman working there. She imagined she would be the first person to be fired when they finally found a buyer. She wasn't going to just lie down and die, however. She stopped eating sweets, started walking during lunch every day, and made time for a haircut, a dye job, and a facial. She felt better about herself, and that was half the battle. Of course, her husband didn't notice, but she wasn't doing it for him, anyway.

The office they assigned her had a window, which looked out on a parking garage. *Does every building in this neighborhood look out on a garage?* But beyond the garage was the Empire State Building. She called her mother to tell her she could see the iconic structure from her office, and she had a project that her boss's brother-in-law had generated. It had been a while since Carolyn felt so good about her life. She actually felt...hopeful.

Marie knocked on Carolyn's door and then opened it without waiting for a reply.

So there would be a warning of sorts...

"Well, what did you think?" she asked.

"I think it will be a challenge, but one I'm up for," Carolyn replied. "I can't thank you enough for trusting me with your brother-in-law's project." She made eye contact with the young woman and wasn't sure if her comment was well received or not. It was okay. She was going to like it here.

17

Tom Adams lived in Brooklyn, where all good New York cops come from. When he left Sandra's apartment on Sunday night, his partner, Jim took over, parking the unmarked car in the alley behind her apartment. When Jim got there to relieve Tom, they walked the perimeter of the building together, making sure that the basement windows were secure and that the other apartments on the ground floor had locked windows. Jim brought flyers that he had typed up, and they slid one under the door of each apartment. The flyer said simply that the building was under surveillance because of increased robbery in the area and to make sure windows and doors were locked and that any suspicious persons were to be reported. If that didn't scare the hell out of the tenants, nothing would.

Now on the way to Brooklyn, Tom felt an anxiety he had not felt before. Always conscientious about the citizens of the city and protective of them, the feeling was beyond duty. He was worried about Sandra. Obsessive thought and behavior was foreign to him, and he knew this bordered on the irrational. He didn't even know her. They had been in each other's company a total of less than twelve hours. She was beautiful, smart, and pregnant. Beyond that, he knew very little. He was slowly learning her personality; she was somewhat of a smartass, but kind. Her concern about the old lady who lived in the mansion was evidence of her caring. He didn't know who Bernice was yet. Sandra was also part owner of some kind of business. He'd have to investigate what it did. The more he knew about Sandra, the easier it would be to protect her from whatever threat Bill Smith was.

His commute from the precinct was usually about fifteen minutes to make the four-mile trip to his apartment in Williamsburg. It would take at least twice as long to make the ten-mile trip from the Upper West Side. Traffic was horrible, bumper-to-bumper on the Henry Hudson Parkway. He'd go through Central Park next time. As he finally drove over the Williamsburg Bridge, he remembered his recent concern about his life. He was in a comfort zone that he didn't think possible. Compared to his friends and family, and for a guy his age, he was way ahead of the game. He had a great apartment in a cool neighborhood, had reached a place in his job that he would be happy with for a long, long time, and had hobbies and friends to keep him busy when he wasn't working. Everything was perfect, except for one thing: He was lacking a relationship. He was the favorite guy in his crowd to fix up with single cousins and friends of girlfriends. He could have blind dates twice a week, if he were interested. His sister bugged him constantly about Internet dating sites. Wasn't he curious to find out who they would match him up with? Not having anyone important in his life bothered everyone else more than it bothered him. And now he thought he knew why he had been alone. The timing wasn't right, because Sandra hadn't needed him until now.

Her office was close to the downtown precinct; he knew right where it was. She said she could see Trinity

Church from her office window. They probably walked past each other all the time.

When he reached his street, there was a parking space in front of his building. The apartment was one of the best things he had done for himself. It was in an ancient building, but completely renovated. There was a great grocery store in the neighborhood, a laundry, restaurants, and a view if he looked between buildings. He could see Lower Manhattan lit up at night; it was breathtaking. His mother was about six blocks away, so he could see her and take advantage of her cooking as often as she would tolerate him. She had been praying for his wife since he was born, she told him. She begged him to take his sisters' offer of fixing him up with a date.

"Oh Tommy, how long must I wait for a baby from you? I'm no spring chicken! Get moving, will you kid?" She would lower her eyes and look at him out of a slit at the bottom. "Is there anything you want to tell me?" she would whisper.

"Ma, give me a break, will you? Ellie, you been filling Ma's head with lies about me?" He'd look over at his sister, make a fist, and shake it at her. It was all in good fun. However, he couldn't see Sandra in that milieu. She belonged uptown in that mansion he took her to that morning. He didn't know yet about her parents who raised their two daughters in the center of Manhattan, in a tiny apartment near the Lincoln Tunnel.

Tom didn't turn the lights on as he entered the apartment. He liked seeing the lights of the city before him. The computer was in a small alcove off the kitchen, and he turned the coffee pot on as he made his way to turn on his computer. He was going to do some investigative work on his new friend, Sandra Benson. There wasn't much he could do from home short of googling her, which didn't turn up much. She had stayed below the radar until her late boyfriend gave her his half of the very lucrative real estate development firm. He didn't want to go there, looking at the business. If she ever found out, she might think he was pursuing a relationship with her because she was wealthy—or going to be. Pouring himself a cup of coffee, he walked to the expanse of windows and looked over the rooftops to the lights of the city. She was right there, uptown. He picked up his phone and dialed her number.

She answered on the first ring. "What are you doing? Are you home already?" she asked.

"Got in a while ago. What's Jim doing?"

"He's in the alley," she answered. "I'm going to leave the bedroom shade up a little after I get into bed tonight so I can see him."

"Can you talk?" Tom asked. He wanted to begin to get to know her, even if it was just over the phone.

"Sure! I am getting ready for work tomorrow—ready or not, here I come! We have a new client, a builder from Riverdale who wants to do something in my neighborhood."

If ever there was a segue into a conversation, this was it. He asked her about the project and what it would entail, and then about the company itself. It turned out it wasn't much of a development company, after all, but more of a demographic research firm that found property for investors to develop. She willingly talked about the value of it and then the shock that it was left to her as part of her boyfriend's will. Knowing that Bill would be a pest for the rest of his life, the wisdom of leaving the business to Sandra instead of the man's wife was clear if Sandra's safety wasn't an issue. Tom began to wonder about the boyfriend, this Jack Smith. *Was he trying to make life difficult for Sandra?* Maybe leaving her the business wasn't such a generous act, after all.

They talked until almost 11:00. Tom fixed his dinner and ate it while they chatted; Sandra got her clothes ready for the next day and packed a lunch. He found out that her father had died at her mother's funeral. She found out that he came from a long line of New York cops, but that his father had made the unforgiveable mistake of being the first Adams to get a divorce when he left his mother for another woman. No one in the family would speak to him except for Tom, and he had to do it on the sly. Even his own mother and father—still alive, but pushing ninety—refused to take calls from their only son.

When his dad left Tom's mother, a tiny Scottish woman with a thick brogue, she fell into a deep depression—for about a week. She said later that she had allowed herself that amount of time to find out if she really minded that he was leaving. And it only took a week to discover that it was a huge relief, a blessing, a gift. She had at least twenty years to make it up to herself, God willing, twenty years to redeem the pure boredom of being married to a drunk for the previous twenty.

"Why'd you stay, Ma?" her son and daughters asked her.

Her daughter Faith confessed to her, "I used to lie in bed at night and hear him talk down to you, and I would pray that he'd leave."

"I stayed because that is what you do where we come from. If the man wants to leave, you hope the door will hit him in the behind. But you don't leave if you are the wife." He was a drinker, and both policeman and drinker make a tough husband to deal with. She grew tired of the Al-Anon meetings, making excuses for his bad behavior, his drunken fights, and his absence in his children's lives.

It was a mystery to all of them why Tommy wanted to become a policeman. He would tell them that he wanted to show everyone that there was a different way to act as a man and a cop. He didn't drink, didn't let the stuff touch his lips, and had no desire whatsoever to try. When the group of his friends went out, he would order a coffee. He knew where to get the best in town, which bars served the freshest coffee or ground their own beans. He was a fanatic about it. When Sandra had offered him a cup, and he saw it was instant, he swallowed the gag and took tea instead. He could get into tea drinking; it had huge possibilities for becoming an obsession. But he would let that be her thing; he liked coffee best. So Tom knew that falling for a pregnant woman was so much the act of a child of an alcoholic; here was someone who needed his care. He was immediately attracted to her, and he knew he had to find a way into her heart. He was going to ignore all the warning signs and fall in love with her.

When Tom had gotten back into his unmarked car and pulled away from the front of Sandra's building, Bill hid behind the Sunday paper he was reading as he sat at the counter. He'd been there for almost two hours, waiting for the guy to leave. Once Tom was out of sight, Bill left the bagel place and started down Sandra's street. When he got to her building, he saw what was obviously a cop car parked in the alley before he turned to walk up to the building. He kept walking straight, head down, resisting the urge to run. *What the hell was that? Were they waiting for him?* Walking around the block, he found a place on the next street where he could look between buildings to get a better idea of what was going on, and sure enough, there was a policeman there in the car, reading. Bill wouldn't be making any visits to Sandra's this evening, after all.

18

For the second time that week, Pam woke up confused, this time thinking it was early morning, when it was nighttime. She groped for the clock to see that it was after 9:00. Sunday night, dark, she was alone. She started to cry. *What is wrong with me?* She felt around on the table for her glasses, putting them on, hoping the reorientation of her room would help sort out the confusion of her life.

No one had told her that this would happen; there were no widow police, no grief experts, standing outside her door ready to guide her. She went to one grief support meeting, and it was horrible. The whining and complaining drove her tolerance level into the ground. She lost her compassion within the first several minutes. Every story was different, but no one had a story like hers, and she wasn't about to divulge the ugly details. No, she would try to work through it alone. Sandra and Marie appeared to have moved on with their lives already and weren't struggling like Pam was. She stifled a tiny bit of anger when she thought of those two. They had gotten away with a lot.

She missed Jack; it was as simple as that. No matter what he had done, the sins he had committed had nothing to do with her. It didn't assuage the love she had for him or that she believed he had for her. It was flawed for sure, maybe not even real. But it had been her life. It had occupied every breath she took, the life she made with him.

There was nothing else. And now, outside of her children, there was a void. She had no desire to start over. No pressing need to save the world during her free time. Her empty life didn't fill her with guilt. It made her angry. She wanted to die herself. Knowing full well that she was probably depressed, she made the conscious decision not to end her life because of the pain it would bring her children. For them, she would carry on. But until they returned home, she would suffer miserably.

Seeing Andy wouldn't help; she had made the decision as she lay in bed earlier that she would not see him again until she was able to resolve her heartache. She didn't want him as a sounding board; he couldn't help her because his own relationship had been vibrant and forward moving. She didn't want anyone to critique her relationship with Jack; her sister and Sandra probably did that on a minute-by-minute basis.

Even the baby coming was no longer enough to keep her engaged. As the days stretched away from the funeral, the baby's importance in her life was diminishing. She might even decide not to tell her children, or if she did, to minimize what its impact would be on their lives. It might mean the end of her relationship with Sandra, but she was so exhausted mentally and emotionally that she couldn't benefit her right now anyway. Seeing Sandra with the young man was really sweet. She could sense that Tom was enamored with Sandra. She wondered when the truth about the baby would be revealed to him.

She got up from the bed and went into the bathroom to get ready, once again, for bed. After showering, she put on sweatpants and a T-shirt, an outfit she rarely wore, and the clothes hung on her. Digging in the bottom of the bathroom linen closet, she found Jack's scale. He had become a fanatic about his weight the past year, weighing himself each morning and adjusting his diet. She had always been a stickler about her body and didn't need to weigh herself that often. At five foot four, 118 pounds was about as perfect as it got. She got on the scale and gasped. She was down to 110 pounds. *When did that happen?* No one had mentioned her appearance. Her mother, usually a pest about such things, hadn't said a word. *Were they worried that I would resent it if they commented?* She would have to ask when she saw her family again.

She left the safety of her bedroom and went into the kitchen. Although it was after ten, she got an open bottle of wine out of the refrigerator and poured herself a full glass. She could afford the calories. She was so tired all the time lately that she hadn't been drinking like she had in the past. *Could that have attributed to my weight loss? But I didn't drink that much, for God's sake!* She walked to the sliders that lead to the veranda and opened them. The effort took her breath away. She wondered if she wasn't coming down with something. *Just what I need*, she thought. *The flu or a cold.* Abandoning her wine glass, she walked back into the house, leaving the sliders open, and got into bed again. The minute her head hit the pillow, she was asleep.

19

When Marie finally got home from work on Monday night, she felt revitalized and refreshed. She immediately thought of her sister, who she had never called back when she got home from Jeff's on Sunday night. Submitting to the tyranny of trying to find something to eat, she pulled a can of SpaghettiOs out of the pantry and worked on opening it and getting it heated. While it was on the stove, she went to her bedroom and changed out of her work clothes into sweatpants. She picked up her phone and keyed in Pam's number. After about six rings, she finally picked up with a weak hello.

"My God, what is wrong with you?" Marie asked. "You sound horrible."

"I am," Pam admitted. "I don't know what's wrong with me; I've been in bed all day. Glad Mom isn't here." She pulled the covers up to her chin.

"Maybe the old lady should be there to take care of you," Marie admonished. "Are you eating?" The tables had turned; it was Pam who had asked that of Marie in the past.

"I don't have an appetite. Would you do something for me?" she asked and didn't wait for answer. "Call Sharon and see if Mom can go down there for a week. I'm not ready for her to come back from Susan's on Friday."

"Just wait, okay? You might feel differently by then." Marie was not going do any such thing. Nelda should be there, taking care of Pam. She might even call their mother and tell her to get back right away. "I'll come after work tomorrow. There is a flu going around that lasts for ten days. Do you think you could have it?"

"Could be. It feels like the flu. Look, Marie, I need to hang up. Call me tomorrow, okay?" She hung up.

Marie looked at the phone. She couldn't not go to work on Tuesday. For the first time in a long, long time, she wanted to go, was excited about being there and doing her job. Of course, it would stand to reason that the onetime Pam would really need her she wouldn't be able to go. She decided to do something that she had resisted in the past; she would call Sandra. Her SpaghettiOs were bubbling away, so she went into the kitchen to turn off the stove. She had Sandra's number on little pieces of paper from times that she had called after Jack died or when Pam tried to get them to interact. There had never been any positive communication between the two of them. Sandra didn't trust Marie, and Marie was jealous of Sandra. But this was for Pam. She'd make the call for her sister. She found the number and keyed it in.

Sandra picked up on the first ring.

"This is Marie. I feel sort of stupid calling you out of the blue like this." She paused, trying to formulate her request. "But, first of all, how are you? How's the baby?"

There was silence, and then Sandra responded with the pat answer. "I'm fine, and the baby is fine. What can I do for you?" Sandra was definitely not in the mood for any of Marie's foolishness. If she started accusing her or talking about Jack, she would hang up. "I'm sort of in the middle of something right now."

"Okay, well, I won't keep you. I have a favor to ask. Pam is ill. She said she hasn't felt well for days, and she said she didn't get out of bed today. Is there any way you can get to Babylon tomorrow? I am totally swamped at work. Our merger moved over yesterday, and it's a zoo there."

"Oh boy, that will be a tough one." Sandra paused. She wanted to help Pam out though. "I might be able to swing by first thing. Do you think that would help?"

"I appreciate it so much. Don't tell her you're coming because, you know Pam, she'll tell you she's all right and will refuse the help. I'll go after work—or earlier, if things are organized enough."

"Okay, no problem, Marie. Thanks for letting me know."

They said good-bye and hung up.

Sandra was concerned, though. She wondered why she hadn't heard from Pam and her phone calls had gone unanswered. There was nothing pressing for her in the office. She left a voicemail for the receptionist that she would be in at noon and that she could be reached on her cell phone. She was a partner; if she wanted to take half a day off, she would do so.

When she got home that evening, Tom was not far behind her, coming to watch over her apartment from the alley behind the building. He explained that it was not that unusual for the police to keep an eye on a victim for a few days after the perpetrator was released from prison, and they had it on record that Sandra was at Pam's the day of the attempted murder of Nelda. Sandra blanched slightly at the word "murder." She went downstairs and opened the door to the alley. He looked up from the work he was doing and stuck his head out the window of his cruiser.

"What's up?" he asked.

She explained about the call from Marie and that she would be going to Babylon in the morning.

"Do you want me to take you? I'm off duty when you leave here, anyway."

"Don't you need to sleep sometime?" She imagined driving with him after he had been up all night. Her hands went protectively to her belly.

"I'll sleep in the afternoon. I never go right home and go to sleep. Besides, I am off tomorrow, remember? Jim will be here."

"Okay, if you're sure you don't mind. I wasn't looking forward to taking the train, anyway."

The next morning, they got on the road by eight. Rush hour was coming toward them, so it wasn't a bad ride. They talked more about their history, although Sandra avoided telling him too much information about her friendship with Jack's family. She didn't know him well enough yet to reveal the details. When they got to Pam's, Sandra tried calling her to let her know she was just outside. She was not expecting what she would find when they got to the door.

20

Shortly after Pam hung up on her, there was a knock on the door of Anne and Bill's brownstone in Greenwich Village. She peeked out the blinds and saw a plainclothes policeman and a uniformed officer. *Oh crap*, she thought.

"One minute!" she yelled through the door. Picking up the phone, she dialed Bernice's number. Of course the maid answered the phone. Anne willed herself to stay calm. She asked for Bill. Several minutes later, Bernice came on the line.

"He's not here, Anne. I thought he might be headed downtown, but that was hours ago."

"Would you tell him I called, Mother Smith? Let him know I am on my way to jail and have no one to pick up our children at daycare. Possibly you could enlist that driver of yours to get them?" Anne stuck her tongue out at the phone. "I have to go now; the police are at my door." And she hung up.

She opened the door and stepped aside to allow the men to come into her house. It didn't make any sense to her not to let them in. Calling an attorney now would just delay the process.

"Hi, I know why you are here. Should I bring anything?" she asked. "Like my purse?"

The policemen introduced themselves. They explained that they had a warrant for her arrest and then read her her rights.

"You can leave any valuables here. Do you need to make arrangements for your children?"

She shook her head yes, and it was then, and only then, that she felt near to tears. In actuality, it would be a relief to be physically separated from Bill. She wasn't afraid anymore, and the feeling was wonderful. But she was worried about her children. She decided to speak out. "My kids may be in danger with their father. His mother is aged, and there is no one else." She bowed her head, determined not to cry. But it meant not speaking again.

The officers looked at each other and nodded their heads. "Okay, we'll take care of them."

She didn't ask how. They let her go through the door first and then waited while she secured the door. The neighbors on either side of their house were home, peeking through the blinds. It would baffle them why the wife was being led away and that brutal bastard of a husband was free.

"Are they at school right now?" the plainclothes officer asked her. "We can wait until the end of the day to pick them up so they aren't so frightened with police coming into their classroom. How old are they?" He slid in beside Anne in the backseat of the car, keeping a conversation going with her as they drove to the jail. She had a horrible headache. Prison loomed ahead as a beacon of safety. She hoped they would find her guilty and keep her there for a long, long time.

Bill had become the new "annoyance" customer at the bagel store on the corner of Broadway and Eighty-second Street. He left his mother's house early Tuesday morning to stake a place at the counter by the window. He watched for Sandra to leave her apartment building to go to the subway entrance on Broadway. Instead, he saw her in the front seat of an unmarked police car, headed east. *What the hell is going on?* he asked himself again. It was the same car he saw in her alley when he walked by her building on Sunday night. *Are the police protecting her?* His anger was palpable. *How the hell did she rate? And what does that mean for me?* He walked out shortly after he saw Sandra drive away, to the relief of the staff.

"He's creepy. Don't we have to deal with enough creeps around here?"

But he would be back before long. *Sandra can't hide forever*, he thought, walking back to his mother's house. He'd continue organizing the junk and artwork he wanted to sell. That afternoon, someone from one of the big art auction places was going to come and take a look at the first load of stuff they had gathered up. Bernice was going downhill so quickly it frightened him. If something happened to his mother, he would have to be in charge and would have to take over. Bill didn't want that; he liked being the child.

Those worries would end however, because a warrant for his arrest had just been issued, and as soon as the officers could locate the defendant's wife to find out where he was, they would have him in custody.

21

Slowly, and without warning, a life may spiral out of control. For Sandra, the downward motion started the day she walked into the offices of Lane, Smith & Romney. At the time, she had no idea that there would be devastating consequences to the simple act of making eye contact with a handsome, charming man.

On Tuesday, Sandra returned home from a day of dealing with Pam's health issues and then more drama at the office. Tom dropped her off at the front door of her building and drove around to the back, where he would be doing surveillance in the alley for the next twelve hours. He had been so wonderful, driving her all the way to Babylon, staying with her all morning, and then taking her downtown so she could work for a few hours. Expecting Jim, the other detective, to pick her up at five, she was surprised and pleased that it was Tom again. He said he wouldn't have been able to relax or sleep anyway, and Jim was happy to trade days off.

She threw her purse down on the chair and went into her bedroom to slip off her work clothes and put on her beloved spandex. The waistband was getting tight. The prospect of wearing maternity clothes scared her because it meant exposure. She would have to "come out" at work.

The mail was on the hallway floor; she bent over and scooped it up. It was mostly junk except for her electric bill and a business envelop from her obstetrician. She went into the kitchen with the ads under her arm. Turning the teakettle on, she got a knife out of the silverware drawer and slit the envelope from the doctor's office open. There was a computer printout of her blood work and a short typewritten letter signed by the doctor. She put the mail down on the kitchen table and got her mug out and put a tea bag in it. She stood by the stove, one arm crossed over her midriff, the other resting on it, with her hand up by her mouth. It was a posture of concern, which she automatically assumed whenever something worried her.

The teakettle whistled, and she poured hot water over the tea bag and took her mug with her. Sitting down, she put her mug down on a coaster and picked up the letter. It said simply, "Call the office as soon as possible regarding your lab work. Additional blood tests are needed to confirm your results." Her heart did a little flip-flop; she could feel the irregular beat. Looking at the printout of lab work, but not yet picking it up, she said out loud, "What could it be?" Sandra often said she was as dumb as a rock when it came to medical things. And she had no nurse friend or doctor buddy whom she could call to get an interpretation. Afraid to touch the paper, but wanting to see if she understood any of the numbers, she forced herself to pick it up. Starting at the top, she read, "Hemoglobin-11gm/Dl. Iron-50." She continued on down the page. None of it made any sense to her. There was no indication that any of the numbers were abnormal.

Picking up her tea, she blew into it to cool it a little and took a sip. Tom was right out there, and she suddenly wanted to see him, to talk to him. She went downstairs and out the back door. He was reading, as usual, but stopped when he saw her coming toward the car.

"Can you come in? I'll make you some tea." He had confessed his love of coffee, but that he may become a tea drinker as well. "Would that be breaking the police rules?"

And then she saw him.

As she was bent over, looking into the car through the passenger-side window, she saw Bill. He was looking over at them from between the buildings on Eighty-first Street, right around the block from her building.

"Don't look now, but guess who is standing right there on Eighty-first?" She stayed ducked down, as though there was nothing more natural than having a conversation with a cop in a back alley. Tom picked up his radio as inconspicuously as he could and radioed in for another car.

"Stay here and talk to me. What were you asking me? Did I want some tea? Tea would hit the spot."

Tom's radio beeped; the officer answered that they saw Bill and were going to question him. Bill was still standing between the buildings, watching Sandra talking to Tom. Just then, they heard the trill of a siren, and the car stopped right where Sandra could see it. Once again, she hoped she wasn't overreacting. *Is pregnancy making me hyper paranoid? But why is he spying on me?*

"Watch yourself. I'm going to go over there." Sandra stepped out of the way so Tom could get out of the car. "Go in the house, okay?" He looked at her and, putting his hands on her shoulders again, turned her around and pushed her gently toward the door. "He might have a gun.

I'm not taking the chance that you'll get hurt. Shut and lock the door behind you."

She did as he said and went to the window with the chest of drawers barricading it. She could see the other officers talking to Bill and watched as Tom hopped over the six-foot-high fence as though he were a pole-vaulter. He spoke with Bill and then to the other officers. Tom frisked Bill and then, shockingly, produced a gun that he had strapped to his leg. One of the officers got his handcuffs off his belt and cuffed Bill with his hands behind his back. It would be illegal for him to carry a gun if he was on parole, Sandra surmised. She was off the hook.

The phone rang. The caller ID showed the name and phone number of Sandra's obstetrician. Her heart jumped once again. She didn't want to miss the show out her window, but this was too important. If she didn't answer, she would be up all night wondering what was going on.

"Sandra, this is Dr. Martin. Am I getting you at a bad time?"

How could she know? "No, this is fine. I was trying to make sense of the list of lab tests," she answered.

"You should have never been sent the report. I have to call several patients who received them. I apologize. We have some new procedures in the office, and sometimes old ones slip by." She paused for a moment and then continued. "The reason I am calling is because your ELISA screen was positive. It's a test that screens for HIV antibodies. Having a positive ELISA doesn't mean you are HIV positive. We need to run another test to be certain."

Sandra had gone to her recliner to collapse. *HIV?*

"Can you come into tomorrow morning and give us another tube of blood?" Dr. Martin knew she had given Sandra what would have amounted to a death sentence a few years ago. There were medications now that were safe and effective. HIV was still dangerous, still worrisome for the baby, unless the mother took medication.

"I'm still back at HIV," Sandra responded. "Everything else went in one ear and out the other."

"Come in tomorrow morning, and we will talk then. We aren't sure you have HIV until we do a second test. Most likely, you are fine, so don't worry. Okay?"

Sandra thought she might be in shock. Thank God she hadn't slept with Tom on the first date. She had wanted to. "All right. I'll come in tomorrow morning before I go to work." They said good-bye, the doctor repeating the order not to worry. Sandra hung up. *How can I get rid of Tom tonight?* As though he were reading her mind, there was a knock at the back door. She struggled to get up out of the chair. She was not going to tell him this latest news. Opening the door for him, she saw him looking into her eyes. *Oh God, one of those intuitive men.*

"You are as white as a sheet. You don't have to worry anymore. He has broken parole and will be shipped back to Rikers Island tonight." He kept looking at her. "I have to go downtown now to process him, but you'll be safe. If you feel nervous, I can ask Jim to come back."

"No, I'm fine. It was really shocking to see him there and then see him be taken away," she lied. He hadn't tried to hug her again, which she was grateful for. She would have surely broken down crying if he had.

"I'll call you later," he said. He got into his car and, waving at her, drove off down the alley. As she locked the door behind him, a vision of Pam went through her brain.

22

Earlier that day, when they got to Pam's house in Babylon, Tom went up to the door with Sandra when Pam didn't answer the phone. The door was unlocked, and they found Pam on the hallway floor. She was a mess. It was obvious she had been ill a while. Tom called 911 and identified himself as an officer with NYPD. Within minutes, the ambulance was there. Sandra was on the floor with her friend, holding her head, trying to rouse her. Sandra got Pam's purse and keys on the table in the hallway, and she and Tom followed the ambulance in his car. She thought of Andy. Tom called the Babylon precinct and left a message for Andy to call him. Just as they pulled into the emergency room parking lot, Andy called back. Tom briefly told him the situation, and Andy said he would meet them in the waiting room. Sandra decided she better call Marie, too. Marie said she would leave right away and meet them in one to two hours.

Andy arrived at the hospital shortly after they did. Sandra told him what had happened and that she didn't have any idea what could be wrong with Pam. Andy shook his head in understanding, but said nothing. Sandra couldn't determine if he was in agreement with her or in shock. *Hadn't they just seen each other?* She decided to do her sly investigation.

"How did she seem when you saw her on Saturday?" She looked right at him. There was no way he would be able to deny seeing her.

"Fine! I mean, she seemed okay. She was a little depressed, but that's to be expected with what she has been through." He didn't add the unspoken *you know all about it*. He seemed totally ignorant of what Sandra's relationship was with Pam. They stood together in a silent circle. "Why don't I find out what's going on?" He pulled out his badge; Tom smiled. It was sometimes beneficial to be a policeman. He left them and went to the nurses' station.

Sandra watched him show his badge to the nurse, who gestured toward the room where Pam had been taken. He disappeared behind a curtained area.

"Let's sit down," Tom said, taking Sandra by the hand. "I wonder how long she would have been on the floor like that if you hadn't offered to check up on her." He shook his head.

"She wasn't expecting anyone that I know of. Why was her door unlocked? Not that the area is dangerous, but since the Bill thing, she is careful about securing the house. One thing I am certain of, Pam is going to have a fit when she finds out Andy saw her looking so awful." Sandra laughed cynically. "God forbid." *Why the derision?* Sandra thought. Pam had never done anything to her, and now Sandra was feeling a bit smug that Pam was being exposed. She felt a little guilty. *Maybe I am jealous of her, after all*, she thought.

She glanced over at Tom. He was really handsome. His jaw was chiseled, and he had huge blue eyes and dark wavy hair; she could sense Jack's jealousy from the grave.

Oh well, you're dead, aren't you? "Look, Tom, if you need to get back to the city, I can take the train home," Sandra told him. "You really don't need to wait here with me."

"I don't mind waiting. You can leave when her sister gets here, correct? I can wait that long. I need to make a quick call, though. Will you be all right?"

She nodded yes. He got up and walked out to the parking lot. She guessed he was making a call to work. Then Andy came back to the waiting room. He was ghostly white.

"She is still unconscious. The doctor said they are going to move her up to the ICU, and then we can see her. They suspect she may have a virus of some type, so she will be placed in isolation until they know for certain. She's dehydrated and has a high fever, and that could be why she passed out. They have IVs started now." He sat down next to Sandra. "So you're Sandra?" he said.

She smiled at him. "Yep, that's me."

They sat in silence for a while, and then Tom returned. Sandra was grateful for the distraction; he took over the conversation with questions to Andy about his job.

In record time, Marie got to the hospital. She parked her car in a no parking zone and busted through the automatic door, pushing aside an older couple who was talking in front of the door.

"Oh my God!" she screamed when she saw Sandra. "Where the hell is she?" Sandra got up and went right to Marie.

"Stay calm now, Marie. The doctors aren't sure what the problem is yet." Sandra talked in a low voice. She placed a comforting hand on Marie's arm and made eye contact. *It's as though I am talking to an insane person*, she thought. "As soon as they know, they will tell you. Why not go up to that person," she pointed to a nurse at the nurses' station, "and tell her you are the family member. They will tell you more than they'll tell us." Marie did as Sandra suggested, running up to the desk and yelling, "Where's my sister? Where's Pam Smith?"

The nurse pointed to the room behind the curtain, and with a growl said, "Right in there." She thought, *Let that doctor deal with her. I'm sick of the family already.* Marie went into the room without knocking on the door. Sandra could hear her screams. *Oh no*, she thought.

"What are you doing to her?" she yelled. "What's wrong with her?" In the next moment, Marie was being led out to the waiting room by a very grim-looking nurse.

"Stay here. When we are done taking care of your sister, someone will come and get you. Don't come back again, do you understand me? If you do, I will have the security guard escort you out." Then she looked at Andy. "You know better. Keep her outta that room!" She turned and walked back to the door behind the curtain.

Marie broke down, her head in her hands, and started sobbing. "Oh my God!" she yelled again. "What is wrong with her? They had her legs spread apart and were putting tubes up into her! She had tubes in her nose! Oh my God!"

Sandra couldn't help herself; she snickered loud enough that Tom heard. "Marie, for God's sake, be quiet. They were putting a catheter into her. You should have knocked before you went in. Poor Pam! Have some respect for your sister." Then Sandra decided that she had

had enough. "Come on Tom, let's get back to the city," she said, standing up. "Marie, please call me when you hear anything, okay?" She forced herself to bend over and embrace Marie, who put her arms around Sandra and sobbed louder than before.

"Good-bye, Andy," Sandra said.

"I'm sorry! I'll pull myself together!" Sandra handed her a tissue, and Marie took it from her and blew her nose. "Poor Pam!" she yelled and began wailing again.

Sandra looked over at Andy, and with her eyebrows up and finger pointed down at Marie's head, she said simply, "Andy?" And then, "Come on, Tom, time to go." She picked up her purse and walked out, hoping Tom was following her. She knew she couldn't stay there another second. When they got to the automatic doors, she looked back and saw that Andy had moved next to Marie and had his arm around her while she cried.

Tom and Sandra walked to the car together, not saying anything. Sandra thought he was probably surprised at how harsh she had been with Marie. *That was too bad.* Andy would soon see that unless he was firm with Marie, she would work herself up into such a state they would have to sedate her. And then she thought back to the afternoon that Jack had died. Marie was calm then. *Why? Did she want to stay alert in case she missed something I said?* Sandra thought. She didn't want to be left out of the gossip.

"Wow, that was intense," Tom remarked. "Does she have mental problems?" Sandra looked at him surprised and then laughed out loud.

"You could say that." They reached the car, and he held the door for her while she got in.

When he sat next to her, she said, "That family has been through a lot this year. She usually doesn't get nuts like that, but on occasion, watch out!" Silently, she thought, *If anything happens to Pam, I don't know what I will do. I'll be the crazy one.*

Tom put the key in the ignition, but before he started the car, he leaned over, taking Sandra in his arms, and placed his hand on her chin. He turned her head toward him and kissed her.

The ride home went fast; there was so much to talk about, so much to share. But the day would end as it began—in total chaos.

23

By midnight on Tuesday, Pam woke up. At first, she didn't know where she was. Once she figured it out, she realized Andy was standing over her. She saw Marie in a chair next to the bed, howling away.

"Oh, Pam! You're alive! Thank God!" Marie wailed.

"Marie! Shut up! Good lord! You need to go to the beach and get my makeup bag right away, do you understand me? And, Andy, I am going to have to ask you to please wait out in the hall until I fix my face."

Marie got up, snorting unattractively, but she grabbed her purse and almost ran out the door. Andy argued with her about leaving; he had been there looking at her all evening. She actually looked pretty good, all things considered. But then something told him that if he wanted to see her again, he would leave and would never, ever say anything about having seen her ill. He pressed the nurses' button before he left.

"Well, hello!" A young, pretty nurse said as she came in to see that Pam was awake. "Do you know where you are?" she asked.

"Am I at Mercy?" Pam looked around the room.

"Right! Did your family tell you why you are here?" She was standing at the side of the bed, adjusting a blood pressure cuff on Pam's arm, pushing some buttons on a scary-looking monitor that hung above the bed.

"No, I didn't give them a chance. I hardly know that man and am angry that he saw me without any makeup." Pam was going to be her usual honest self, no matter how silly it sounded to others. She shuddered, thinking about Andy standing there, towering over her bed, looking down at her with unbrushed teeth and uncombed hair.

"He is very concerned. You don't look that bad, anyway! You were unconscious. Your friend found you on the floor in your home when she came to check on you this morning. They called 911, and you were brought here. I'll go out and let your doctor know you are awake, okay? Can I get you anything?"

Pam was back at "your friend." *Who found me?* She'd ask Andy. Or Marie. She shook her head no in answer to the nurse. Letting her head drop back to the pillow, she thought over the past three days, or was it longer? She wasn't sure what day it was. She felt better though. Looking at her arms, she saw the IVs. She felt the catheter in her bladder, the oxygen cannula in her nostrils. *Real attractive.* She was more than a little annoyed at Andy for being there.

Marie was back with Pam's makeup within fifteen minutes. She got her sister a basin of water with a toothbrush and washcloth and helped her freshen up. Pam put on enough makeup to feel human again. Marie brushed her hair for her and then helped her put it up in a clip. She felt better than she had since...*Saturday?* She remembered asking Andy to leave. Something must have been brewing in her body then. It was so unlike her to just give up like that. Marie was telling her about asking Sandra to check up on her.

"I knew I would have trouble getting away from the office, so she said she would come out first thing. They found you on the floor! And why would you unlock your door?" Marie asked.

"I don't remember. It's so strange that the door wasn't locked." Pam frowned.

Then the doctor came in, Pam's chart in his hand. The nurse was with him. She turned to Marie and asked her to please step out for a moment. Marie did as she was asked, reluctantly. The nurse shut the door behind her. Pam was nervous. The doctor held out his hand for Pam's.

"I'm Dr. Kempa. Do you remember anything about being sick?" He gave Pam time to think about the days prior to this and listened carefully to her, writing down everything she said.

"What do you think I have?" she asked. Her voice was shaking so badly it gave away her fear.

"I think what is making you sick may be nothing more than a common, run-of-the-mill virus. Your blood work is not too bad; you're slightly anemic, but the rest of the labs are normal, if not in the low range. However, we did run an ELISA, which is a screening for HIV antibodies. Your test was positive. We ran a second test to double-check, and it was also positive. You have AIDS, Mrs. Smith. The viral load is light so far, so I think it has just converted from HIV to AIDS. I'm sorry, I know I'm throwing a lot at you. I want you to know that it is not as bad as it sounds." He stopped, waited. "Can I sit down?" Pam looked through him, but nodded her head yes.

168

He pulled a chair up to her bed. The nurse took the bed controls and lowered the bed so the doctor and patient would be eye to eye, then stepped out of the room.

"Can I go on?" Pam nodded her head yes again.

"Your CD-four cell count is very low. These are the cells that fight infection in your body. Have you had a lot of stress lately?" he asked.

Pam nodded yes for the third time. "My husband died right before Memorial Day. I've had a lot of stress since then." *An understatement.*

"That could definitely contribute to getting sick." He didn't like using that term, but didn't want to use the word AIDS again. He didn't think she could take it. "The new medications are wonderful, Mrs. Smith. We have a specialist here who will customize a regimen of drugs just for you. She'll draw labs again in the morning and use those results to determine the drugs. The fact that you are ill now is concerning because it may be evidence that you are immunosuppressed. The key to staying healthy is taking the drugs exactly as they are prescribed." He stopped talking and waited for her to react.

She was looking right at him, but not focusing her eyes on him. It was a little unsettling. He didn't like to make generalizations about patients, but couldn't help himself. Something about this woman shook him up. The diagnosis alone was horrifying. She said her husband had recently died. She wasn't a drug addict. She had been married. He hated to think what a diagnosis of AIDS would mean to her as she grieved for her husband. She finally spoke.

"When can I go home?"

"Probably tomorrow, after you talk to Dr. Toms. Is there anything I can do for you now?" He felt responsible for her state of mind. He'd do just about anything to make her feel better.

"Yes, there is something."

He stood up and waited for her to continue.

"Could you tell my visitors that they can't come back in? That I am going to sleep?"

"I can do that." He put out his hand to her.

She took it and grasped it.

"Good night, Mrs. Smith. I'll see you tomorrow."

"Goodnight, Dr. Kempa." She put her head back on the pillow, dismissing him.

He left and closed the door behind him. He must have told Marie and Andy to leave, because they didn't come back.

24

Jack, you did this to me. Now I have to tell our children that I have AIDS. Then she thought of Sandra and Marie. *If I have it, they must have it, too. Or would they be spared? Marie was screwing him almost as long as I was,* she thought. Pam thought of Sandra's baby. *Oh God, please spare that little innocent life.* A chill went through her body. She rarely allowed the visions to encroach her thoughts but allowed them in now. First, the sexual embrace between Jack and Sandra, he in his favorite missionary position with Sandra's long legs wrapped around his waist. And next a baby, a boy baby, perhaps. One that looked like Jack. As she imagined this baby being cradled in Sandra's arms, she saw the vivid physique of Jack, so tall and handsome, posed behind her to the left, gazing down upon the Madonna-esque figures.

She looked up at the ceiling. *Jack, you're an asshole.*

The ICU nurse had to threaten Marie with security if she didn't leave. Dr. Kempa had made it clear that Pam wasn't to have any more visitors; she needed to be allowed to sleep. They had already broken the rules allowing Marie and Andy to stay because he had flashed his badge. Now the nurse felt terrible about it; her patient's dignity had been violated. It wouldn't happen again on her watch.

She softly tapped on Pam's door and then opened it so she could see it wasn't her visitors.

"Can I come in?" she asked. "You've had a rough night." She said it as a statement. "What can I do for you?"

Pam was lying back on the pillow, looking up at the ceiling. "I never, ever thought my life would turn out the way it has." She turned her head to look at the young woman. "Why would someone as beautiful as you are choose to be a nurse? I would think you would want to be something that was more glamorous—or at least cleaner."

The nurse laughed out loud. She sat in the chair Dr. Kempa had vacated. "I always wanted to be a nurse. I saw nurses taking care of my sister when she was very ill. I loved that they had some control over her destiny. They advocated for her. They did what they could to take away her pain. They fought to maintain her dignity. I wanted to do that, too."

"Are you able to do all those things?" Pam asked.

"No," the nurse answered without pause. "I found out quickly that I have little control over anything anyone else does. I can only practice within parameters set by the patient's doctor. But the things I can do—try to make you comfortable, be your advocate, keep your dignity, protect you—I do with a vengeance. By the way, I owe you an apology for allowing that gentleman in here tonight. We have a strict rule about family members only. It won't happen again, I promise you."

"That's okay. He meant well. I don't like people seeing me looking a mess. A pretty package. I'm a vile disease tied up with a ribbon. How am I going to tell my family that I have AIDS?" Pam put her head back on the pillow and closed her eyes. She sat up again. "I thought of something you can do for me. I would kill for a pepperoni pizza right now."

"You haven't eaten today, have you? Let me see what I can do."

A half hour later, a lovely young nurse sat at an AIDS patient's bedside, sharing a pizza with her.

The next morning, Dr. Toms came in first thing and gave Pam an in-depth education of the drug protocol they would have her on. She couldn't offer any psychological support for her. The issues that Pam was faced with—having to tell her children and her mother, warning her sister and Sandra, and her own mortality—would be dealt with in the days to come. For now, she was in survival mode. It was still a minute-by-minute surrender to stay sane. Over and over, she reminded herself to stay focused, not to worry about anything but what was needed at that moment. Once the doctor left, Pam made her exodus from this room her main goal. She needed a ride home; Andy, in spite of her anger at him for invading her privacy, was the only option. Remaining civil was in her best interests.

The nurse came in with Pam's discharge papers. She was free to go. She would begin taking the drugs immediately; the hospital dispensary would give Pam the first weeks' worth. Getting there before Andy arrived was crucial; she was *not* telling him her diagnosis! The pharmacist went through each drug in detail and then offered them to Pam with a huge glass of water. He was a kind man, but she noticed him looking at her curiously. She supposed she would be susceptible from now on. People would want to know how someone who looked like she did would have

AIDS. They were dangerous generalizations. Everyone was vulnerable. Picking up the drug bottles, she stuffed them into her purse. All she wanted to do at that moment was get home. When she got there, she planned on unloading a fresh barrage of hatred toward her late husband. Fighting the urge to start screaming in the hospital lobby, she put all thoughts out of her mind. An empty head was crucial.

Andy met her in the lobby, and as much as she hated to admit it, she was happy to see him. She was still a little guarded; after all, he had seen her at her worst. She would take that up with Sandra, too, although Sandra would be getting bad news soon enough. Pam thought of all the possible relations, people who were joined together by the commonality of Jack Smith's DNA, his HIV virus. Before she put these thoughts out of her head, she screamed silently, *Fuck you, Jack!* She put her biggest fake smile on.

"Hi, Ja—Andy!" She almost slipped. "Thank you so much for helping me out!"

He hugged her, and she gave in a little. *Let him think I'm stiff from being sick.*

"What would I have done without you? Taken a cab? Oh my!" She giggled a fake Pam giggle. They walked to the curb, where he had left his patrol car. "Do I have to sit in the back?"

"Not today! Right here in the front next to me. I'll even turn the lights and the siren on, if you would like."

She slid into the car, surprised at how awful she still felt. Was this the story of her life? She had a terrible disease. It was a brand, almost. To the world, *My husband was a reprobate.*

"Do you want to get a bite to eat first?" He was looking at her.

Was he crazy? "No, thank you. I'm not feeling well enough to go out yet." She looked straight ahead.

"Of course! What am I thinking? Sorry. Home it is!" He sped out of the hospital parking lot onto the road that led to the beach.

Pam was counting, *One, two, three, four, five...Hold on, girl,* she thought. *You are almost there.* They didn't speak the rest of the way. Pulling up to the front of Pam's house, she gave out a sigh of relief. *Home! Thank God!* Under no uncertain circumstances was he coming in.

"Please don't get out; I really need to be alone. Thank you so much for coming to get me! I will be forever grateful." She then turned to look at him. "Please."

Andy looked at her and said nothing. He could sense this was it; it was the end of their relationship. Their friendship probably wouldn't grow into anything else as he had hoped. "Okay, Pam. But if you need me, or if you need anything from me, please know I am waiting to do it for you. Tell me you understand that," he said.

She nodded yes and got out, trying not to struggle. A week away from the gym had taken its toll. She closed the door and looked down through the window, waving a little good-bye.

He waved back at her, but didn't take off until she was inside.

So that was that. Pam felt liberated walking up to her front door. She wasn't ready to be in a relationship, AIDS or no AIDS. She wanted to be alone, to process her life and what had been revealed to her. Up to this point, nothing really had been *done* to her short of lies and betrayal. Now, the virus that was attacking her body, that was real. It was something horrible that was tangible. Jack had given this to her. *Where did it came from originally? Oh God, what a horrible thought.* She thought of Harold or Bernice. She wasn't about to suggest to Bernice to get tested for HIV. So she would never know. She bent over to pick a weed growing out of the gravel sidewalk. She would call the gardener today; he had been slacking off since Jack died.

Out of nowhere the thought came, *How was Jack's business?* A meeting with Sandra and Peter might be due as well. They certainly were not including her in the loop. She unlocked the door to her house and didn't turn around one last time to wave good-bye to Andy. She could hear the car slowly pull away from the curb. He should have known better than to ask a woman whose husband had died two weeks prior to go for coffee. It wasn't her fault. She felt released from guilt over Andy.

Her house smelled musty, closed in. It was Wednesday. *Had the cleaning ladies come on Tuesday?* She didn't think so. *Or was that why I had gotten up to unlock the door? And then fainted? Could I have been there on the floor all night?* Her answering machine message light was beeping away, evidence of many missed calls and messages left. She thought, perhaps, she shouldn't be home alone today, but having her family there, Sandra, her mother, it would just be too overwhelming. She would shower and do her hair and makeup, get out of this dirty sweat suit.

Immediately afterward, she felt better than she had in weeks. She remembered the doctor and nurses reminding her to drink plenty of fluids. She went into her kitchen pantry and found six-packs of Gatorade and put one of them in the refrigerator. *What is my routine, anyway?* She knew she had one, a meager one, but it was almost a liturgy. It would be the way she would continue to live her life, boring and self-absorbed, alone.

25

Marie tried to call her sister at the hospital, only to find out she had been discharged. *To whom and to what? An empty house?* She was going to finish what she had to do at work, and then if she could get away she would go to Babylon. The new members of the staff where experienced self-starters and were capable of working without her breathing down their necks. Pam shouldn't be home alone. She tried calling again and still no answer. She debated calling Sandra but decided against it. *What could that snake tell me? That my sister is sick? No fucking kidding!* When Sandra called her after calling the ambulance, Sandra was so condescending that Marie thought she might be blaming her for Pam being unconscious.

"Did you notice anything unusual when you talked to Pam?" Sandra asked. "I find it difficult to believe that she sounded normal."

Marie ignored her and asked for details.

"I don't know anything," Sandra replied. "I found her out cold on the hallway floor and then called 911. I just hope we got her help in time."

Sandra's comments resonated in Marie's head; she wouldn't make the same mistake twice. This time, she would go to her sister whether she needed her or not.

While Pam was settling in at home, Sandra was headed to her obstetrician's office to have a second blood test. HIV. It was such a loaded acronym that hearing it yesterday and repeating it through the night and over and over in her head had made her ill. Well past morning sickness now for at least a month, she awoke retching first thing that morning. She had never been so frightened in her entire life. The doctor said it meant nothing. The test was probably a false positive, and they would solve the mystery by taking more blood that morning, and by the afternoon, have an answer for her. No one had asked her yet if she had unprotected sex, if she shared needles, or if she had a high-risk lifestyle. What did that mean? Working like a demon day after day, barely having a social life, and then a weekly meeting with the man of her dreams, who just happened to be married and now, it would appear, was also a child abuser, whoremonger, or worse? For a split second, she thought she might know what Pam had been going through for the past weeks—the betrayal, the total lack of respect, the horror that had been Jack. As the cab pulled up to her stop, she thought of Marie and Pam.

She got out of the cab and threw some money down for the tip and the fare. The cab sped off. She stood on the curb, petrified to take that next step, to walk through the door and face her doctor. Traffic was horrible, cars whizzing by, cabs narrowly missing pedestrians; she was taking her life standing there. *Go do it*. She got up on the sidewalk and went to the door of the office.

She was the only patient in the waiting room, but the receptionist refused to make eye contact with her and was short and curt. She pointed to a seat and told her to sit down; the nurse would be with her in a minute.

The door to a back room opened, and a smiling nurse said, "Follow me."

It took less than two minutes to draw the blood.

"The doctor will have the results after lunch, and if there is anything to hear, she'll call you. I doubt it, though." She patted Sandra on the back.

Sandra had to control the urge to swing around and throw the offending hand off her body. *Why do you doubt it?* she wanted to ask. *Don't I look like someone who might have HIV?* Sandra could feel the irrational outburst forming in the back of her throat, and unable to make eye contact, she simply said, "Thank you," and left the room quickly.

She decided to go across town and go back home; she wasn't going to work today. In spite of rush hour, she got a cab right away. It was already hot, and the cab smelled like body odor. Tears were near the surface, and she fought them and took control of her body. She would not decompensate in the back of a stinking cab. The streets of the East Side of Manhattan flew by as the driver broke every traffic rule. Sandra reached behind her and found her seat belt. The Pakistani man looked at her in his rearview mirror when he heard the click and gave the gas pedal an extra push. Sandra screamed at him.

"My boyfriend is a cop, and I'll call him right now if you don't slow this damn cab down!"

"I'm not driving fast," he argued.

"SLOW DOWN!" she yodeled. And she got her phone out with a sweeping gesture, sitting forward and slamming it up against the glass partition, but not touching the filthy thing with her hands. "And I am warning all my friends to stay away from your filthy cab! HELP!" She screamed.

The driver slowed down.

She told him to stop in front of the grocery store on Broadway; under no condition would she allow him to see where she lived. She threw money down on the backseat and slammed the door. She held her phone up so he could see it. "I've got your number!" she yelled.

"Someone got up on the wrong side of the bed," a woman whispered as they passed by.

"I wish I had the courage to tell a cabbie off," her companion replied.

Sandra went into the store and got a few things to get her through the rest of the week. She couldn't stop eating. She had to go on living because of the baby. The four-block walk home was grueling, the heat, the worry. *It is probably for nothing* kept going through her mind. *But was it?* Jack could have easily given her something, knowing his history.

After she reached her apartment and let herself in, she finally exploded, throwing her purse across the sitting area. She was so angry at Jack. "Now I can waste a day waiting for the doctor to call me. Thanks!" she yelled at the ceiling. "Thanks, Jack! You asshole!" The still, small voice said to Sandra, *He can't hear you.* "Well then, thank you, God! This is just what I needed!"

She went into her bedroom to change from work clothes into her spandex. She would get a jump start on her housekeeping for the weekend. *I sure as hell am not going to the beach. NO WAY!* And then she thought of Pam. *Gen-*

tle, sweet, forgiving Pam. She immediately calmed down. Maybe she better give her a call, make sure she was okay.

She got her cell phone out of her purse and keyed in the hospital number. The operator told her Pam had been discharged. *Well, that is good!* Dialing Pam's house number, she thought, *She must not be too ill if she was sent home already.*

"Hello?" was the timid whisper of a greeting.

Sandra's heart sunk. "Pam? It's Sandra. How are you?"

Pam wanted to tell Sandra the truth, but over the phone? Maybe not. "I'm better! Thank you for asking." Pam said and remembered how she ended up in the hospital. "By the way, thank you for what you did for me yesterday. What would have happened to me if you hadn't come?"

You would have probably been fine, just sore from lying on the floor. She gave a simple "you're welcome" instead.

"So what do you think about this weekend?" Pam asked.

Sandra thought she might be able to tolerate a day there, but not more if Marie was coming; Marie was getting on her nerves lately. "I think I can come. Will Marie be there? The three of us haven't been together in quite a while!" she added, hoping the statement hid the real reason she was asking.

"I'm going to ask her today. So we'll talk later?" Making small talk was exhausting her. Not exploding with facts about AIDS, warning Sandra, apologizing to her. She had decided she wanted to tell both Marie and Sandra together. She had to tell her family, her mother, and children. But she was not telling Andy. They hadn't exchanged any bodily fluids that she could remember, limit-ing their kissing to closed-mouth pecks. She'd check with Dr. Toms. Suddenly overcome with fear and worry, Pam didn't want to talk on the phone anymore. "I'm so tired! So good-bye for now."

"Oh, I forgot already that you are ill! Yes, we will talk later. Good-bye, Pam," Sandra said and hung up. She stood at the dining table and looked out her window. There weren't many birds lately; they must be finding plenty to eat in the park. She stared at the empty birdfeeder. *Was Pam dismissive with her? Was there something underlying that Sandra was missing?* She thought that Pam was too good to be true and that, one day, the real Pam, the human Pam, would burst out, spewing hatred and unforgive-ness all over the place. Sandra caught herself in what was becoming a more frequent inner dialogue, one in which she blamed Pam for her predicament. If Pam had been a better wife, Jack wouldn't have looked outside of his mar-riage for companionship. If Pam hadn't been so kind, she could vent her anger at Jack against her. And then came the about-face; schizophrenically, Sandra covered her face with her hands and started crying. It was no one's fault. The affair just happened. She was to blame if anyone was, because she slept with a married man. Finally, her inner voice said, *GIVE IT A REST.*

She got busy cleaning up, trying not to look at the phone. But when she ran the vacuum, she picked up the receiver and carried it in her pocket. At 1:00, she stopped for lunch. She was making a sandwich when the phone rang. Her heart started pounding against the wall of her chest. The caller ID said it was the doctor. She reluctantly answered it, pressing the talk button.

"The results of your last test are in, Sandra. It was positive for HIV." She didn't say anything else for a moment. "There is a doctor here in the building—Dr. Mathur—who specializes in treating HIV and AIDS patients who are pregnant. Can you see him tomorrow? Taking antiretroviral drugs will help keep you and the baby safe."

"I can see him. I hardly know what to say. Should I start screaming now or after we hang up?"

"Sandra, I promise you it isn't as lethal as it sounds anymore, if you take care of yourself. You are healthy and young, and that is great start. See Dr. Mathur as soon as possible, okay? He'll give you the latest information. I would like to continue to be your primary, though. We will see you weekly, if you are agreeable to it." Sandra choked back tears. She had been fully ready to be judged.

"I'll call him as soon as we hang up."

"Good-bye, then, Sandra. I'll see you next week, okay? Call the office after two, when the receptionist gets back from lunch, and make an appointment. We'll work through this together."

They said good-bye.

Sandra sat at her dining table and put her head down and cried. She was so alone. Thank God her parents were dead. She would never be able to tell her sister, who didn't know about the baby, either.

Tom. He had kissed her full on an open mouth. She would have to tell him. Lowering her head to the table again, she wept for the embarrassment of it, for the futility of the relationship she thought they might have had. She had just given it a death sentence with the diagnosis of HIV. *Fucking Jack!* But it was her fault as well. She was reaping the fruit of sleeping with a married man. *Boy did he ever not fit the mold! Jack, HIV positive!*

And then she thought of Pam and Marie again. Certainly, she got the virus from Jack. She'd had a negative HIV/AIDS test after her last "real" boyfriend. It was something all of her friends in New York did. So it had to be Jack. That meant that both his wife and her sister had been exposed. She didn't know enough yet about the virus and its incubation. They may have built up immunity to him after all these years. *Was that even possible?* In spite of her Pam-bashing thoughts just minutes earlier, now she wanted to talk to Pam. She *needed* to talk to Pam. There was no one else.

26

Marie and Pam finally caught up with each other. Pam had to talk to Marie about getting tested for HIV/AIDS right away. Pam knew it had come from Jack because Marie had been a virgin when she met him and had claimed never to have been with anyone else. Somehow, she would find the courage to tell her sister the awful news. It was yet another affront to her life and what she had mistakenly believed it to be. Her husband had had sex with her own sister and possibly infected her with HIV. What could be worse?

"Do you think you can come by before this weekend?" Pam asked. "We need to talk."

"What do you have in mind?" Marie asked in return. "After work either today or tomorrow is all we have."

"What about Friday night? And then you can stay if you want," Pam replied, leaving out the part about Sandra possibly being there on Saturday.

"I was supposed to have dinner with Arthur on Friday night. I haven't seen him all summer because he has a new boyfriend." Marie thought there was a good chance her friend would cancel on her; it had already happened twice in August alone. "You tell me," she told Pam. "You're the ill one."

Pam had never begged for anything in her life, and this was starting to feel like "a beg."

"Are you okay? I mean, I know you're sick, but it's not more than 'sick,' is it? You're starting to scare me."

"Well, come tonight, then," she replied. "I don't want to talk about it over the phone."

Marie's heart missed a beat.

Then Pam added in explanation, "More news about our beloved Jack."

Okay, I can handle that. Marie thought. *What could be worse than what we already know?*

They hung up.

Pam was relieved that step one of the big reveal was going to be over in few hours. She sat at the kitchen counter, looking out the big windows that opened out to the vast dunes and beach grasses and then down to the water. No matter what happened in this house, that vista never changed. It was the one and only constant in her life. The momentary fear that she might not be able to afford to stay there after Jack died taught her that she would have to stay no matter what. The beach, not the house as she had once thought, was her lifeline. It was the stabilizing force in a sea of drama for which she had no control. The things that scared her a few months ago were resolved; she no longer felt like the sand would suck her in, that the undertow would take the house out of her reach. Those manifestations may have been a response to stress. Lately, she spent many nights out on the veranda, falling asleep and waking up there in the morning, which was stupid of her, because vagrants and social misfits were known to canvass the beach at night, looking for loot left behind by day-trippers, sleeping on the sand, or looking for an un-locked garage to steal from or get out of the weather. Her neighbors had barking dogs, thank God, and they were roused by the passing of a fly. She would be safe as long as they lived next door.

The ringing phone disturbed her revelry at the window. She picked it up and saw Sandra's number. She must have decided when she would come.

"Hi again," Pam said. "So will you come this weekend?" She was trying to get her old enthusiasm back for company in spite of the reason for the gathering. "The weather is supposed to be gorgeous again." And then she heard it—a soft moan, sniffling. Sandra was crying. "What is it Sandra? Are you okay?" Pam stood up with the phone and started pacing.

"No, Pam, I'm not okay. I'll never be okay again. And I'm afraid you and Marie won't be, either." And then was crying in earnest—*wailing* was a better word—and snorting.

"Sandra, what is it?" She had already forgotten about her own diagnosis. "Please tell me!"

"I'm HIV positive! The doctor just called me not five minutes ago. I was going to wait to tell you, because of you being sick now and everything, but I am so worried about the baby! I have to start taking all of these drugs and going to a different doctor. Jack gave it to me, too! So that means you and Marie have to be tested." She launched into a new wailing. Possibly for the first time, Sandra sounded like the twenty-something woman she was.

Pam had stopped pacing and walked into her bedroom, pulling the covers back and getting into bed again. She waited while Sandra's crying seemed to be calming down somewhat; she wasn't crying out loud, anyway. "Sandra, are you there?" Pam asked. "Answer me, dear."

Sandra mumbled into the phone that she was. "I found out last night I have AIDS," Pam admitted. "I wanted to tell you in person. It didn't occur to me that they test for it in pregnancy now. What I am sick with right now is just the flu. The doctor thinks I may have converted this summer because of all the stress with Jack dying. They can tell by the virus load and some other things."

"You have AIDS?" Sandra asked, incredulous. "Not just HIV?" *How could this be happening?*

"AIDS." Pam fell back against the pillows again. She was exhausted. "I still have to warn my sister. She's coming here tonight." *Oh God.* "She'll need to be tested right away. Sandra, I have to hang up now. I'm completely wiped out. I'm sorry this happened to you. It's the worst. It was Jack's fault, entirely his fault. Please accept my apologies. But I have to rest. I hope you'll visit this weekend." She didn't wait for a response from Sandra. "Good-bye, my friend." And then she was gone.

Sandra looked out her window again. There was a momma Cardinal on the ledge of the feeder, looking in at Sandra. She was very still, as to not scare the little bird away. Time was moving on. Two people in the world had received devastating news, news that would connect them in yet another macabre way. They had gotten an everlasting gift from the same man. Yet a baby would be born in less than four months who would bear the worst burden of all—the possibility that he or she might also be sick through no fault of his own but his mother's sin and that he might be orphaned at a young age.

In spite of the tragedy, people were still making reservations to dine out tonight. Someone was preparing for their wedding this weekend. The minister at the Methodist church on the corner was writing his sermon for Sunday service. The cabdriver she had yelled at that very morning was getting ready to go home to his family for dinner. About eighteen million people in New York City were coming or going, working or sleeping, fighting or loving, being born or dying. Life was going on. It wasn't affected by Sandra's melodrama. It was of her own making. Ego, pride, loneliness, all of the things that made up why she slept with a married man she didn't know very well, after all. A beautiful face in a smoldering, putrid body, riddled with a virus he had picked up from who knew what, maybe from his own father.

When she had first discovered she was pregnant, she had praised a God she didn't worship. How had her situation changed? She was still pregnant. The huge unknown was a possibility for prayer, to put her faith in something that she had relied on in the past, only in the direst times. So without wasting another minute, she slid off the chair onto her knees. She blubbered once and caught herself. She leaned over the seat of the chair and grasped her hands together.

"Dear God, please help me," she said out loud. "Please don't let this hurt my baby." The tears came swiftly and violently then. She yelled out to a god she didn't know and wasn't sure existed, but she was desperate. "Please, God, please!" And then quietly, with head bowed and jaw clenched she growled, "Punish him, Lord. Punish Jack."

27

Work was crazy busy all afternoon, and by the time Marie was able to leave, it was in the middle of rush hour. She had to go to the garage at her apartment building and get the car first before she could leave for Pam's. The possibility that she would end up staying the night loomed, so she ran into her apartment and threw clothes into an overnight bag. Traffic in town had started to die down by the time she pulled onto Thirty-fourth Street, headed toward Long Island. For some reason, she started to count up the number of times she had made this trip over the years. Not counting the times she had taken the train or driven with her brother-in-law, it might have been close to a thousand times. Most of the trips were loaded with happy anticipation. Even now, knowing that she may be getting more crappy news about Jack, she was excited about the trip. She wanted to see that her sister was safe, and it would be good to see the ocean midweek.

She remembered when Jack was alive. During one of their many rendezvous for lunch at a hot dog vendor, he would say to her, "I think I am going to go home tonight. I miss my girl." Marie had never told Pam that; she didn't want her to know all the times that she and Jack had lunch together. It was several times a week until he started to fuck Sandra. Maybe she would tell her sister the story tonight. He had missed his wife. He had loved her in his own way. He expected nothing from her because she was all that he thought he needed outside of his sexual escapades with Marie. When she refused him, not wanting to come into the city, he never, ever said a negative word about it. "It was just Pam," he said. He would do whatever it took to make her happy, even if it meant not living with her throughout the week. Of course, it backfired. He was incapable of being faithful to her. Sex was just something that you did to relieve yourself from an urge that wouldn't go away. If he saw something on TV that aroused him, he had to take care of it soon after. The weekends were filled with sex for him, both his wife and his sister-in-law, if necessary. What Marie knew of him was miniscule, the tip of the iceberg.

Marie was aware that he had a sexual addiction of the extreme kind. He was a compulsive masturbator. He admitted to jacking-off in the toilet stall of the train on the way home on Friday night, never worrying about getting caught, about having his reputation destroyed. It was habit, jacking-off in the shower. He probably did it at work in his private bathroom as well. She remembered the many times he came to her bed when they were still in the apartment on the Upper West Side, the chances he took getting caught molesting her, she just a young girl. The urge was greater than the fear. Who knew why? He had something wrong in his brain, some wires crossed. Of course, she didn't know about his own terror, his father torturing him. She was obsessing over the thought. *Did Pam know? Did she know he was masturbating?* Maybe she thought it was normal. Marie couldn't know just yet how

trivial masturbating was; if only that was all Jack was doing.

 After the molestation began, he would come to Marie's room at night, after they had already had sex once or
twice or three times that weekend, and he would ask her
to use her hand. She was mesmerized watching him, his
facial expressions. She became addicted to the power she
had over him. He didn't ask her for oral sex until she was
older, out of high school. "It's not appropriate," he told her
when she asked to do it to him. All the girls at school were
doing it. You didn't even have to be dating a guy to do it
for him. Jack was appalled. "Never, ever let a boy make you
do that! Promise me!" He'd take her by her shoulders and
shake her gently. "You are too good for that, too lovely and
too pure. Besides, I would kill whoever made you do that,
and you wouldn't want me to go to jail, now would you?"
He would take her in his arms then and hold her, murmur-
ing over and over, "Never ever, never ever." It didn't occur
to him that what he was making her do was much worse,
the long-lasting effects devastating.

 "Poor Jack," she whispered. The memory of the first
time she gave him oral sex floated through her mind like
gossamer, elusive and delicate. She loved doing it to him
and the effect it had on him. He actually cried. He would
moan out loud, writhing in ecstasy. Soon Marie thought
that might be all that she had to do for the rest of her life,
give blow jobs. She imagined getting paid for it. But then,
wasn't that what a prostitute did? Oh well, it was a good
idea while it lasted. He would ask for it whenever they
were together in the city, often coming to her apartment
nightly just for that. Now she realized that, of course, it

meant nothing to him outside of the physical sensation. He was saving money, getting her to do it rather than a whore. He cared nothing for her. He used her. These thoughts occupied her mind until she got into Babylon and arrived in front of Pam's house. She would make it an act of her will to be loving to her sister and only say loving things. She would definitely tell Pam tonight that Jack loved her. Loved her as much as he was capable of loving.

Pam was still looking out the window when her sister pulled up. It was after 8:00 p.m. She was exhausted, but had thought to get something for Marie to eat. She could only have imagined what her day at work had been like and then to be summoned to the beach like this in the middle of the week. Opening the front door for her, she waited as Marie got her suitcase out of the passenger side of the car and walked up the path to the house. They embraced, Pam reluctant to let go.

She took Marie by the hand. "Come have a little dinner. I ordered in from Romeo's."

"Yum! Let me change into my sweatpants, okay? How do you feel? You look better, that's for sure!" She walked toward her room, Pam following.

"Can you believe that Andy saw me looking like that? I don't mind telling you I was a little annoyed that he was even called."

It was a rare thing for Pam to criticize Sandra to her. Marie resisted commenting. Maybe Pam just needed to vent.

"I sort of told him I can't see him anymore."

"Oh Pammy, you liked him! You deserve to have someone in your life." She didn't add, *Who isn't a jerk.*

"Oh well, as Jack used to say, 'it is what it is.' Get changed, and I'll fix you a plate. Chicken parmesan. I might have a bite myself."

Marie changed into her sweats, and the two women got their food and went out on the veranda. Pam had candles lit and wine poured for her sister. Pam shouldn't drink anymore. She didn't feel well enough to that night, but knew the day might come where she would miss it, that having a glass of wine would be all she desired.

"No wine for you?" Marie noticed right away.

"No." There was plenty of time for explanations later. Pam wanted her sister to eat. "Can you believe the weather we have had? It's been perfect here at the beach every day."

"I miss it here. It's so hot and miserable in town; my air conditioner was on the fritz on Monday. I thought I would suffocate, and of course, the windows don't open up on the high floors. This breeze feels great."

They ate in silence. Marie was tired, and Pam was about ready to keel over.

"Honey, I have something to tell you." Pam made the decision that she had to tell her sister the truth and had to do it right then. But the second it was out of her mouth, she lost her nerve, petrified, couldn't find the words. *How do you tell your baby sister that she might have AIDS?*

Marie was looking at her, waiting. "What is it Pam? Please tell me." She put her fork down and reached over, grasping Pam's arm. "You can tell me anything, you know that. You *have* told me anything."

Pam looked down, resigned. Her entire body language spoke of defeat. "I have AIDS." There. It was out.

The words hung in the air, alive, dangerous. She had said it out loud for the second time that day. AIDS.

"What do you mean?" Marie was clearly confused, in shock. *I know what she just said, but it isn't registering. Pam can't have AIDS. Whores and drug addicts get AIDS. Poor people. The immoral.* All the unfortunate generalities trailed through Marie's mind, and none of them fit Pam. Her beautiful, healthy sister, perfect in mind and body, obsessed with fitness and nutrition, and loyal! She would *never* have had an affair! "It's a mistake!" she stated. "There is no way! Who could you have gotten AIDS from, anyway? You don't shoot up; you never cheated on Jack! There is no way!" She repeated it again and again, *No way, no way.*

Pam didn't expect this reaction. She thought Marie would rail against Jack, throw things, and possibly go berserk in rage against him. But she wasn't even thinking of him! "Marie! Listen to me! Jack gave me HIV! You could have it, too! Sandra has it; she found out today! Jack gave Sandra HIV! You have to get tested, Marie. You have to pull yourself together so you can get a test tomorrow. Do you understand what I am saying? It was Jack."

Marie was in shock, her face bright red, mouth hanging open like a crazy person. "But Jack loved you, Pam! He wouldn't give you AIDS! I know he loved you! He told me many, many times!"

Pam couldn't believe what she was hearing. Marie must be losing it. Pam started laughing! She was screaming laughing, with her mouth wide open and no sound coming out. "Jack didn't love me! It was impossible, Marie! He wasn't capable of love. You have to pull yourself together," she repeated. "You have to go tomorrow so you can get

tested. You might just have HIV, not AIDS. They think I
have AIDS now because of the shock of the past months.
It's new, the AIDS is new. It is much better to have HIV if
you have to have this. Do you hear me? But you have to get
treatment. I'm sorry, Marie!" Pam started crying. "I'm so,
so sorry. This is my fault as much as Jack's. I drove him to
you. I neglected to see it. I ignored the signs. It's my fault.
I can't live with myself if I don't face this right now. I have
to face my responsibility in the horror of it." She blew her
nose on her napkin. "I have to tell my kids. I have to tell
my kids that their beloved father, the man they worshiped,
gave their mother AIDS. They will figure it out for themselves that he was the worst kind of monster, because they
aren't dumb, those two children of mine. When they find
out you have it, they will figure it out, you can be sure of
it. The baby and Sandra, you and me." She bowed her head
and, in anguish, sobbed. Her heart was broken now. She
had heartache before, sadness beyond anything she could
have ever imagined, but now she knew her heart was damaged beyond repair.

"I had to give Andy the boot, more for his safety than
anything else, but also because I am so damaged. I doubt
if I am capable of love anymore. I can't even imagine it.
The thought of sharing my life makes me sick."

Marie listened to her sister ramble on and on, knowing that what she was saying was important, even meaningful, but it really was worthless now. Jack had betrayed
her with Sandra. He had a cruel streak that was for sure.
*But this? To knowingly give another human being HIV, with
the entire stigma? What a motherfucker!* She was glad he was
dead so she wouldn't have to kill him. She thought she

might be capable of it right this minute. She imagined shooting him with a gun, in the head. She saw the bullet tearing through his forehead, slamming him backward, and pieces of skull with gray hair attached to it flying all over. Or grabbing a huge knife, like the one Bill used on her mother, and stabbing him repeatedly in the chest. She could imagine the resistance of the tip of the blade, going through his clothes, skin, bones, and then plunging into him right up to the hilt. She saw the paper, the headlines: "LI Man Stabbed By Sister-in-law Forty-two Times. The arrest and then the trial, with her sitting at a table in front of the courtroom, her hair pulled back in a ponytail with a black barrette. Andy Andrews would be there as the detective on the scene. He would testify on her behalf. *Your Honor, he gave her AIDS.*

"Marie! Oh God, Marie, wake up, honey, wake up! Marie!" Pam was yelling at her, slapping her face, hard. "I should have killed Jack before he did this to you!"

"Stop hitting me! I'm awake!" She opened her eyes to find her sister kneeling over her, hysterical crying like she had never seen Pam. "I'm okay, Pam!" She struggled to sit up and grabbed her sister. "I'm okay! Pull yourself together, Sis! For God's sake, this isn't good for you to be so upset."

They sat on the floor together, holding each other, and Marie finally let loose and began to cry, too. They cried for Brent and Lisa, for Sandra and her baby, and for each other, but mostly they cried for Jack, because he was already dead.

28

Tom Adams got off his shift at 7:00 p.m. and decided to take the subway up to Sandra's. It was easier for him to ride the train than drive up to her apartment. Traffic would be horrible in the morning if he stayed the night. He knew he was pushing things with her. They had only known each other for four days. The connection between them was instantaneous, and she had felt it, too. How two people find each other at a certain time of life, regardless of the circumstances, was a miracle. Although he was raised Episcopalian, he started going to the Catholic church around the corner from his building. The liturgy, the mystical, magical part of what the Catholics believed in appealed to him after the brutal way he spent his life, tracking down thieves and murders, putting rapists and cheats behind bars. He believed that the timing was perfect, that Sandra had appeared in his life at the moment that God wanted her to be there. And it was up to him to accept it as a wonderful gift. Whether she was pregnant or not made no difference. He would adopt the baby if she would allow it.

He imagined their life together. In his mind's eye, he saw a combination of their two apartments. It would have her homey decorating touch, spare and comfortable, with his flair for contemporary art. Her kitchen was too small, not much more than a closet. He would need a larger space, a cook's kitchen. Cooking was a passion of his, along with his love of coffee; he'd work at putting some meat on Sandra's bones, cooking for her. She was a slender little thing. He got a shiver thinking about her.

The train was hot and smelly. He didn't ride that often, and even though he had spent his life in the city, every time he rode it the smell of urine shocked him. He was not a snob, but public urination was something that he couldn't tolerate. He never gave offenders a second chance. His father told him not to glamorize being a police officer. His job was to protect the laws of the land and that was it. He wasn't going to change anyone by ignoring his main directive. New programs in the department that focused on teaching wouldn't make any difference in the long run. It wasn't up to them to teach.

Tom thought about his dad and how he changed after he had retired from the force. He lived in a perfect little cottage on the water with roses growing up a trellis in front, which he tended with precision.

No longer drinking, he was a sought-after speaker at AA meetings. Tom thought it might have been the most difficult part of him leaving his mother; someone else would be able to help him find his stride when she had been unable to. The "other woman" was a lovely person in her mid-forties, attractive, athletic, kind. Tom liked her, although he was careful to never mention her name around his mother and sisters. Gwen may have been his father's soul mate.

What did those words mean? Tom remembered from childhood Sunday school that you were soul mates with God. But didn't He want "woman for man" so He would not be alone? His mother and father had never been together. They may have slept together and planned what was the best for their household, but they weren't friends. If he was going to spend his life with someone, that person better be his friend, he decided.

The urine smell in the train was permeating his nostrils and, he was afraid, his clothes. Finally coming to his stop, he sprinted through the door and up the stairs to the cooler, but still hot and muggy air of an August night in New York. Walking up Broadway to Eighty-second Street, he understood what it was about this neighborhood that people loved. There was everything you needed, every cultural and spiritual venue within walking distance. Every ethnic food offering, fresh veggies and fruit stands, organic food stores and restaurants galore were there for the asking. If he were lucky enough to end up with Sandra as his lifetime mate, they would live up here if she wanted to.

He crossed Broadway and starting walking down Sandra's street to her building. She didn't know he was coming, and he understood the risk he was taking by surprising her with a visit. When he got to her building and knocked on her door, there was no answer at first. He looked at his wristwatch, thinking she might have been delayed. But it was past 8:oo p.m. He rang her bell again, and a very annoyed sounding Sandra said, "What do you want? I wish you would have called first." But she did release the lock with its accompanied buzzer. Tom was instantly regretful that he had made her angry, but he was there and inside, no turning back now. Walking down the hallway to her door, he was a little nervous about seeing her. Standing at the doorway with the door open, he expected a frown. But he was immediately concerned, if not a little surprised, that she was waiting there with a tear-stained face, holding her hand out to him. He took it and followed her inside, preparing to take her in his arms again to comfort her for whatever it was that had upset her so badly.

"*Don't* kiss me," she said, closing the door as she went into his arms.

"What's wrong?" He looked down at her, trying to see into her eyes, but she wasn't cooperating.

"Come and sit down in the kitchen with me. I will make coffee; I bought a pot today." She held up a shiny percolator coffee pot that made one cup at a time. "After I tell you what I have to tell you, you may not want me to make coffee for you. Tomorrow would have come soon enough; I had a plan. But you coming unannounced like this changes everything." She looked him right in the eyes, finally.

He had gone from ecstasy at hearing that she cared enough about him to buy a coffee pot to fear that she was going to tell him to hit the road. *What the hell is going on?* In spite of whatever it was she had to say to him, he wanted to know. "Come sit next to me." He pulled her over to the table and then onto his lap. "What is it? You can tell me anything, Sandra. What could be so bad?"

She covered her face with her hands and started crying again, standing up and moving away from him. She went to her bedroom and got a box of tissues. Now everything put him at risk, her runny nose, her tears. She had to tell him.

"I found out last night that I am HIV positive. My former boyfriend gave it to me." Sandra put her head in her hands again and started sobbing, with shoulders heaving.

Tom was aghast. "What about the baby?" he asked.

"We won't know until it's born if it was passed on, but I will start taking the drugs tomorrow morning, and I'll have a C-section. There will be just a slight chance then that the baby will be infected." Uncharacteristically, she began to sob. Real heart-wrenching, choking sobs. "I am still so worried about the baby!"

Tom got up and tried to take her in his arms.

She resisted, saying, "My tears can infect you!"

He pulled her to him. "I can't get HIV from your tears! Or from kissing you. I'll be safe. You come here." He held her for a long time, patting her head, hugging her. He kissed the top of her head, smelling her shampoo. Eventually, the sobs became less and less, Sandra reaching over for a tissue for the tenth time.

"I don't expect anything from you. You can leave now and never speak to me again. I wouldn't blame you."

He continued to pet her, rubbing her back, kissing the top of her head. "No, I don't think I will. Leave. I'm a cop. I know all about HIV and AIDS. I'm also a responsible adult man. I know how to protect myself from sexually transmitted diseases. If I did get it, I can't think of a nicer person to get it from."

Finally, she reached her arms around his waist and held him tightly. In four days, she had bonded with this remarkable man who didn't flinch once when she told him about another man's baby and now a deadly disease, all part of her package. *Here I am! Take me as I am! How do I rate, having such a great guy who hasn't run in the opposite direction?*

Tom was there. He wasn't going to run from her like he probably should. From now on, she would take what he was willing to give her and try to give as much as she could in return.

29

Summer nights at the beach were the best of any nights in Pam's memory. She enjoyed them alone this summer, sitting on her lovely veranda by candlelight until the early hours of the morning. Before Jack died, she would spend it thinking of him. After he died, she found she could simply enjoy the passing of time for what it was—a rare, momentary freedom from worry. Marie had made the decision to go back to the city after the revelation of Pam's AIDS because she wanted to see her doctor first thing in the morning. So instead of sharing this time with her sister as she had planned, Pam was once again alone. She always dressed, even though no one would see her. Tonight she put on a flowing pants and top outfit made of white gauze. Her hair was pulled up into a loose knot on top of her head with perfect makeup. She felt like a prop in a movie. There would be no dialogue or interaction with other players, although the stage had seen its share of dramatic reenactments in the past months.

A large crystal glass of iced tea with a lemon slice took the place of wine. The briny smell of the sea was strong tonight, the tide was out, and the heat from the sand added to the intense summer atmosphere. Lost in thought, she was startled by the "Hello!" that echoed from the dune that bordered her property.

"It's Jeff Babcock, Mrs. Smith. Can I come up?"

Pam stood up and was able to see Jeff's profile in the moonlight. "Absolutely!" she responded, walking down the path to meet him. She offered her hand, and he took it. They began talking like old friends who had just been reunited, first about the type of grasses she had planted in her garden and then an offer from Jeff to take her to see his award-winning landscaping. He had heard all about hers, being well known in Babylon because she designed and planted most of it herself, and she had read about his in the Sunday *Times*.

"Come have a seat. Can I offer you a glass of wine?" she asked. "It's such a lovely night; I don't want to go inside."

"What are you drinking tonight?" Jeff asked, looking at her iced tea with suspicion.

Pam laughed out loud. "That's tea! I have a bottle of wine in the fridge that I opened about three hours ago; you just missed Marie. I opened it for her." He didn't respond to her revelation, and Pam found that a little strange. *Hadn't he introduced her to his family two days ago?* Maybe Marie was reading more into their relationship than met the eye. Pam took the bottle out and handed it to Jeff, who made a face.

"No thanks, I'll pass! I'm not drinking anything from France these days. If it doesn't come from the United States, I don't buy it." He went into a long diatribe about French wines.

Pam wasn't hugely knowledgeable about wine, but thought some of what he said was ridiculous. She decided that moment to change her modus operandi and speak her opinion. "For me, it has always been about the taste. If I don't like the way a wine tastes, I can't drink it!" Then she laughed. "It's the simpleton's wine philosophy."

Jeff caught himself in his snobbery and laughed along with her. "Good point! Give me a glass!"

Pam poured one and gave it to Jeff. She took the bottle out to the veranda so, hopefully, he would finish it off, French or not. She wouldn't be drinking it and hated wasting good wine.

"This is pretty good. My humble apologies for the lecture back there."

They sat down and spent the next hour chatting about gardening, living at the beach, his love of cooking, and how it saved him from clinical depression. Pam asked if the depression might have stemmed from his divorce.

"No, the divorce was mutual. Mindy and I are best of friends now. We had to be for our girls. In retrospect, I think retirement was a shock. And it was a contradiction. I couldn't stand the courtroom anymore, yet I missed it in theory. A dear friend suggested I try cooking classes, and that is how I ended up going to the CSI. I have a house in Rhinebeck, within walking distance of the school. I often say it saved my life." He glanced over at Pam, noticing for the first time how slender she had become and stopped himself before he mentioned it. Not everything needed to be said. She had just lost her husband. No wonder she lost weight. "I'd love to cook for you sometime! What are you doing this weekend?" He noticed the suspicious look in her eyes and then, with horror, remembered Marie was her sister. "Is Marie going to be coming?" He was hoping to spend more time with this interesting woman, and Marie would put a damper on it. But that couldn't be helped. "We could make a party of it!"

Pam visibly relaxed. "She is supposed to be coming Saturday morning! How nice of you! I feel like it's been a long, long time since I had fun." *What is fun?* "What can I do to help?"

"Oh no, this is going to be my opportunity to pamper you. I'm sorry I haven't been a better neighbor."

Pam recalled that his food offerings on the day of the funeral were among the only that could be eaten. "Your gifts were wonderful lifesavers. We received some pretty nasty stuff! Oh! That was so inappropriate!"

Together, they laughed out loud as Pam related some of the food they received, including a casserole that was made of canned peas and bologna. Jeff told stories about his dogs and their antics. Pam relived her childhood adventures at Coney Island. Before either of them knew it, time had flown by, and it was almost 2:00 in the morning.

"Thank you for a lovely evening," Jeff said, putting his hand out to Pam.

She took it and they shook. "It was," she said. "I can't tell you the last time I laughed so much."

They walked together down the path to the end of the dune, continuing to talk. Jeff walked backward toward his house so they could continue talking, and they finally said goodnight. Disappointed that the night was over, Pam walked back up her path and resolved to call it a night herself, although she could have stayed up until sunrise. AIDS, Jack, lies, and betrayal had not entered her thoughts since Jeff Babcock's visit. She cleaned up their glasses, thinking about him. There was no physical attraction at all for her, and it seemed on his part as well. She found herself wondering if he was gay. And she felt badly about reducing her evaluation of him to stereotypes; it was the entire package that made her think that. His grooming, interests, mannerisms...*But wouldn't Marie have suspected it?* She was dating him. Most of her friends were gay men; she should have picked up on it right away. Well, Pam decided she was not going to question her about her boyfriend's sexual preferences. It was not her business.

She locked up the sliders and made sure the front door and the door to the garage were secure before she got ready for bed. While she was taking the makeup off her face, she had a pang of worry about Sandra, which she quickly squelched. She would not be taking on that burden. Jack got her pregnant. Jack gave her HIV. Not Pam. It was so like her to start thinking about something like this right before it was time to sleep!

Once again, her bed did its magic. The cool sheets and the darkness pulled her in, and she was sound asleep within seconds. But it wouldn't last, because at 5:00 in the morning, her phone started ringing, waking her with a start.

"Hello?" Her heart was pounding so loud she was sure the caller could hear it, but there was no answer. "Hello?" she said again. "Who is this?"

And then a recording, "This is an automated call from the New York State Prison System. Please press one to continue." *Oh crap*, Pam thought. She had a choice here: respond with pressing the key that could lead to a verbal boxing match with her brother-in-law or hang up and let the peace of the day continue. She hung up.

"Your party hung up," a recorded message said. "God damn it!" Bill Smith yelled into the phone.

"Pipe down, Smith," a prison guard said.

Bill thought, *Now what the hell am I going to do?* He needed Pam to vouch for him while bail was being set that morning. *She owes it to me to pay up. Her late husband was my brother, for God's sake!* He started pacing. A court-appointed attorney was due in by 7:00 that morning. The guard came and unlocked the phone room and took Bill by the arm, his hands cuffed in front of him, shackles on his ankles. He shuffled along with his head down, embarrassed. *How did I get into this mess again?* He vacillated between remorse that he had so little self-control and rage, wanting to kill his sister-in-law. She was the only one who could help him. His mother was dependent on Pam as well and had no money of her own. He didn't know if she was following through on the art auction because he was unable to talk to her until visiting day. He'd ruined his chances of getting Sandra on his side. The police had informed him that she had taken a restraining order out against him, and that is why they were parked in back of her building. *Don't they have anything better to do than be lookouts for that whore?*

The attorney, a pimply faced, twenty-something girl found out for Bill that Anne was being held in a lock-up downtown instead of bringing her to Rikers, for her own protection. Unless Pam dropped the charges against her, she would be going to trial early next week for theft; she had pleaded not guilty. His attorney was supposed to have asked his mother to call Pam and beg her to drop the charges. Their boys were being cared for by Anne's sister, and Bill cringed every time he thought of it. She was a lazy pig of a woman with an unkempt house and drunk for a husband. He laughed out loud! *Sounds like my own family*, he thought.

The guard unlocked his cell and let go of his arm. He walked in and didn't turn around, for fear that he would lunge at the guard and tear him from limb to limb, controlling his normal aggression. There was nothing he could do now but wait—for Pam to make a move on his behalf and that of his wife.

After just two days, Anne Smith loved prison life. She was told when to bathe, all her meals were served to her on a tray, sex with Bill was the last thing she had to worry about, and there were endless expanses of time with nothing to do. No phones ringing, no television blasting away, no shopping to be done, and she didn't have to think about bills to pay and lack of money. It was the ideal life. She made the decision to plead not guilty because she wanted a trial. The longer she could drag out this stint in the city jail, the better. There were only six women in her block—five prostitutes and Anne. She didn't have to go outdoors if she didn't want to, and there were no work details. Being there was like having a long vacation, and she hoped it would last the rest of her life.

30

First thing the next morning, Marie found herself sitting in one of a long line of plastic chairs at a public health clinic in Manhattan. There was no way she was going to her regular doctor with this problem. She'd become a ward of the state first. Arthur had taken the day off from his stage-setting job at the Lincoln Center to be with her.

"You always call at just the worst possible time," he told her the night before. "We were just getting ready to consummate our love," he said, speaking of his new boyfriend, Peter.

"Yes, well, I figured you owed me," she reminded him.

"Will you ever forget that?" he asked, making reference to the night he called her many years ago, a victim of Rohypnol and stranded at a club in the Meat Packing District.

She had been lying in bed with Jack, who wouldn't wait for her if she left the apartment, ensuring that their night together would be over. He left while she got into her car and drove the short distance downtown to pick up her pathetic friend, standing on the corner of Hudson and Jane. *Poor Arthur*, she thought. *If ever there was a candidate for sexual reassignment surgery, it was Arthur.* When she told him that, he lit into her.

"That is a tacky generalization, if I ever heard of one. I love being a man! I love my package! You are the one who wants me to be a girl. You! Because then, if I'm a girl, you'll stop lusting after me."

"Keep dreaming, asshole," she said to him, and they laughed together.

Now, at the health clinic, Marie understood what a friend she had in Arthur. Who else would be here with her? Pam? She didn't even offer. "You should be tested right away," she had said. Marie was on her own, only this time she couldn't do it by herself. She'd gotten home from Pam's close to midnight and called Arthur right away.

"Someone better be dead," he said when he answered the phone that night, slightly out of breath.

"Why'd you answer?" she asked him later. "That's what caller ID is all about."

"I knew if you were calling me that late, it must be unavoidable. I was right," he said, putting his arm around her. He recognized her cry. She was wailing into the phone, "Pam has AIDS," over and over again. Arthur was the one person in the world who knew the truth from the beginning. He quickly figured out that if Pam had AIDS, his girlfriend could be in trouble, too. He was a regular at the clinic and knew what she needed to do. And that included taking a strong friend with her.

"So did you and Peter complete the act?" she asked him.

"No, I told him not to take his Viagra...Usually when one call comes in for help, another is right behind it. And I was right, his mother called. It was a bust all around."

They were interrupted when a woman in a blue scrub outfit called Marie's number. Arthur pushed her to go, starting her on a journey she didn't want to take.

"Come with me," the woman said. Marie followed her through a hallway that had five or more doors leading off of it. She took Marie to the farthest door, which led her to a tiny room.

"Have a seat," she offered, taking one across from her. "My name is Joanne. I'd like to ask you a few questions, if you don't mind. It isn't required to answer to receive the test, do you understand that?" Marie shook her head yes.

"Okay then, first of all, why do you want to have an HIV screening test?" Marie shrugged her shoulders. *How much information should I give?* She'd word her answers carefully.

"I just found out that a man I had been sleeping with for many years gave HIV to another woman. He's dead now, not of AIDS." It sounded so trite to her, like she was a run-of-the-mill whore. Maybe there was some truth to it.

"When did the other woman find out about the HIV?" Joanne asked.

"Yesterday," Marie answered, and then, "she has AIDS." Joanne wrote it down, but didn't flinch or make any sign that she was passing judgment.

"I'll draw some blood, and we send it off to the lab with no identifying marks except your number. No one will know anything but you and the person who runs the test. When the results come back, I'll call you myself, and we will invite you to come back and get the results, whether they are positive or negative. We don't give any results over the telephone. Do you have any questions?" When Marie shook her head no, Joanne smiled and said, "Well, roll up your sleeve!"

"Let's go to lunch," Arthur said, looking down at his skinny friend. He had also been through bouts of anorexia with her. "I've got a hankering for Middle Eastern food, what do you say?"

"Okay, if we must." He accepted that as a yes and wasn't going to argue with it. He was afraid that she would stop eating until the results came in. He wondered what he would do if she was positive. He felt paternalistic toward his friend, even though he had never had a child and wasn't sure he would know what paternalism was if it hit him in the head. But seeing her suffer was difficult, and keeping her safe was important. When she was screwing her sister's husband, he used to live in fear he would have to beat the guy up for being such a prick. He almost did once.

It must have been about four or five years earlier, when he got a late-night hysterical call. Marie was pregnant. She had just run a test.

"Don't tell him! This might be your last chance, you idiot! Just have the baby! You never have to tell your sister whose kid it is, and he is certainly not going to out himself!"

But, evidently, Jack watched Marie's menstrual cycle carefully, afraid she would purposely try and get pregnant, and when her period was late, he took her to a friend of his and the baby was aborted. It was a horrible experience; she got infected and was later told she might never conceive again. Now this. He should have killed Jack when he had the chance.

They decided to walk, the restaurant just a few blocks away. Arthur kept up a running dialogue about food, Peter, the latest show at the Lincoln Center. Marie listened and was grateful for the chance to simply be and not have to think or engage. When they arrived, they were seated right away. Arthur ordered for them—eggplant and lamb and rice, glasses of wine, and flaming cheese appetizers. Marie would have to go to work sometime; she said she would be late, and it was almost 11:30. *But was it that important?* She had been working late nightly for the past two weeks, barely acknowledging that the workload had increased exponentially when she became a manager.

"I think I am going to call out sick. Or maybe I shouldn't. What should I do?" She looked at Arthur beseechingly.

He laughed and pulled her into a bear hug. "Call them and tell them you will be there after lunch." He dug out his own cell phone and gave it to her.

She did as she was told.

"Now you can relax and get there with plenty of time to catch up this afternoon. I'll go in to work for a few hours. We've been busier lately after five, anyway."

Their lunch came, and Arthur watched Marie eat, enjoying her food, talking comfortably, and having seemingly forgotten about AIDS. Out of the blue, she started talking about Sandra and the baby.

"That damn baby! I can't stop thinking about how angry Jack would be. He'd have to tell Pam about this one, wouldn't he? Would he get away with another aborted baby?" She shook her head. "I'm guessing mine weren't the only ones. Ha! I bet there were others."

"You know you are not too old to have a baby. Even if your test turns out positive, God forbid. Women do it all the time. I'm here for you, sweetheart!" Albert and Marie had conspired when they were young that if neither of them had a partner by the time they were forty, they would have a child together.

"You're kidding, right? I have a hard time recovering from a heavy meal. How the hell would I survive a pregnancy? No, my friend, this body is shot. Besides, I can't give up my nightly bottle of wine. It's not happening, no matter what the results." Marie never thought she would want a family until Jack died. Now it was too late.

After lunch, they caught the uptown bus together, Marie getting off near her office in Hell's Kitchen and Arthur going farther uptown. She took her time walking and was revived by the time she got there, ready to work.

31

At 5:00 the next morning, Tom Adams crept from the lower level of Sandra's apartment, where he had slept on the couch, and let himself out the door to the alley. He'd have to get home to Brooklyn, change clothes, and get back downtown by 7:00. It would be a close call.

After he learned the news that Sandra was HIV positive, all he wanted to do was stay with her and comfort her. He made her dinner, wrapping a kitchen towel around his slim waist for an apron and, with a few fresh vegetables, a package of dry pasta, some parmesan cheese, and a little cream, made a fabulous primavera. They sat next to each other, watched TV in her den, and around midnight, he went up to bed with her. They held each other, kissing and stroking, and finally, he left her there, tucking her in. He told her he wanted to make love to her, but they agreed that it was way too early in their relationship. He insisted that her HIV status had nothing to do with them not doing it right then.

"How long should we wait?" he asked. "When do people do it nowadays? If it isn't the first date, then how many have to pass until it's not too soon?"

"Well, it has to be longer than four days!" She was laughing now, too. "We haven't had a real date yet, have we? I mean, shouldn't we go to dinner? Or walk in the park? What about a gallery opening?" *Did he even like art?*

And as if he had read her mind, he answered, "I love gallery openings! You have to come to Brooklyn to see my apartment. It will give you a greater understanding of who I am as a person."

"What? You think you know me because you have seen my apartment? Tell me who I am," she challenged.

He thought about it for a moment, looking around at her spare, comfortable decorating.

"The first time I came here, when we were questioning you about Bill Smith, I liked this place very much. Everything I see I think that you may have placed there for a purpose. There is no frivolous 'stuff.' Does that make sense?" He was weighing his words. "But what is here, I get the feeling, is very meaningful to you. The books, the few trinkets, they are important to you. So that tells me that you are thoughtful. Intense. No nonsense. And that you haven't decorated to impress anyone. Am I correct?"

She was smirking at him. "Yes, I guess you're right. So what? I already know that you are obsessive compulsively neat, that you like more contemporary decorating, and that you can't stand knickknacks. And I haven't seen your apartment yet!" Then Sandra got serious. "Just so you know, Jack was never here. Never once, not even to pick up me. I wouldn't allow it. As a matter of fact, I have lived here for four years, and I have never had a man here. I just thought of that! Oh my god, what does that make me?" She started laughing hysterically! "Wow, I guess that must make you feel pretty lucky?" She asked it as a question, lifting one eyebrow his way.

"I do feel lucky! Lucky you would even look in my direction," he said.

"Because I am such a catch," she said sarcastically. "How is this going to work? I mean, are we 'seeing' each other? What are you going to tell your family about someone like me?"

He looked at her a little shocked. *Can't she see what a great person she is?* "Well, for one thing, if you will have me, I am going to tell my family that the baby is mine."

Sandra lost her resolve to stay strong and started crying.

"What? What's this for?" he asked. "I believe what I feel for you already is love, although we aren't saying that out loud yet. But we don't have much time to mess around."

"I'm already five months almost." She snorted, still crying but trying to control it. Her hormones were messed up, she had recently gotten bad news, and now this wonderful guy was being kind to her. It was almost easier to be treated badly. *Denying the baby's paternity in any form wasn't an option, was it? Sorry, Jack.*

"Right, but my family doesn't know every single thing I do. As a matter of fact, I keep them in the dark as much as possible. For all they know, we have been together since last Christmas." She looked at him like he was exaggerating. "It's true! I don't date much, either. See, we should be able to sleep together because we have been dating for almost ten months."

"This is so unbelievable! How can the worst day of my life also be the best? Everything is happening so fast. I think we better slow down. It won't matter if the baby comes and we aren't 'public' yet. Very few people know I am pregnant, and if I can continue to hide it, it will stay that way."

They talked until almost 1:00 in the morning. He had little sleep, but felt revived and ready to take on the world. He got on the subway at the same place Jack had said his final good-bye to Sandra and went downtown to get his car.

Sandra woke up an hour later, exhausted but happy. She knew he had planned to leave early, but went down to look, just in case. She felt lonely for him when she saw the empty couch, the blankets and sheets folded neatly, a note left on the pillow.

Call when you can, it read. She took it and put it in her treasure box on top of the dresser down there, the one she had dragged in front of the window. She looked out and saw the sun coming up over the buildings already. It would be another summer day.

32

Labor Day weekend was just a week away. Lisa and Brent Smith would return home from school for a short break before fall classes began. Pam woke up on Friday hoping she would have the energy to drop the AIDS bomb on her mother when she returned from Connecticut today. Her sister was bringing Nelda back home, and Pam would tell both of them together. Her sister from Cherry Hill was going to come on Saturday morning and take their mother back home with her. After this was accomplished, she could look forward to her children's homecoming with some excitement.

Following her usual beauty routine, she bypassed the gym and took a long hike on the beach instead. She put the strap to her hat under her chin to help keep it on her head while she walked. The morning was cool with a breeze from the ocean. The tide was out, and she brought a bag along to hold the glass and shells she might find. She recognized people as she walked.

A young man with two German shepherds, who ran on the beach like they were training for something, would throw a stick, and the two dogs would sprint beyond it, circle back, and one would pick it up, returning it to his owner. The scenario was repeated over and over again, everyone stopping to watch them, laughing together. Their advancement on the beach was slow going. There was also a chubby, middle-aged man with a metal detector who was on the beach every morning. He arrived in his car at sunrise and combed the beach before most people were awake. Pam didn't like it, but thought how ridiculous she was being. He had as much right to the beach as anyone. Her neighbors on the north side of the house were a devoted couple, he debonair, she regal looking, even in their beach-strolling attire. Every morning they walked together and always stopped when they saw Pam to inquire about her well-being. She appreciated it but knew that it was a superficial kind of concern, that they would never be there if she really needed them. Conveniently, when Jack died, they were going out of town for a long weekend. That was fine because it left her off the hook. Jack used to say, "A friend in need is a pain in the ass."

Her bag was getting full of stuff, some shells, one piece of glass, but mostly debris. She'd empty out the trash in a barrel not far from her house. She and her neighbors took great pride in keeping the beach clean. People could be pigs. She had turned around and was heading back home when she saw him. Andy was watching her from the street that ended at the beach access. He waved to her and she back to him. Of course, that wouldn't be enough for him. He would have to take his shoes and socks off and sprint down the dunes to join her. She would just have to be guarded. *How did I get to this point in my life?* she asked herself for the umpteenth time that week.

"Hey! I was hoping I would see you today," he hollered as he ran toward her. He wasn't even out of breath. "How are you doing on this beautiful day?" He grabbed her by the shoulders and kissed her cheek. "You look like you might be feeling better."

"I'm feeling better, thank you." Pam felt guilty about being annoyed, but what was she going to do? She couldn't have a relationship with him; it would mean revealing the AIDS thing, and she wasn't ready for that. She would work at finding that balance he seemed insistent on and move from there. She remembered she had just told him that she needed to be alone. Evidently, what she needed wasn't really that important to him.

"Mind if I walk with you?" he asked as she continued walking.

Am I being rude? Maybe I better stop. "We can stop here and talk," she said. "What are you up to today? Are you parked up there?" she asked, nodding her head toward the street at the top of the dune.

"I'm not working today, actually. I was hoping I would see you because we need to talk. Or I need to talk to you. Would that be possible?"

He looked so hopeful that she felt horrible being firm, but didn't see any other way around it. "When I told you that I needed to be alone, I was serious. We should have never started seeing each other so soon. Whether it seems important or not, I need to mourn Jack's death. It seems too difficult to do it when I am with you. My pain finds a different way of coming out, and I find I get annoyed at you. You deserve better than that kind of treatment."

"I understand that. It doesn't bother me," he replied.

"But it bothers me. I don't think you understand that I want to be alone now. I don't want to be involved, to worry about superficial things that are natural to worry about when you are in a new relationship. I think I need to pamper myself a little bit." He either was going to get it or not. She decided to let it go. She wouldn't see him again if she could avoid it, but would be pleasant in cases like this where he sought her out. She would refuse him otherwise.

"Okay, when you put it that way, I guess I get it. But I didn't think I was asking that much of you," he said, putting her on the spot.

"Just by saying that puts me on the spot. I don't need to feel guilty about not wanting to see you." There. She said it out loud. She didn't want to see him. By the expression on his face, she thought he must have finally got the point.

"Not even as a friend?" he asked. He was not going to take no for an answer. He stood there on the beach in the sun, his hair blowing in the wind, handsome and rugged. What was there not to like? But she didn't have it in her.

"Oh, don't look at me like that," she said as she laughed. "Right now, I just need space. Someday, I think you'll understand. I need my privacy. I don't want the exposure that intimacy would force on me right now."

He looked down at the sand and then up again. "Is this because I came to the hospital?" He was a quick learner.

"Yes, in some ways, it is. I know you were called, but if you had known me well, you would have protected my pride by not coming into the room when I looked like I did. We hardly know each other! The nurse told me you flashed your badge to gain admittance to my room. That really stung." She had spilled her guts, now to see the way he would respond to her accusation.

"I am so sorry," he said without sarcasm. "I wasn't thinking. All I knew was that you were ill and might want someone there. You looked lovely in spite of being so sick."

She laughed out loud. "Lovely? Well! Thank you, I guess!" What to say to that? He hadn't gotten defensive or angry. "I'm getting tired. Can we end the conversation? I just need more time, okay? I want to walk back home now, so I am going to say good-bye." She started walking backward, away from him, smiling at him, and waved bye.

He didn't follow her as he could have. He waved back and started up the dune. She turned around and kept walking toward home. The walk and the encounter had a positive effect on Pam. She would prepare for her mother and sister, fixing lunch for them. Puttering in her kitchen gave her a renewed sense of her value. This was her kitchen, in her house. She was a member of the community, a neighbor who could be depended on, and although she could count the friends she had on one hand, she knew many people who had been the recipient of her husband's generosity during his lifetime. There were some good things about Jack, and although he had made it difficult to dwell upon them, she would make it an act of her will from now on. She had a few painful scenes to go through in the coming days, revealing the disease to her family and outing her husband. But she would remain loyal to him and not allow any Jack bashing to take place in his own house. How this would play out was yet to be seen. Staying positive and refusing to give in to self-pity would determine a lot. She was totally alone, and keeping optimistic might be a challenge. It would be a test to see how strong she really was.

She heard a car pull into the driveway. It was Susan and her mother. Thankfully, she left her children behind. Pam went to the door to greet them and could see her mother's concern right away.

As she embraced her daughter, she whispered, "You're so thin."

Susan wasn't as graceful. "Jesus, Pam, how do you stay so damn skinny?"

They had a group hug, Susan breaking away first to go to the veranda and look out at the ocean. "This view always takes my breath away." She turned around and looked at Pam. "You deserve to have this to look at every day."

Pam smiled at her, turning to dish up the fruit salad she had made them. *Oh God.* "Let's eat outside, okay? Mom, can you get your plate? I'll bring the tea." She had hot biscuits made from a mix just out of the oven and fruit salad with cheese. *A light, healthy meal to protect one's stomach after hearing bad news*, she thought.

They sat around the smaller table on the veranda and began eating.

Nelda talked about what a great time she had with Sue and her boys in Connecticut. "It gets so quiet around here! Those two boys never stop! I got some great exercise." It was a nice change from the loneliness of the beach.

Pam hadn't mentioned Sharon coming to get her. She hoped the need would be obvious after her revelation. She would serve coffee and pie, and then tell them. When they were about done with the salad, she got up to get dessert, taking coffee orders.

Susan got up to help her. "Are you okay, Sis? You seem a little frail." Pam hugged her.

"Let's talk out on the veranda," she answered. Susan immediately began to worry. Pam got the tray of coffee things, and Susan followed with the pie and plates. Coffee poured and dessert passed around, they could relax again.

"Mom, while we were in the kitchen, Susan asked me if I was okay. On Tuesday night, or early Wednesday, I passed out. My friend Sandra came Wednesday morning to check on me, found me on the floor, and called an ambulance." Nelda gasped.

Susan said, "I knew there was something wrong."

"Let me finish," Pam said, smiling. "At the hospital, they ran some tests and found out I have AIDS. It sounds terrible, but it's not as bad as it used to be." There. It was out.

Her mother sat looking at her like she had two heads. Susan was fighting the urge to be dramatic and run to her.

And then Nelda started. "Where in God's name would you have gotten AIDS?" She sat with her mouth agape, completely unprepared for this news. "It must be a mistake."

"It's not, Mom. They double-check all results. I have AIDS. That's all you need to know for the present. I found out that you can't catch it by kissing me or touching me. But if you are uncomfortable being around me, I totally understand it. I am feeling a little punkie right now, so if you don't mind, Sharon is coming up tomorrow to take you home with her for a week."

The two women sat in silence, in shock.

Susan hadn't said anything because she didn't know what to say. If Pam was saying that it wasn't as bad as it sounded, she would grasp that and run with it. "Whatever you tell me, I'll go with that, okay? I won't go berserk worrying if you say there is nothing to worry about. What did Sharon say?"

"She doesn't know yet. I'll tell her tomorrow. I think it should come from me, don't you agree?" she asked, looking directly at her mother. "I know the temptation is to call everyone you know and tell them, but I am asking you to keep my confidence. My children don't know yet, and they won't be home until next Thursday."

"Oh, what are you going to say to them?" Nelda was clearly confused. She wanted more, but Pam would not give in to it, to her need to know all the gory details.

"Exactly what I have told you and nothing more. The how's and why's of this are my business right now. I need the privacy to recover from the shock of it. That is all I ask, that you respect my privacy, my right to give out information as it is needed. I will not satisfy anyone's curiosity." She knew it was killing her mother not to ask, 'Did Jack give it to you?' Or, like Marie, think she got it from someone else! Pam let a laugh escape. "Let's move on, shall we? I'm bored talking about it. If you want more information, look it up online." She stood up and started clearing plates, wishing she had arranged for her mother to leave that afternoon. But Nelda wasn't budging.

"Well, I never! My daughter tells me she has AIDS and I am supposed to simply sit here and not have any questions?" Nelda was enraged. "That is the most unreasonable request I have ever heard!"

"Mom, just let it go, will you? This isn't about you anymore. It's about Pam and what's best for her and her kids." Dear Susan would try as hard as she could to make peace, but Pam knew this was just the tip of the iceberg.

"I will not let it go!" Now she was raising her voice. Pam stayed in the kitchen, fighting the urge to throw the dishes in the sink and get into bed. Her mother would not ruin Pam's resolve to stay above this.

"I want to know why my middle-aged daughter has AIDS! Why?"

Pam calmly walked out of the kitchen onto the veranda. The sun was directly overhead and cast wonderful shadows through the wisteria growing above. "It's none of your business, Mom. Is that the answer you want to hear? I'm not speaking of it with you anymore today. Live with that or leave. It's up to you. If I told you I had cancer, you wouldn't expect to hear any juicy details, would you?"

At that, her mother decompensated. "How dare you! I have every right to know the details! HOW DID YOU GET AIDS?" She yelled this so loudly Susan looked out at the beach. Someone had to have heard that outcry. Nelda stood up and put her hands on her hips, a stance she used when the girls were children. "I will not be silenced!"

Pam looked at Susan, and the two women started laughing. Pam laughed until she had tears running down her face. Susan howled, her mouth stretched as wide as she would open it, with no sound was coming out. Nelda, appalled and furious, stamped out of the room toward her apartment. The sisters went to each other, continuing the laughter, when, as though a switch had been turned, Susan started crying, grabbing her sister, and then Pam lost it.

They held each, crying for what might be, the scary unknown, and a mother who was as unfit to be a mother as a woman ever could be.

33

Except for burping up cardamom and cumin after lunch, Marie was having a good afternoon. She was too busy to think about AIDS, and there was so much to do and so many new faces that it was easy to stay focused. Carolyn Fitzsimmons was making progress on the file Marie had given her. She could be found in her office, writing away, reading, checking details. Marie moved on to the next project, which was a demographic report regarding the possible development of property adjacent to the south side of Riverside Gardens. Currently, it was a mess of vacant industrial buildings. She had given that file to the older, handsome gentleman, Steve Marks.

His team was taking their time with it, making site visits and taking photos, double-checking numbers. They had found several contradictions in the research. When Steve came to Marie with the problem, she was not surprised that the researcher was none other than the beautiful and popular Sandra Benson. *Shit.* When the report was returned to Lane, Smith & Romney, the documentation regarding the changes would go along with it for the entire world to see. In the meantime, she would enjoy working with handsome Mr. Marks. She wasn't what one would call flirtatious, at least not before Jack had died, but Marie had learned early to sniff out a lamb or a snake.

Steve Marks was a quintessential womanizer of the worst kind; he was broke, so he lurked around young women of means. He had Marie pegged as an older working girl, not his usual conquest. And then he found out through office whispering that the file he was working on was from a firm downtown whose owner was the husband of Marie's sister. Marie went to their house in Babylon every weekend. The guy was a doting brother-in-law; it was talked in hushed tones around the office that he took Marie to lunch every day, had paid for her car and apartment, and basically occupied her life so that she never dated. Conveniently for Steve, he dropped dead of a heart attack on a train to Long Island. She was so aloof most of the time that no one knew anything more about her. Most of the office gossip came from the secretaries and their sources. His curiosity was aroused.

Marie was in her office playing catch up when Steve Marks knocked on her door. He was using this file as an excuse to get into her head. It was an open vessel.

"Hi, I hope I'm not bothering you," he said when she told him to come in.

"What's up?" she asked. "File causing problems again?"

He turned it around so she could see what he was referring to. "This is the only title here in the file, in spite of there being six buildings in the area. We ran a tax record search, and four of the six buildings are up to date. That might pose a problem, unless the developer has already approached them about selling. Not sure if we even need to go to this depth. Are we thinking too hard?"

She looked through the file, closed it, and handed it back to him. "Sit down. I have to think about this, okay?"

She stared at her computer screen for a few minutes. "Those buildings are already owned by the developer," she said. "You're thinking too hard." She smiled at him and returned to her computer screen, dismissing him.

He wasn't going to let her off that easily. "Would you have a cup of coffee with me?" *What the hell!* he thought. *I'm going to either get in or not, might as well find out right away.*

Marie hesitantly looked away from the screen. "You're kidding, right?" She did not look amused.

"You only have to say no. Can't blame a guy for trying, can you?"

She wanted to reach across the desk and slap the smug look off of his face. "Go back to work, Stevie, break time is over." She went back to her computer screen. "Oh, and by the way," she dug around under her desk and pulled out a small device that looked like a phone, "just in case you feel the urge to try to use this against me or pull any crap with that file, you're on tape." She stuck it back where she got it (he couldn't see the source) and went back to whatever was fascinating her on her computer screen.

Steve Marks was concerned. He was a rogue, not a criminal. He'd be more careful around Miss Fabulous, but he wasn't through with her yet. He got up and slightly bowed, which she did not miss, either.

"And close my door," she told him.

After he left the office, Marie sat back in her chair, her hands shaking and teeth chattering. She had a vision of herself as being totally vulnerable now that Jack was dead. Arthur claimed to want to protect her, but she often felt like it gave him a sexual thrill to see her talking to other men; he wanted the man! So now, in her very own office, the enemy was circling. She missed Jack. He would tell her to call the cops if she felt the least bit threatened. Steve Marks didn't threaten her, but she thought his ballsy disrespect unnerving. Her thoughts were interrupted by the phone ringing; she had a call on line two. She hit the button and said hello.

"Miss Fabian, this is Joanne from the clinic. Am I getting you at a bad time?"

"No, not at all," Marie answered. "I'm just surprised you are calling me already. I thought it would be weeks."

"Because of your special circumstances, I pushed your case through as an emergency, and it is back already. Can you come back this afternoon?"

Marie already knew that nothing would be said to her over the phone, so she agreed to come over in a half hour.

"I'll see you then," Joanne said and hung up.

Maybe because asshole Steve Marks had already upset her, she was surprisingly calm for someone who was about to get what could be life-changing news. She cleaned up her desk, slipping her phone back into her purse, it having proved its value in the harassment department, and headed out the door. She decided to walk downtown. It was a beautiful day, and she needed the exercise. The upbeat mood persisted until she got to the building. Its official-looking facade was a grim reminder of the business that was conducted within.

Joanne was waiting for her, saving her from having to register again. She held her arm out in a gathering posture, inviting Marie to come in. She would be there to try to protect her. But, in the long run, there was nothing Joanne—or anyone else, for that matter—could do to protect Marie. The damage had been done. She, too, had full-blown AIDS. Only, hers was worse than Pam's. Her nutritional status had led to the vulnerability that would allow the disease to take hold, and she was really sick. Joanne had made arrangements for Marie to see a doctor that afternoon; they would prescribe the drugs she needed to get started right away, and she would give Marie a referral slip to have some scans done. There were opportunistic diseases that she was wide open to contract, and they wanted to make sure she didn't have any of them yet.

Joanne read down the list of do's and don'ts for the disease: Don't have sex without a condom, or better, practice abstinence; use a rubber dam if she was going to engage in oral sex; don't share needles; be careful kissing if she had any open sores in her mouth. She was appalled as this stranger recited intimate things that Marie should refrain from. She hadn't intended on ever again having sex with a soul after Jack died, but that was her melodrama talking. She fully intended on getting Jeff into bed as soon as possible. Now this! When their talk was over, Marie stumbled out of the clinic and started walking back uptown toward her apartment.

Each step closer to home brought her to the realization that someone who she had devoted her life to, even more so than her sister had, had betrayed her in the worst possible way. It meant giving up the promise of having her own children, a husband, and a life. By giving her AIDS, Jack had sealed their love with an unbreakable bond. She was bound to him forever by the virus. No matter what,

Jack's DNA would always dwell within her. No one could possibly love her because of it. She was ruined completely.

That night, she had horrible dreams about Jack being alive and refusing to see her or marrying Sandra and flaunting the baby in her face and divorcing Pam. She had one in which Pam changed into a demented crone, a hermit who shunned even her own children because they continued to worship the man who was their father. Twice, Marie woke up screaming. The next morning, she walked to work as usual but in a fog. Her life wasn't going to change much. She had these drugs to take, and aside from practicing safe sex, if she ever found a mate again, there was nothing that she had to do differently except try to have a healthier lifestyle. She kept to herself when she got to the office, closing the door, as was the practice now, and getting down to work.

Around 11:00, Steve Marks knocked on her door again. *What is this guy up to?* she thought. He was looking at her through the sidelight, so she wriggled her finger for him to come in.

He slid through the door like a snake and closed it behind him. "I'm sorry about yesterday," he started. "That was tacky of me, for sure. Can we start over?"

He looked sincere, but she didn't know. She was getting a vibe from him that he was a player. She had been sleeping with one since she was a teenager; he couldn't hide it from her.

"What exactly is it that you want from me?" she asked.

"Nothing, really. I'd just like to get to know you better—outside of the office."

She frowned. "Haven't you ever heard the old saying, 'Don't shit where you eat'? You should practice it," she said to him. "Plus, aren't you a little old for this?"

That comment threw him, and he started laughing, a boisterous, hearty laugh. "You really know how to hurt a guy!" he responded.

"Well, you have been here a week and you are hitting on someone who has more seniority than you. I would think you would have more common sense," she said.

"There are no laws against asking a coworker out for a drink." He had a grin on his face that said, *No matter what you say, I am going to hound you.*

"It's obvious from your arrogance that you don't realize what sexual harassment is." She had a smirk on her face now.

"I'm not harassing you!" he said.

"If you keep making unwanted advances toward someone at the workplace, that is harassment," she explained. "This isn't anything new, for God's sake."

"I don't feel like this is unwanted." He smiled his smirky smile at her.

"So now you can read my mind? You better get the hell out of my office before you get reported, and trust me, I will not hesitate to take it as far as I need to."

He didn't move, and that pressed the wrong button.

Marie screamed at the top her lungs, "GET OUT OF HERE!"

Steve flashed her at dirty look and got out of there quickly.

The receptionist and employees who were in the area came running. Marie stood up from behind her desk and straightened her clothes.

"Are you okay?" the receptionist asked.

"Just a misunderstanding," Marie said. *Why are men such assholes?* she wondered.

34

Peter was on the warpath at Lane, Smith & Romney, and it was all Sandra's fault. Since she took over Jack's clients, they were down a researcher, and she had been trying to do both jobs for months. Several important files should be near closing, yet she was nowhere near finished with them. He had been hiding in his office for weeks, and finally, that Thursday, he came out looking for her. The receptionist had warned Sandra the day before.

"Just an FYI, Pete is in a snit about the Riverside Garden file. It's still out."

Sandra knew just what she was referring to; it went to Marie's office weeks ago. Then they had some trouble with it because it was incomplete. Sandra felt like Marie wasn't doing enough to fill in the gaps and said so. That caused hurt feelings, and now she was afraid they were sitting on it.

"I'll call over there," Sandra said. She dialed Marie's direct number.

She picked up with a loud "What!"

Oh great! Sandra thought. "Marie, is that you? It's Sandra." She waited, and there was no response. "Are you okay?"

"I'm sorry. Yes, I'm okay. What can I do for you?" She knew it was probably about the Riverside Gardens file and said so.

"Yes, my secretary just told me Peter is having a fit about it. Is there any way you can release it today? I'm sorry it has caused so much trouble. I don't know what I was thinking when I did the research on that file," Sandra confessed.

"Peter can be a real asshole. I'll find out where they are with the file and bring it down to you. I have to get out of this office right now, anyway."

Sandra was grateful and said so. There was no reason not to be nice when it was warranted. It seemed like Marie was having a rough day, yet she was willing to go out of her way.

They said good-bye, and Marie hung up, got her purse, and left her office, locking the door behind her. She wasn't taking any chances with Mr. Personality. She went to the office where they were working on the file she needed.

"Gather everything up. The client wants the file back now. You did a great job in the time you had it; it's not your fault that it was so much extra work. Trust me, they will be billed for those extra hours by all these extra people." Marie stood there as Steve and his team put the file back together.

He came to her and held it out like he was offering it for a blessing. "What do I get if I give it to you?"

The other staff members in the room looked at him like he was nuts.

"You get to keep your job," Marie said. She held out her hand, and Steve reluctantly handed it over. "It's almost five, so you all go ahead and leave early today. Thank you so much for your effort on this file; it will mean a lot to the client." She put the file in her briefcase and left the office, happy for a chance to get out in the fresh air, but nervous about seeing Jack's office; it had been a long time since she had been there.

What a hell of a day, she thought as she rode the elevator down twenty floors. Between learning she had AIDS and then being harassed by that creep, she was surprised that she had handled it all so well. "Maybe I am finally growing up," she said to herself. She hailed a cab; it was too close to rush hour to take the train downtown. Traffic wasn't great, but she still got there before 5:30. Jack's offices were in a beautiful art deco building. The view from his personal office was breathtaking, encompassing all of New York Harbor. She wondered who was using it now. When she was in her twenties and just out of college, she met him there on a Saturday afternoon, the excuse was to sort through some old files. She remembered walking across the threshold of the office and him dragging her into his arms, kissing her passionately like he rarely did because they were always hiding or sneaking around. This would be the first time that they had freedom, and they took advantage of it. It was total abandonment, complete and utter joy. She had loved him, of that she was sure. Of course, none of it meant a thing anymore. It could have been the love affair of the century, and it still would have been looked upon as a torrid, disgusting, and illegal union, almost incestuous. And now she knew that it meant nothing to him. He was using her totally, and there had been no feeling in it for him at all.

The cab turned onto Exchange Place, and she got out, looking up at the tall building, trying to get some of that excitement back that she had years ago when she was going to meet him there. She walked into the lobby and felt nothing. It was gone for her, thank heaven. It had been banished, along with memories at the beach. He killed it. She rode up the elevator and got out on his floor. The reception area was small, but there was a huge brass sign spelling out Lane, Smith & Romney. Mr. Lane had sold out to Peter and Jack years before, but they kept the name. It just sounded right. The sign was imposing, well lit, and large scaled. The receptionist was new and didn't know Marie. She approached the desk and asked for Miss Benson. Within sixty seconds, Sandra came out to get her. Marie was surprised that her belly wasn't very big. She was hiding her pregnancy well. Sandra asked her to come back to her office. The carpeting was new, soft and thick. There was recessed lighting down the length of the hallway, which gave the space the feel of an airplane. She wondered if they had done that on purpose. She didn't remember it from her youth.

"You look good for being as far along as you are," Marie whispered.

"Thanks," Sandra whispered back. "I haven't gained much weight. Now, with this new problem, I have to be careful about my diet." She raised her eyebrows at Marie, and they nodded in agreement. Marie followed her into the office, and Sandra closed the door and locked it. "I know you know about me, so we can talk freely, correct?"

Marie shook her head yes, near tears but fighting it.

Sandra continued. "There is no one else but you and Pam. No one." She then thought of Tom, but didn't mention him. "I have never felt so alone in my entire life. And it is of my own doing. How could I have been so stupid?" She looked at Marie to gauge her response and decided she had said enough. The poor soul was on the cusp of breaking down. Sandra remembered that she was supposed to be tested. Most likely, no results had come back yet.

Then Marie made an attempt to get herself under control. "I found out today that I have AIDS—full blown, worse than Pam's. I have a printout of the blood work; it's probably advanced because of my anorexia. My eating disorder is a big family secret, but I don't care if you know about it. My mother would have a fit if she knew I was telling you this. We can either accept each other or not. I haven't told Pam yet about the test being positive. There is no point. She is as fragile as a human being can be. It can wait." She dug through her briefcase and pulled out the file. "Here is that God forsaken file. What is with this guy, anyway?" They shook their heads. "The reports are finished but not edited; I'd appreciate you explaining it to Peter. There are new photos and a large file of spreadsheets that need to be printed out. Tell me if the format works for you, and if not, I'll send them to you in an email. There were just a few original documents missing, but we didn't have any trouble getting copies from a new title search. It looks like a wonderful development, really keeping the flavor of the area. The neighbors should be happy." She smiled at Sandra and then, with some difficulty, said, "Nice job," to her. *Where had all the animosity gone?* she asked herself.

They spoke at length about another project file, and Marie told her about the new woman, Carolyn, who loved working on it and would do a bang-up job with it. She would be done by the end of the month.

Marie was going to the beach for the weekend; Sandra still had not made up her mind. She wanted to feel out what Tom expected of their first weekend together. Maybe Pam would let her bring him, give him a chance to meet all these people she talked about all the time. Marie got a cab to go back uptown and, instead of getting off at home, had the driver stop at a little bar that she and Jack had occasionally gone to for lunch and she now went to after work. Having forgotten already that she shouldn't drink, she ordered a glass of wine. She sat in the dark at a table in the back, sipping her wine, and then ordered another. It was past sunset by the time she was finished, but she lived just a few blocks away and spent years walking home in the dark. It would be okay.

As she was walking toward the door, she saw her new "friend" Steve with his back to the door, practically licking his chops as he watched her. He put his hands up in front of his chest.

"Can I say hi to you? We're not at work, so it isn't workplace harassment, correct?" He had a disarming smile on his face, but she still didn't trust him.

She did manage a smile. "You can say hi," she answered. She kept walking, more nervous now that he would follow her outside and toward home. So she said bye and kept walking. Her heart sank when he slid off his bar stool.

"Wait, have a drink with me."

"I can't. I have to get home and get some work done tonight. But thanks, anyway. Maybe I'll take a rain check."

She opened the door before he could get too close to her, but he jogged up and grabbed it above her head. "Please," she said when they were outside of the bar. "Please leave me alone. I really don't want to have a drink with you, or a cup of coffee, or an office romance. I'm begging you to leave me alone."

"Why? What's wrong with just a little friendly drink once in a while?"

She wondered whether or not he had something wrong with him that he couldn't take a hint. She'd have to approach her boss in the morning, play him the recording of this jerk bugging her.

"I am just not interested, okay? Does that explain it for you?" Marie was getting a headache. *What the hell is wrong with this man?*

"Come back inside and have one drink, just one, and then I'll leave you alone."

She knew it was dangerous, but this guy didn't get it, and she was tired. "Okay, I'll come back and have just one drink. Do you understand me? Just one!"

He almost jumped up and down. He was thinking to himself, *One drink is all I need.*

But she was wise to him. She came in and sat down at the bar. The first thing she did was give the bartender her business card.

"If anything happens to me tonight, if my family or my employer come here looking for me, here is my information. I don't know this man very well. Meet Mr. Steve Marks. So can I count on you to remember me?"

The bartender shook his head yes and then said out loud, "Miss, if you would like, I'll call the police for you.

There is usually an officer sitting at the bar over there."
The bartender liked Marie, felt sorry for her drinking
alone night after night.

"No, just don't forget my face." She looked over at
Steve, and he was as white as a ghost.

This bitch is crazy! he thought to himself.

She ordered another glass of wine, keeping her hand
over it unless she was looking at it. She wouldn't put it past
this guy to drug her. When she was done with the wine,
she said to him,

"Okay, I had the drink. Now I am going home. I
want you to stay here. Don't follow me, or I will call the
police. This is the last time you are to bug me about drinking with you, do you understand me?"

He looked at her and nodded yes. But he was thinking no.

35

New York City policemen must prioritize their days. In the morning, between bank robberies and assaults, they had complaints that a former cop conned some Brazilian tourists, and a young woman said that a stranger had touched her breast. Tom and his partner, Jim, went from one call to the next all day long. He found the time to call Sandra during a short break before lunch and again around dinnertime, when she would be taking the subway back uptown to her apartment.

In the five days he had known her, he was never surer of this one thing: She was meant for him. No matter what her current situation, bad by any standard, he was in it for the long haul. He wanted to integrate her into his family as soon as possible, let her meet his sisters and mother, and then his dad and Gwen. He was going to lie to them. They traveled in different circles, her late boyfriend's family and his family, so the chance of the truth ever getting to them was slim. Sandra's own family knew nothing of her pregnancy yet. He would encourage her to tell her sister, the only living relative she had. He hoped his sisters would embrace her. Granted, Sandra was on a different path than anyone he knew in Brooklyn. She wasn't a snob, exactly; she'd be the first to say that it would be difficult for an unmarried, pregnant AIDS victim to be a snob. But there was just something about her. He couldn't put his finger on it, but it was one of the things that attracted him to her. She was aloof. For being so young, she had a haughtiness about her that he found extremely attractive, like she was born and bred on the Upper East Side, and not right next to the Lincoln Tunnel.

Sandra left Exchange Place after Marie brought the file in and she handed it off to Peter Romney. He was waiting in his office, and she brought the file to him rather than having the secretary be the recipient of his wrath. Peter grabbed it out of her hand and didn't thank her.

"Peter, stop being a dick, okay?"

The uncouth statement was so foreign to him and coming out of her mouth of all places was so shocking that he burst out laughing. "What did you say?" he asked, trying to control himself.

"You heard me," Sandra replied. "We're all sick and tired of your histrionics, Peter. Get over yourself. We have all had a rough summer, not just you. You acting like a jerk around here day in and day out is not making it any easier. And before you pick the file to pieces, there is still some work that may need to be done on it before we hand it over to the client. I'm giving it to you to get you off my back. I'll work on it this weekend, and it will be ready to go out Monday."

He flipped the cover open and thumbed through the work. Then he looked up at her. "Okay, whatever you say."

Sandra turned around and walked out. It was more interaction than the two of them had ever had. She fell to wondering how Jack ever got involved with such a zero personality.

She left the office and walked up to the subway station. The train was packed, and she had to stand up the whole ride. Her car was full of rowdy young men who didn't offer their seats to anyone, but yelled and pushed each other back and forth. Finally, from a forward car, a middle-aged, gruff-looking cop came back and stood near Sandra, holding on to a strap, staring at the boys. He took his nightstick and pointed it at them, sweeping it toward the center of the train.

"Act like a gentleman and offer your seat to a lady," he said to the boy he had pointed out. "You know better than to act this way."

The kid shrugged his shoulders and got out of the seat.

"Now, offer it to a lady," the cop said.

The kid looked at Sandra. "You can have my seat," he said, looking at her and then down at the seat.

She thanked him and sat down. The others followed him, standing up and offering the vacated seat to a woman standing on the train. She found herself wondering about the young men, if the experience would be lasting. It was doubtful. Someone like Jack who had every advantage turned out to be rotten to the core. If the information she found hidden in his desk were true and Jack had been molested by his stepfather, it was sad and awful. But it was still no excuse for him to do what he did. He made the choice to be depraved and to use people. She remembered him saying to her that she was the one person who didn't cause him any problems. *What did that mean? What problems could someone like Pam or her children give him?* She didn't expect anything from him because she knew he wasn't able to give it. He was a taker. And, at the end, he gave a gift that would keep giving.

That morning, she took her handful of pills with her breakfast of cereal, fruit, yogurt, and tea—more than she usually ate all day. She snacked on carrots and raisins during lunch and would pick something up for dinner from Zabar's. She was hungry now, the baby flipping around inside her magnifying the growling of her stomach. *Too many sensations at one time!* she thought.

She got to her building and gave a sigh of relief. It was a haven of rest and protection, always had been and always would be. She remembered the first time she saw it. A rental agent had taken Sandra and her father around town all morning, and each place was more depressing than the last. Finally, her father said to look at something in the next price range, almost too much for her, but he would help her out if she needed it. This apartment was the result. She fell in love with it right away. Each thing she brought into it was something she loved or was necessary. There was nothing superfluous to take up room or collect dust.

She struggled with the key; it was getting harder and harder to turn. She'd have to get the building manager to take a look at it. The door opened, and she smiled. "I'm home!" She hollered. *Wonderful, safe home.* She threw her purse on the chair and took dinner into the kitchen. She would change into spandex and a T-shirt first and then read her mail. Her routine, sacrosanct when alone, was comforting and grounding. Before Jack, she often included a short prayer. But since Jack, the guilt and remorse over being his instrument to cause so much pain, she felt a distance from a higher power. She could thank Him for all He had done, but ask Him for anything? No.

Sticking her dinner in the microwave, she would take it downstairs and eat while she watched the news. The food smelled so delicious—garlic and basil on chicken with pasta. It filled up the kitchen with the scent. Tonight, she planned on going to bed early, to make up for last night. She went down and put her food on the coffee table. She picked up the remote and turned the TV on, the sound blasting away. Before she could turn it down, she was grabbed from behind.

Her assailant threw his left arm around her chest and shoulders and, with his right hand, stuffed a wad of something, paper toweling or toilet paper, into her mouth, gagging her. Then he took something that was rough, hemp rope or something similar, and tied her hands behind her back. She was passive, trying not to hurt the baby. She didn't think she could have fought him off, anyway. He was huge—arms as big around as melons and taller than she was by at least a half foot. He covered her eyes with something, a piece of cloth either from her closet or something he brought with him. Every once in a while, as he struggled to tie her up, she got a whiff of his body odor; it had been in this very room before. She was so petrified it made her gag again. This was not the first time he had been in her house. She was hoping that he would be there to steal from her or rape her, at the very worst, but not to kill her. He dragged her over to the recliner and pushed her down into it. Reaching over her, he grabbed the handle and pulled it so the bottom of the chair rose up and her legs with it. She was immobilized. Then she heard him pick up the remote and turn the TV off. He had purposely turned it up loud so her neighbors couldn't hear any scuffling or in case she screamed.

"I hope I didn't hurt you," he said. It was Bill.

But how could that be? He was in jail again and was unable to raise the bail money. It was in the paper that morning. She remained still. She couldn't talk, and there was no reason to piss him off by struggling against the ropes he had placed around her wrists and ankles.

"I'm sorry this is necessary at all, believe it or not. My brother would be so angry at me. I can hear him now, yelling at me, 'Goddamn it, Buddy-boy, what the hell have you gotten yourself into?' I hated it when he called me that. Buddy-boy. Our dad called me that. 'Come 'er, Buddy, give your old man a hug,' he'd say. He always wanted more than that. You knew about that, right? About me and my old man? I was pretty sure Jack must have told you about it. You knew that we were lovers, right? Jack and I were lovers. It's okay, between brothers. My dad told me it was okay from the time I was a little boy, just learning to walk. 'It's okay because I said it's okay.' He'd say that, and then he'd make Jack and I do it, and he would watch and beat off. It was better than doing it with our dad. He was cruel, our dad was.

"Our mom knew all about it, too. Don't kid yourself. She drank herself into a stupor each day so she didn't have to face it. Face what her great husband was doing to his kids. Of course, he's an icon now. She has him so far up on a pedestal that she can barely see him. 'Your father was a great man,' she says all the time. 'He loved you so much.' Or, my favorite, 'You were blessed with a great father, and

I had a wonderful husband.' Bernice has organic brain syndrome. Did you know that? Full-blown dementia. From alcoholism. I am not the smartest guy around, but I can read. She started showing signs of it right around the time my dad died. I figured it was stress. Her taking you in like she did, that is a clear sign that she is not right. Why in God's name would you befriend a slut who is hell bent on ruining your family?

"That was your goal, wasn't it, Sandra? You sure as hell didn't have any real interest in us. Did you call us once after Jack died? Reach out? See if we needed anything? You have his business now; you could have helped me out several different ways. I didn't even ask for money, just for the clients my brother had promised he would send my way. I was a good business man. My dad is the one who fucked everything up, not me. He stopped doing any real business years ago. My brother was to blame. My dad loved my brother. And when Jack stopped talking to him, it about killed my dad. He would come home at night and practically rape my mother. I would hear them in their room. She would be screaming, and he would be going to town. It took me a while to figure out he wasn't beating her up. He was using her instead of Jack.

"Jack threatened my dad with exposure. Did you know that? You do, don't you? You know that Jack was going to file a fake lawsuit, expose my dad to all that humiliation and then me and my mom. Jack didn't care about himself. He was ready to go public. He thought it would cure him of his obsession with whores. You knew about that, right? You were in a long line of whores, the only difference being that he took you out in public. He thought that if he went public, he'd stop. It had gotten out of hand. We had women coming to my parent's mansion looking for Jack. His attorney did a great job covering up the lawsuits against my brother—charging him with rape, for one thing. Or women who were pregnant, just like you, who he had abandoned. He paid through the nose, over and over again. Ask around, you'll find out I'm telling the truth.

"He was so worried his wife and kids would find out the truth about him. Don't you think it's strange that his kids go to school as far from Long Island as possible? One in Los Angeles and one in Oahu? And that wife of his! What a fucking dimwit. Pam was a looker in her day, and all he wanted was someone who would look good and blend in with the family. My mother had to take care of her when she was pregnant. Did you know that? Get cooks and cleaning ladies to their apartment so my brother wouldn't starve to death or suffocate in the squalor. It was awful. I still can't believe he stayed with her all those years.

"Ever try to have a conversation with Pam? She doesn't have a thing to say. She'll ask you all about yourself and then sit there like a bump with not a word to say for herself. Their kids are brilliant; they sure as hell didn't get it from Pam. No wonder my brother strayed; she'd bore you to death!

"My brother loved me. He protected me from Dad as much as he could. He used to whisper to me, 'Just close your eyes and pretend you are on a beach somewhere.' Finally, when he got old enough, he told my dad he would kill him if he touched me. Kill him or expose him to the city. 'I'll ruin you,' he told my dad. He saved me from my dad." Bill started to weep.

Sandra was taken aback, thinking there was a woman with him, because it sounded like the whimpering of a young girl.

"Jack! Goddamn it! Why'd you have to go and die on me? I need you, Buddy! I need you! Why didn't you tell your bitches to take care of me? Why, Jack? I thought we loved each other!" The sobbing was horrible, loud and choking.

Sandra was afraid he would have a heart attack and she would die by starvation, tied up in her basement. Finally, after what seemed like an hour, he stopped. She could hear him go into the bathroom and pull toilet paper off the roll, yards and yards of it, and he blew his nose. She heard the toilet seat be thrown up with a slam and the stream of his urine hitting the water. He didn't flush the toilet. *What a pig*, she thought. *What did I expect?* And he continued whining after he peed. She could smell his urine coming from the bathroom, and her gorge rose. She would choke if she puked with this wad of mushy paper in her mouth.

"My mother is in denial. I know Jack confronted her last year after Dad died; he told me he was going to. 'I'm not going to my grave letting the old lady get away with it,' he said. 'She's going to apologize for letting that fucker abuse us, or I am never speaking to her again.' I guess she refused to say she was sorry, because he never did. He never saw her or spoke to his own mother again. She is heartbroken about it. You know that, right? She won't mention it, but it's clear to me. She's got you up on a pedestal now, too. You, Jack, my dad. You're all up there being worshiped.

"She can't stand Pam. Ask my mother about Pam sometime; she can't win, that girl. She'll give my mother a huge check, and the next words out Bernice's mouth will be, 'She is a real dummy, that one.' When Jack told my parents he was marrying Pam, my mother took to her bed for a week. I don't know what she expected of Jack, if she thought he would come back home someday or stay single and keep doting on her. He did that, you know. Every week, I don't care if he was overwhelmed at work and had things going on with Pam and the kids, he would come uptown and take my mother out for lunch. He would purposely run into her at the store or in the park if she was out for a stroll. He'd call the house, and Mildred would tell him where she was, and he would seek her out. When I got home from school, I could always tell if Mother had been with Jack. She was kinder to me then, more motherly, if that makes any sense. He brought the best out in people, Jack did. No one could make my mother laugh like Jack did. It was almost embarrassing the way she worshiped him.

"I don't know, to this day, what his breaking point was, why he had to confront Bernice, why he stopped helping me out. Something happened right before my dad died. And then, after he died, Jack began his downward spiral. He got a young girl pregnant. I bet you didn't know that, did you? She came to the mansion, hysterical, demanding to see Bernice. She was sure that once she confronted her, Bernice would convince Jack to allow the girl to keep the baby, even marry her. She was a college student, an art major. When Pam told me about you, I thought she was referring to this young girl. We had paid her off. I denied to

Pam that Jack would ever be unfaithful. And then I found out that he had given the business to you, and I knew then that he had someone else. You are the first 'normal' woman I can remember him being with. You know what Pam said about you? She said you were 'a lovely woman, a professional business woman.' What kind of weak-spined person would refer to her husband's mistress that way? She never did have any pride. When she was pregnant with Lisa, she told my mother that she didn't know if she could take care of two children. Imagine being pregnant, purposely getting pregnant, and admitting that to someone? My mother was appalled. She said she was going to watch Pam like a hawk, and if she did one thing inappropriate, she would have those kids taken away from Pam. Even then, even when I was in the worst denial, I thought, 'Jesus Christ, if any kids should have been taken away, it should have been my mother's kids.'

"She was a horrible mother. How Jack could have forgiven her like he did, being gentle and kind to her year after year, is a mystery. My mother never took care of us; Mildred did. She started drinking before I was born, Jack told me. He remembered the first time he noticed there was something not right with our mother. He came home from school, and she was nowhere to be found. He went up to take a shower before my dad got home and happened to notice her bedroom door open. He went and peeked in; she was face down, sprawled across the bed snoring. He went in to see if she was okay, and he could smell the booze on her. He tried waking her up, but it was futile. She was out cold. Later that night, during dinner, she came down, apologetic for not being there when he got home from school. Jack said my dad hollered at her and called her a lush. Jack looked the word up in the dictionary and said that was how he knew the old lady had given in to the bottle. I often wondered if I didn't have fetal alcohol syndrome. She drank during the time she was pregnant with me. I have trouble reading and 'impulse control,' they call it. In other words, I am a fuck up. My dad used to yell at me when he coached my little league games and tell me it wasn't my fault I was uncoordinated. 'It's from too much booze in the womb.' I laughed every time he said for twenty years, but now I wonder if he wasn't correct. My mother is a smart woman; she graduated magna cum laude from Barnard. Did you know that? She was a philosophy major." Bill started laughing when he said that, screaming laughter. "Oh Jesus, what a waste of money."

The phone started ringing. Sandra prayed that if it was Tom, that he wouldn't say anything incriminating. The answering machine picked up, and he simply said, "Hi, call me when you can." He gave no name. She could hear the faint bell of her cell phone in her purse and then the beep that told a message had been left. She felt her bladder getting full. *Is he planning on keeping me tied up all night?*

"I guess your friends are looking for you. Humph. Not good for me. I'm not even sure why I came here. I don't think I can kill you."

She could hear him moving toward her, and she flinched when he picked up her T-shirt. He placed his hand over her stomach. "You're not very big yet, are you?"

She shook her head no. Then, as if on cue, the baby started to move, rolling moves that surely showed through her skin.

He laughed and added a little pressure to his hand. "Oh God! How cool! I had forgotten how cool it is to feel a baby moving. My two boys aren't that old. I haven't seen them since June. Anne wouldn't let them near me when I was home last. Now my fat-ass sister-in-law has them. Did you know about Anne's family? I met her at school. She was there on a full scholarship. Anne is a better athlete than student. Don't kid yourself, it was no academic scholarship. She wouldn't have been interested in me if it had been. The only reason I even got into school was because my dad was an alumni and Jack went there, too. He got his master's in business there. My dad made him work for it. He had to pay his own way. Did you know that? I probably got more handed to me than Jack did. Jack was always a worker. He said he knew early on that his one way out of the mess we were in was to be independent of my dad. He said, 'Don't worry, Buddy-boy, I'll take care of you.' And for years, he did. He paid for my apartment when I finally got the nerve to leave home. You knew we both had to go to school in the city and had to commute. We weren't allowed to stray too far from Columbus Circle. My dad had huge appetites, too." Bill cried out then, scaring Sandra, who jumped slightly in her chair. "Why! Why did he do that to us? It was torture, I tell you, not just the pain, but the constant drama! He was so mean to us. Jack said that he got beaten once because he hid me from my dad when he got home from work. I was a toddler, and Jack hid me to protect me. Jack started screaming so the help could hear him, and Mildred came running. I thought my father would explode he was so pissed off. 'Don't you EVER yell like that in this house again, do you understand me?' Then Jack took his own life in his hands because he said, 'Leave Billy alone until he gets older. Do it or I'm telling.' He said my dad laughed in his face, but evidently, he did leave me alone for a year or so more."

Sandra could hear Bill sit down on the daybed down there. He blew his nose. Then the phone rang again a second and a third time, but there was no message left. Sandra's feet were starting to hurt, so she tried to move ever so slightly. There was no sound coming from the daybed, then very soft snoring. He had worked himself up into a nap. *What the hell am I going to do?* She couldn't push the foot of the chair down without making a racket. She didn't want him to wake.

She didn't know how much time had passed when she heard a very slight rattling of the door that lead to the outdoors. And then, in seconds, there was a ruckus, and she was rescued. She felt hands on her face pulling the wadding out of her mouth and the blindfold off her eyes, and there was Tom. Uniformed officers had Bill on the floor; he was bellowing for all he was worth.

Tom helped her out of the chair and picked her up gently, carrying her upstairs, out of view of Bill. He put her in a chair in the sitting room and was just about to ask her if she wanted some water. There was a pounding at the front door, and Jim let in emergency medical technicians, who came to Sandra and asked her if she was all right.

"Be careful," she whispered to them, telling them her HIV-positive status, and the woman patted Sandra's arm, with a "that's okay" look on her face. They took her vital signs, got a fetal heart monitor out, pulled up her T-shirt as Bill had, and started looking for the baby's heartbeat. Tom was kneeling next to her, and Jim was standing nearby, trying to hide the surprise on his face. Suddenly, the strong and rapid heartbeat of Sandra's baby filled the room and the entire apartment. Tom reached over and kissed Sandra passionately on the mouth. She put her hand up to the back of his head and kissed him back. Their secret was out.

36

Once again, Marie's apartment, the same one she hated and didn't appreciate having much of the time, delivered. She opened the door, stepped in, and the first thing she saw was the panorama overlooking the nighttime skyline of New Jersey. She closed the door behind her, put her things down on the couch, and walked to the window without taking her eyes off of it. The very edge of the sun could be seen as it sunk below the earth, the turquoise sky fading into indigo. *Lucky.* She walked backward into her kitchen to grab a bottle of wine that she had opened the day before and a glass and went back to sit on her couch and watch the spectacle out her window. *This glass of wine will make four for the evening. Am I drinking too much?* She had conveniently forgotten that she was not supposed to drink with the antiretroviral drugs, among others that she would be taking for the rest of her life. *Too bad*, she thought as she took a slug of the wine, a delicious French wine she bought to spite Jeff Babcock. He had not called her since the family meeting at TGI Friday's, and that was Monday. Four days. "Fuck him," she said out loud, slurring her speech. For some reason, out of nowhere, she thought of her viral load. It was extremely high, the doctor had said, and she was extremely infectious.

"It's imperative that you take your drugs as directed and that you abstain from any form of sexual activity, especially intercourse. If you absolutely must do it, please, please, please, use a condom!"

She didn't particularly like the doctor, who was trying so hard to stay neutral and not categorize Marie that he failed miserably. She felt like a twelve-year-old who had gotten caught having sex with the next-door neighbor. He asked her what she did for a living, and when she told him, he seemed shocked, like she was better suited to selling dope in an alley. *Oh well, I'm probably being hypersensitive. Do I have a giant A on my forehead for AIDS?* No one could tell; it was her secret. She poured herself another glass of wine. More lights had gone on outside, and now they were visible all the way to the horizon. New Jersey was a beautiful state; it was called the "Garden State," after all. Its rolling topography was clearly seen at night by the layers of lights. Her door buzzer rang. For a split second, she thought of Jack. Then she said out loud, "Arthur." She pressed the intercom and said hello and couldn't believe her ears!

It was Steve Marks!

"Surprise! I got your address from Switchboard.com! Gotta love the Internet!"

"Go home, Steve, before I call the cops." Marie was tired of him, but she was also angry. *He has a lot of nerve.*

"Don't be mad at me," he said. "Let me come up. If you talked to me, you would learn to like me."

"Okay, I have about had it with you. If you don't leave right now, not only am I going to call the cops, but I will report you to my boss in the morning. GO HOME!" she yelled into the intercom. There was silence. She wished there was a way she could alert the other tenants so no one let him in. Suddenly frightened, she got a dining room chair and wedged it under the door handle and then dragged the couch over in front of the chair. He wouldn't get into her place, even if he got through the front door.

Seconds later, her phone rang. She picked it up, but didn't speak. She heard Jeff's voice.

"Hello? Marie?"

She let out a sigh of relief. "Hi, Jeff. Sorry. I'm being stalked by a coworker who showed up at my door tonight, and I was afraid the call might be him."

"Oh! How frightening! I would be petrified!"

Marie looked at the phone in disbelief. *Is this guy kidding?*

"Make sure your doors are locked!" he advised.

"So what can I do for you?" Marie asked, anxious to hang up. She was having suspicions about Jeff.

"I have a formal affair to attend in town next weekend. Would you be my date?"

"Can I get back to you?" Marie answered. "Work is crazy right now because of the merger. I'm going to Pam's tomorrow, though. Are you at the beach or Rhinebeck this weekend?" She hoped he was going to say Rhinebeck.

"Oh! I am cooking for you at Pam's Saturday! Won't that be fun? The weather is supposed to be gorgeous!"

The issue was becoming clearer and clearer; she could almost see him simpering. *Oh Lord, no. Am I his beard?* "You'll be at Pam's? What? As her date or mine?" Marie was pissed off. *Who is this guy, anyway?* She had all the male friends she needed. Whatever was going on, she wanted truthfulness out of him.

Jeff giggled, which fueled her anger. "Both. Neither. I like both of you! Do we need to define our friendship in 'date' terms?"

So that was it, she thought. *He is such a weasel!* "Yes! I don't want to waste my time with someone who I was hoping to be romantically involved with. If you are gay, for God's sake, say you're gay! Why the hell are you still in the closet?" She was yelling at him. *He has a lot of nerve!* She understood why he felt it was necessary to introduce his brother and sister-in-law to a woman. He was hiding who he was from them, and it made her sick. "Wait, I get it. Your family is a bunch of religious fanatics and you have to keep your real self a secret. Am I correct?"

There was silence.

"Answer me, Jeff!" She thought about the wasted weekend where she was force-fed and the trek to Friday's to meet the family and be cross-examined about her religious beliefs.

"No, not exactly. I mean they aren't religious fanatics. They're just passionate about Jesus." He didn't say anything else.

So this is the way it is going to be, she thought. She would have to yank everything out of him. "Are you gay?" she asked, more of a statement than a question. Waiting for him to answer, she thought of Arthur, how wonderful and honest he was about everything, himself, his friends, life. She found herself wondering if this type of blatant denial was more common than not. And then she calmed down quickly. The poor man was at that cusp of the generation that had to hide who they really were, whose family would disown them if they didn't measure up in every way. It wasn't enough that the guy was a successful attorney who had raised two lovely children. She decided to take a different approach. If he had to hide behind her, so be it. He still hadn't answered her, so she would change tactics.

"I'm sorry I'm beating you up here, Jeff. I just don't like to be lied to. I thought there might be something happening between us, and now I see that is impossible. So I will do what I can to help you out when you need it, but if you don't want at least an honest friendship with me, then forget it." She listened to his breathing. "Hello?"

"Okay, I'm sorry. I didn't mean to lie," he confessed. "I'm so used to living behind a veil that I forget that it's possible to hurt people. I'll be honest, okay? But I need your discretion. One hundred percent."

"One hundred percent," she echoed.

He took a deep breath. "Yes, I am a gay man. Yes, I am in the closet. I've been celibate, but think it might be time to change that. Just last month, I started seeing someone. My children are grown, so my ex-wife can't use my sexuality against me. I really didn't know I was gay when we got married. That sounds like a bunch of horse-shit, but it's true. The way I was raised, 'men were men and women were women,' and there was nothing else, no deviation from the traditional roles. The church we were raised in taught that homosexuality was from the devil. Satan. I don't remember now, but if there were any impulses, I would have squashed them. Just once, just a tiny misstep when I was a boy sent my mother into a tailspin. I'll never forget it.

"I was getting ready to go out to play and had taken my Sunday clothes off to put my play clothes on. I was standing in my bedroom in front of my closet in my underwear with my hand on my hip, looking in, trying to decide what to wear. My older sister came in, and I asked her, 'Should I wear the plaid shirt with the blue jeans or the green shirt with the khaki pants?' She reached in to pull out the green shirt, and my mother, who must have been standing there listening to us, screamed. She ran into my room, grabbed my sister by the arm, and pushed her away and then reached out and slapped my hand off my hip. 'Don't *ever* stand that way again!' she yelled. 'Get dressed! Put anything on!' And then she grabbed my sister again and shook her by the arm. 'Don't encourage him!' she yelled. It was awful. My sister started crying, and my mother shot me the death look and went back to her place in the kitchen. After that, if I slipped up doing the slightest effeminate thing or even what they call 'metrosexual' today, she would slap me and yell, 'Stop it!' Of course, this was never in front of my dad. The poor man would have had a heart attack. He was a deacon at the church, for God's sake!" Jeff laughed. "My mother is still waiting for me to come out of the closet. She was mortified when I went to culinary school." He stopped, contemplating what he had revealed to Marie.

Marie was wondering if she needed to come clean with Jeff as well. *How much honestly is required?* He just spilled his guts at her insistence. *Now is it my turn? Is it tit for tat?* She waited for a few minutes to give him a chance to regroup.

"People are stupid, that's all there is to it. I hate it when they use religion as an excuse to be hateful," he said. "The funny thing is," he continued, "I am a Christian. I love God. I believe that Jesus is His Son and reigns with Him in heaven. I do hear the prompting of the Holy Spirit. All of the things I am supposed to do, I do. But, boy oh boy, don't let my sister-in-law get started on the gay men who work in her gift shop. She spews so much hatred. I can't believe she doesn't see the hypocrisy in it."

"I have a few confessions to make myself. Do you want me to start now? It's getting a little late." She was hoping he would agree and hang up. No such luck.

"I have time to listen if you need to talk" was his gracious way of giving her the floor.

"I don't need to talk, but I need to be truthful about some things up front if we are going to be friends." She was still hoping for a way out.

"Go ahead, I'm listening," he said.

"Well, for one thing, I'm an anorexic. Always have been, always will be. Your weekend of food was slightly overwhelming, but I did it because I wanted to be with you. If I had known it was a ruse, I would have refused to eat!" She left out the part where she made herself throw up at the side of the road.

"It wasn't a ruse, I swear! I wanted to entertain you because I liked your company. Go on, I have the feeling there is something more." He was interested in knowing more about her.

"This next part is upsetting because I stayed in your house and used your dishes. I just found out yesterday that I have AIDS." He didn't respond, so she went on. "I was in a very long-term relationship, almost thirty years, and the man betrayed me" was all she was going to admit. "I found out that I might be infected when another acquaintance discovered she was ill. The man is dead now, so he isn't a problem."

"Oh, how awful," he said with compassion. "I'm so sorry. Are you well otherwise?"

"So far, so good. I am drinking, which you aren't supposed to do. French wine, by the way. In honor of you. But what about the dishes and bedding? Aren't you upset about that?" She was hoping he would express his disgust, but he wasn't biting.

"You can't get AIDs from dishes or sheets, so knock it off," he responded. "Besides, if you could, I would dead by now. Many of my friends are HIV positive. I'll tell you the truth; it's the anorexia that bothers me the most. All kinds of research have been done regarding the importance of nutrition in AIDS." Marie yawned. *Oh no, not this. Time to change the subject.*

"And drinking while taking antiretroviral drugs is not good."

"Yeah, well, maybe I'll join AA. Look, I better hang up; glad we had this little chat and all that. I have a brutal day tomorrow, and if I am going to see you at Pam's Saturday, we can chat then, okay? In the meantime, mums the word!"

They said good-bye and hung up.

Another gay friend, just what she needed. Maybe she would try Internet dating. Single. White. Infected with AIDS. *How would that go over?* she wondered.

37

"So how'd you happen to come to my apartment with reinforcements?" Sandra was sitting in the back of the unmarked car with Tom while Jim drove. They were going to Benny's Shakes for burgers and chocolate milk shakes. Sandra could smell them—fried onions on a greasy hamburger patty, mustard and pickles, all on a soft bun. They would get large french fries and giant chocolate milk shakes made with full-fat ice cream and whole milk. She would look pregnant before the week was up, if Tom had anything to say about it. He had been so worried about her today. His protective radar was going full blast, which included feeding his conquest.

"I tried to call you, and when you didn't answer, I got worried. So I called Jim, who was at work, and he got the uniforms involved. I made it uptown from Brooklyn in less than thirty minutes."

She was sucking the ice cream up her straw with all of her might. It was not easy! "How'd he even get out? Bill, I mean. I thought he couldn't make bail?" Sandra was so glad that he would be put away for a long time.

"Mom," Tom answered. She got a big check from some auction house today—an advance on a sale they are going to have. Sadly, she won't be getting that money back. Gotta love New York law. By the way, Billy sends his apologizes. 'I didn't mean to scare her,' he says."

Jim was on the phone with his wife, lying about dinner. He was supposed to be eating salad from the cafeteria tonight.

Sandra was getting ready to stuff the last of her burger in her mouth. Her appetite seemed to increase in the past hour, in spite of the trauma she had experienced. "Would you like to come to the beach with me this weekend? I'm going to ask Pam if it's all right, first thing in the morning. The drama is over, for the most part. Unless Marie tells us she is going to have a sex-change operation, it should be very peaceful." She told Tom about how Marie had gone out of her way for Sandra that afternoon. She thought it was a gesture of friendship.

"You better wait to make any plans. I don't think you realize the magnitude of what you went through tonight. It will probably hit you later. It's a sort of shock you are in right now." Tom was looking at her with concern.

He's probably right, she thought. But it wasn't all that bad. She knew she was lucky Tom and the other policemen got there when they did. *What would Bill have done? Would he have killed me?* They would never know. "What will the charges be?" she asked.

"For one thing, he manhandled you when he placed the gag and tied you up, so we have the possibility of battery. Then he held you against your will, and that constitutes kidnapping. And he got into your apartment without your knowledge. On top of his theft charges, breaking parole, and the restraining order violation, he may be gone for good," Tom said.

"He won't get bail again, that is for sure," Jim added. "Can I take you two home? I have to get working on the case." He turned the car around, and they headed back up-town.

Tom had his arm around Sandra's shoulders, and he leaned over and kissed her again. She felt like she was a teenager, making out in the back of a car and said as much.

"Don't look in your rearview mirror, Jim! We're being naughty back here." Jim went through a charade of adjusting his mirror so he could see the backseat. The car pulled up to her building, and Tom got out first and offered her his hand. She was surprised at how stiff she felt. The EMTs had tried to convince her to go to the hospital to be checked, but she was afraid her HIV status would become an issue. She'd be okay, she hoped. She stood on the sidewalk, her neighbors walking by, curious about how she came to be getting out of the back of an unmarked cop car, while Tom talked to Jim. He would be spending the night, and if they needed him, he'd be available.

The car sped off as Tom and Sandra went up the walk to her building. She gave him the key to get the door open, telling him how difficult it had been to unlock earlier. He thought it had been jimmied by Bill. The creepiness factor, someone with his crazy background stalking Sandra and then roughing her up, hit Tom with a force he didn't recognize. He was glad the man was behind bars now because it meant he was unable to kill him. He understood the potential for police brutality. He'd call in later and make sure the people in charge knew the victim was a policeman's girlfriend.

Friday. *What did Friday used to mean to me when Jack was alive?* Marie thought. She was on a roller coaster again—one minute, glad she was free of him; the next, feeling hopeless. Jeff Babcock had provided a respite for a brief time, a few weeks of hope that she could have a normal relationship with a man. His revelation last night didn't surprise her as much as it pissed her off. *Why? Why do I attract men who are unavailable?*

In the past, Friday meant getting ready for the weekend. She loved going home and preparing for the drive to the beach. She wouldn't leave until Saturday; her gesture of respect to her sister, allowing Pam and Jack one night of privacy before Marie would come and usurp his attention. Pam had no idea of what was going on right under her nose for thirty years. Jack called her his high-maintenance girl, but the truth was she didn't need him for much at all, as far as you could tell by looking at the surface. He was free to live in the city, have affairs, and when he was home, all he had to do was golf and play around with Marie. She put her head down on her desk and fought back tears. What a waste. Then there was a knock on her door.

"Come in," she said reluctantly.

It was Steve Marks. He had a rakish grin on his face, a "you'll forgive me anything" look. Marie stood up as he walked through the door.

"Anyone but you! Get out before I tell my boss about last night."

He put both hands up in the air and started walking backward toward her door. "You can't blame a guy for trying," he whined.

"Oh yes I can! I talked to my sister's boyfriend, who's NYPD, and he said I already have a case for a restraining order against you. Stay away from my apartment! And if you continue to bother me here at work, I'll file a harass-ment charge against you." *So I told a white lie, kill me.*

He giggled at her. "You're not serious, right?" He lingered in her doorway until she started walking toward him.

"Dead serious! Now get out!" She slammed her door, no longer concerned that other employees or even her boss would hear. She had never caused a second of trouble here; he had better stand behind her and protect her. Or she would take matters into her own hands.

38

By early Saturday morning, Pam hadn't heard from either her sister or Sandra about their plans for the weekend. She forced herself out of bed to prepare for Sharon's arrival and the drama of telling her about the AIDS. Nelda may be dead for all she knew; she went up to her apartment yesterday afternoon and refused to answer her phone. Susan finally left, having a two-hour drive home to Connecticut. She had offered to take Nelda back with her, but Sharon was planning on taking her and needed to be told the news. She'd have her week with Mom and then bring her back when the kids were home for Labor Day weekend.

The scene with Nelda had exhausted Pam. She went to bed soon after her sister left, thinking she would lie down for a while and get up to eat something later. She ended up sleeping through the night. She woke up without the alarm, lying on her back and looking up at the ceiling. The telltale light of day was already creeping into her room, just over the closed drapes. It must have been after 7:00.

She was right. Getting up out of bed, she stretched, going to the window to open the drapes. The beach was a clean, white slate, waiting for sunbathers and dog walkers, children with Frisbees, and shell collectors. When she and Jack planned this life, she hadn't imagined it without him.

Does any married couple? Even though he never lived there full time, the thought of him was always foremost in her mind: Jack's house, his office, his car, his golf clubs, his friends, his children. Her own needs didn't factor into much of their life or what they did together. It was usually all about Jack.

Who was she? Who was Pam? While she was in the shower, she tried to remember what her dreams were when she was growing up. Since an early age, she wanted only one thing, and that was to have her own family and home. She would struggle to maintain the picture in her head of what a family should be. Determined to connect with her children, she refused to allow the busyness of life to interfere with what was really important to her. She was successful at it. Her son and daughter were happy, well-adjusted adults who praised their mother. It was true; Pam had just the life she wanted.

And although she would strive to never criticize her own mother, Pam couldn't help but compare her mother's selfishness now, when she was needed by her daughter, to the selflessness she practiced back when she was raising her family. Although it wasn't spoken of anymore, Sharon, the second child, had been born with a congenital spine defect and had to have surgery after surgery. Nelda devoted every waking second to her care, unintentionally at the expense of the other girls in the family. Susan was born one year to the day after Sharon, and although she rarely acknowledged it, her childhood was a nightmare of neglect and chaos. If it hadn't been for Pam, she wouldn't have survived. And then Marie was born. Pam remembered everyone was shocked when her mother started to show with her pregnancy.

"Fer heaven's sake," her grandmother had said loudly, "didja ever hear of a rubber?"

Nelda couldn't cope. She let the baby lay in wet diapers all day, and when Pam got home from school, she took over.

"Go rest, Mom. Everything is under control." The ten-year-old became the mother's helper, and the new baby bonded with the sister, not the mother. Susan bonded with no one. Although Pam tried to care for her, she was so independent at a young age that she didn't seem to need anyone. As much as Pam hated to admit it, she had done the same thing to Marie, only worse. Marie was her mother's helper. She begged to move in with Pam and Jack right after they got married, and Pam would have allowed it if Nelda had. She should have never let the girl come within ten miles of Jack. Pam knew it was her fault—the abuse, the AIDS, Marie's battle with depression and anorexia. Nelda had been a fabulous mother compared to Pam. Her children had at least been protected from vileness until Pam allowed Jack into their lives.

Pam let the tears come while she was in the shower. It was so sad, so wasted. She had to forgive herself. There was nothing she could do now. What was done was done. Hopefully, Sandra and Marie were coming for the weekend. She would concentrate on them and meeting their needs. It was the least she could do.

Sharon arrived to pick up Nelda by 9:00. She was alarmed when she saw Pam and voiced her concern.

"I'll explain. Can we talk before I tell Mother you are here? She is angry with me right now. Coffee?"

Sharon accepted a cup. They went out to the veranda, the preferred place, it would seem, to give and receive bad news.

"Okay, let me preface this by saying it isn't as dire as it sounds. I have AIDS." She waited, looking at her sister search her face.

Sharon started sobbing and grabbed Pam. Over and over she repeated, "I'm so sorry, I'm so sorry," and then she stopped to blow her nose.

Pam explained the circumstances surrounding how she got the diagnosis.

"Why is Mother angry? Wait, let me guess. She wants to know who gave it to you, correct? That's Mom!" she replied when Pam nodded yes.

"My own children don't know yet. I have to be able to have a dialogue that will satisfy them and leave me some privacy at the same time. I don't want Mother knowing all the gory details! It's none of her business," she repeated for the umpteenth time that week. Pam got up to refill their cups. "She probably won't speak to me, so why don't I go into my bedroom when she comes down?" She heard Nelda and left for her bedroom, hugging her first. "Bye," she whispered.

"So hello, Mother!" Sharon said to Nelda. "Are you ready to leave? We have soccer games to go to this afternoon." She took one of the bags her mother brought with her.

"Where's Pam? Is she going to let me leave without saying good-bye?" Nelda was still angry and was whiney and petulant.

"Can you say good-bye to her without making her feel bad, Mother?"

Nelda started to say something and then thought better of it. "I want to say good-bye to her." Nelda was not going to budge, so Sharon went to Pam's bedroom door and knocked.

"She wants to see you," Sharon singsonged through a crack in the door.

Pam came out and hugged her mother, a bright and cheerful smile on her face. "Have a wonderful week!"

"So you really aren't going to tell me anymore?" Nelda said.

"Oh for God's sake!" Pam and Sharon said loudly.

"Good-bye, Mother!" Pam shouted and went back to her room.

Sharon sped along the parkway toward Staten Island, hoping her mother would shut up. The old lady had not stopped complaining and criticizing Pam for the past half hour. She called her lazy and selfish, said she was a terrible wife for not staying in the city with her husband, and that her children escaped to college because they couldn't bear living with their mother. Sharon was never able to stand up to her mother's cloying protection and felt guilty because Nelda had devoted her life to caring for her when she was an ill child. Finally, unable to squelch her anger, Sharon exploded.

"Mother, please be quiet!" she yelled. "I don't want to hear another word out of you. Do you understand me? How can you say those things about your own daughter?" Nelda was livid.

"How dare you speak to me that way? You have always been an insolent, disrespectful child! After all I did for you! Night after night in the hospital I sat with you. You never wanted for a thing your entire life! Everyone else worked while they were in college! Dad and I sacrificed to put you through school! He worked two jobs for years to give you everything you needed! All those years of doing without so you could have everything, and then you talk to me like this? Take me back home right now!" She was leaning forward with her hands on the dashboard, screaming at Sharon.

"You are coming home with me, whether you like it or not. So, Mother, with all due respect, shut up!" The words were no sooner out of her mouth when her back right tire blew out and she had to focus all of her attention and strength on stopping the car at the side of the road before she killed someone.

She got out of the car and opened the back up to get the tire and jack out. Nelda was struggling to get out of her seat belt.

"Mother, stay where you are. Do you hear me? Don't you dare get out of this car!"

"You're going to change it yourself?" Nelda yelled. "Call Triple A!"

Sharon ignored her. It was something she enjoyed doing, being independent, stretching herself to see how much she could accomplish. She had changed tires on the left side of the car in worse traffic than this. If her mother would just shut up, she would be fine.

Shortly after Sharon and Nelda's departure, Pam got a call from Sandra.

"I was hoping to hear from you. Do you think you'll come today?" She asked.

"I would like to," Sandra answered, "but would it be okay with you if Tom came? I'd like you to meet him."

Pam thought for a second and then agreed, knowing that the presence of Jeff was going to completely change the dynamic of their conversation anyway. *What harm would another man do?* Pam was growing weary of the triad of Marie, Sandra, and herself.

"You can say whatever you want in front of Tom, Pam. He knows all about the baby and the HIV and still wants to see me! How often do you suppose that will happen for me?" She went on to tell Pam about all the adventure she had with Bill.

Pam was stunned. "You must be exhausted! How awful, Sandra. Good old Bill," she said. "I wonder when we will hear from him again."

"Never, if Tom has anything to say about it. I wonder what is going on with his wife and kids?"

They chatted about what was left of the Smith family. And Bernice. No one had heard from her. But that would probably be short-lived. Pam hadn't contacted her mother-in-law because she had been sick. And Bernice wasn't one to stay in touch, either. It had always been all about her.

39

There was a knock on the door, and before Pam could hang up and get to it, Marie walked in. Pam said good-bye to Sandra and went to Marie, who was happy to see her sister looking well.

"Hello! You look a lot better! Thank God!" She hugged Pam, then held her at arm's length to see how she really looked. "Definitely better. How do you feel?" She was scrutinizing Pam's face to detect if she was covering anything up. "You have your poker face on."

Pam laughed out loud. "I am truly fine! You just missed Sharon and Mom. Sister, there was a scene here last night with Mom and Susan. Oh my, Mother is in rare form. She is angry with me because I won't tell her who infected me. Before I go off on a tangent, why don't you get settled? Are you spending the weekend?"

Marie said she was and then told Pam the news that she was infected with AIDS and her viral load was extremely high. "What do you suppose Mother will say about that?"

Pam was stunned. She managed to withhold crying again, afraid that she would be unable to stop if she succumbed. "I loathe the phrase, 'Why is this happening to us,' yet I seem to be saying it on an almost daily basis."

"It probably hasn't sunk in yet; that's why I'm not saying it. So tell me? Who's our chef tonight?" She gave Pam a sly smile.

They talked about their expectations for that night with Jeff.

"He came out to me last night," Marie told Pam. "I confronted him, and he was honest with me. Then I was honest with him about the anorexia and the HIV. Don't worry, he doesn't suspect that it's a family epidemic."

"Wait! He's gay? No way!" Pam said. "I can understand why he was keeping it under wraps."

"You do? Why in God's name would you understand that? It's ridiculous in this day and age to be so dishonest about who you are." Marie went to the pantry to see what wine offerings her sister had. "Not that I'm judging him or anything. What do you have to drink around here?"

"Ah, do you think you should be doing that?" Pam asked. "We're supposed to abstain."

"Oh jeez, don't start that crap with me, okay? As self-destructive as it sounds, I am not stopping drinking. Not yet, anyway. If my 'viral load' is as high as they say it is, and all these other 'counts' as low, then I should be dead by now. I'm not changing the way I've been doing things all along. It's more fun talking about Jeff," Marie continued. "I won't divulge what he told me about his family. Whew! I thought ours took the prize for weirdness. His mother and Nelda run neck and neck."

Pam thought of her earlier self-examination; she wouldn't win any Mother of the Year Awards herself if the truth came out. "I am not going to defend Mom, but she did the best she could," Pam said. "That sounds like such a flagrant copout, but it is so true! When my children come home next weekend, what should I tell them, Marie? Isn't

it enough that I am honest with them about the AIDS?
Do I have to tell them about you and Sandra, too?"

Marie thought for a minute. "Are you asking me if
we need to tell them about my AIDS? No. I would rather
not go there with them. It's too much of a coincidence,
unless we lie and say you gave me a blood transfusion or
something. The truth is that I am not involved in their
lives much at all. This summer, I haven't heard from either
kid. It hurt at first, but with Jack gone, it is almost like I
don't have anything in common with them anymore."

Pam looked hurt, and Marie was sorry about that.
She didn't feel like she had to embellish her relationship
with her niece and nephew. It had evolved into nothing,
and she didn't think it was uncommon for that to happen.

"I take responsibility for it, so don't get worked up. I
couldn't very well be myself with them. I mean, facts are
facts; I was in love with their father. I need to be free to
grieve. It's difficult enough to pretend it was something
different around you."

Pam thought, *Well, gee, thanks, Marie! This weekend is
getting off to a great start! I don't think it is necessary to remind
each other every single time we are together that the root of all of
this pain was Jack? But since it is out now, can we let it lie?* Pam
asked silently. She understood her sister's selfishness and
that she wasn't going to change, but she didn't want her
nose rubbed in the relationship she had with Jack, either.
It was still her house. But she opted to say nothing. Marie
was hurting and in denial. She was also mentally unstable,
and Pam was trying to be patient with her.

"I hope you can have a relationship with the children
again someday." Pam let it go. She had been sitting in a

chair by the window in Marie's room, looking out at the plantings along the fence line. Soon, autumn would be here. The days would grow shorter and shorter; the allure of the beach would be gone. There would be no reason for anyone to come here on the weekends.

She'd been struggling with this fact the past few days, since her walk on the beach. She saw a very early sign of fall approaching; the Japanese blood grasses her neighbor had planted along his property line were turning bright orange. It would be a matter of weeks before school would be back in session, the leaves would change, sailors would take their boats out of the water, and the beach would be a vast, quiet expanse for solitary walking. She imagined her life without Jack or the kids, and it loomed unbearable.

"Can I confess something to you?" she asked Marie. Marie looked up from unpacking.

"Of course. What's wrong?"

"I've been thinking a little about moving back to the city, just for the winter. I will have to sell Bill's house because they have stopped paying their payments to me, and Bernice hasn't had a dime to pay her mortgage for over a year, and then there is the Madison Avenue apartment. The thought of being alone here is very...depressing." *And that is a kind word for what it is*, she thought. "I don't like Jack's place, so that will stay rented for now. I'm tempted to rent out Bill's house because it costs a fortune to maintain and the market is horrible; I would probably end up giving it away. So that leaves the mansion. I could take care of Bernice and have an interesting place to live as well. What are your thoughts?" Pam really cared what her sister's opinion was.

The first thing that came to mind was Bernice. "Would she even allow it?" Marie wanted to know. "I mean, I guess Mother and Bernice could feed off each other."

"She might fight it! But if I foreclose, she is out on the streets. I can't do that to the children or Jack's memory. She overtly hates me, but the house is big enough that I would stay out of her way. She and Mother can shop or do whatever it is old ladies do together. I'm sure I'll be finding that out soon enough as my birthday approaches!" She let out a laugh.

Marie was sitting on the edge of the bed, looking at Pam. "I can't imagine you back in town." She was choosing her words.

"What would Jack say?" Pam said, more as a statement than a question. "Honestly, I believed he wanted me out of the city so he could play." She raised her hand to stop Marie's protest. "I see now how he manipulated me. Then he told everyone it was for the good of the family when I had never said a word about it. Being passive was my weakness. How can I blame him when I actively withdrew?" Pam looked at her hands in her lap and shook her head. "I should have insisted we stay in town, even if it meant having to see Bernice every day. Leaving her grip was one enticing reason to leave. Oh well, another mistake on my part! They just keep pouring in!"

"Let's go outside," Marie said. "It's too nice to stay in on a day like this. There won't be many more."

They left Marie's bedroom for the veranda.

"So what time do we expect to be graced with Jeff?" Marie asked, not really caring, but needing to change the subject. She hated to hear Pam beating herself up over what was, for all intents and purposes, not her fault at all. If she only knew how much she had been manipulated! And as much as she hated to admit it, it was much easier for Marie to stay on the continuum of allowing Pam to blame herself for everything than to get her to face the truth.

"We never specified an exact time, just that he would be over to fix our dinner. At first, we were going to his house, for 'the tour,' he said. He kept looking at me like I needed to be fattened up." Pam was beginning to feel a little claustrophobic, even out on the veranda. "Do you want to walk on the beach?"

Marie jumped at the chance. They took their shoes off and took off down the walkway.

"Oh, what if Sandra comes while we are out? Maybe I better leave the door unlocked. Bill's in jail again, so we're safe."

They talked about his latest brush with the law, Marie disbelieving that he had targeted Sandra. *Why?* "I think he must have had a crush on her. Why else keep hounding her?"

"It's obvious. She has the business now. Can you see some wisdom in not giving it to me? I'd have taken him on as a partner by now." Pam gave a sigh of relief. *Thank God the business isn't mine to worry about.*

The sand was cold under their feet in contrast to the hot sun. It was a beautiful day. The two women had their silent and separate revelries about Jack and the walks they took with him on this same beach. He had left no footprint on the sand, but bulldozed through their hearts. Pam couldn't help herself.

"Can I take a little walk down memory lane?" she asked.

Marie moaned. "If you must. Remember, I might choose to have my turn."

"When we first moved here, Jack would pick me up and carry me. He said he didn't like the thought of my feet being on ground that others had tread on. Honestly. I always had to wear shoes on the beach. At least flip-flops."

Marie found herself wondering if her sister was a virgin when she met Jack. *Was he her first, too?* She would ask her another time, when they weren't expecting guests.

When it was her turn, Marie remembered out loud how she and Jack raced each other on the beach in the evening. They would start at the walkway and run to the lifeguard chair. If there was a full moon, they would run back to the house. But on other times, when the night was dark, they would strip and swim nude, often copulating in the salt water. This she didn't share with Pam. Marie remembered the sting of the water in her vagina. Or they would climb up into the guard chair, and she would fellatiate him right there. She would spit his semen onto the sand and then rinse her mouth with the seawater.

Jack tried to force her to swallow it, hating her to hold it in her mouth until he was finished. "Don't spit!" he would command, holding his hand over her mouth. "Swallow!"

But she tried, and it made her gorge rise. They had a horrible fight about it.

"If you loved me, you would swallow it while I am coming. Can't you do that for me?" He'd have this awful, fake, pious look on his face. He tried holding her head down over him, forcing her to swallow it and choking her in the process. When he let go of her head, she came up sputtering and coughing.

In a rare moment of anger, Marie yelled at him, jumping down from the guard chair, threatening him with exposure if he ever did that to her again. "I'll report you, you bastard!" she yelled, crying. She ran from him back to the house, but he caught her in time, dragging her to a shadowy cove to kiss her and calm her down before she went inside the house, Pam probably waiting with questions and suspicion.

"What are you doing to me? Does Pam swallow it?" Marie had asked him afterward, challenging him.

He became furious with her, pushing her away from him. "My wife doesn't do it, period! What the hell do you think she is?"

Marie was completely confused after that conversation. As a teen spying on them having sex, she had seen him go down on Pam with her own eyes. *It wasn't reciprocal? He was lying.* But she let it go. Now, all of these years later, Marie was dying to ask her sister if she performed oral sex on her husband. How would that start out the weekend? She made the decision to save it for another time.

"What do you think he expected of you, not to get your feet sandy?" Marie asked. "Do you think he had you up on a pedestal?" Maybe she could get the answers she sought another, indirect way.

Pam was thoughtful, looking out to the sea while they walked. "I am not sure what his problem was. There were things that were said and done, or not done, that have me question a lot of what I had believed our relationship to be." Pam had tried to forget something that had occurred when they hadn't been married very long, but it popped into her mind as she walked with her sister.

One night, Jack seemed to forget who she was when they were making love. He went wild, banging into her and screaming with no words, tears running down his face. When he finally came, he fell on top of her and immediately went right to sleep. The next morning, when he woke up, he didn't mention it or seem to remember it at all. There were other things about their sex life that may have been abnormal, but at the time, she was so inexperienced that she had nothing to compare it to. How would she know?

There was so much that was good about it that she finally decided that what had happened between Marie and Sandra and whomever else he was sleeping with didn't really impact her at all. She would accept it at face value. All of the betrayal was hearsay. She had never caught him with another woman or in a lie. There was no concrete evidence until her diagnosis of AIDS was made, and he could have acquired it before they were even married. He said he had loved her, and he showed her by giving her a life to be envied, and by making love to her. At the end of his life, he didn't initiate it, but he never turned her down. The only thing she had left of Jack was their private time together, and she wasn't sharing that with Marie.

40

It is expected that Saturday morning traffic to Long Island on one of the last days of the summer will be horrendous. Smart Manhattanites avoid it; those with a house to go to brave it. Tom Adams seemed to have developed advanced road rage since their last trip to Babylon. *In spite of being a police officer, or maybe because of it*, Sandra thought. It had given her some insight into his personality. She was immediately sorry she didn't sit in the backseat. She spent most of the ride staring out of the left corner of her eyes to be prepared in case he did anything really stupid. Would she be able to protect the baby if a quick exodus was necessary? With her arms wrapped around her belly, she could jump from the car to save herself. *Silly*, she thought, *you are being silly.* But her hand was on the door handle, just to be sure. When they finally pulled in front of Pam's house three hours later, Sandra couldn't get out of the car fast enough.

"Hey, wait for me!" Tom yelled with a laugh. His behavior of a driver possessed seemed long forgotten.

Perhaps he isn't aware of the way he acted. She'd make excuses for him as long as she had to. Waiting by the door for him, she reached out for his hand. When Pam opened the door, it would be to these two attractive young people.

"Hello!" Pam said with a big smile. She reached out for Sandra and embraced her. "I am so glad to see you.

Thank you both for rescuing me the other day. Tom, I have to apologize to you for being dragged into my drama!"

He shook his head no. "It was no problem at all! I was happy to do it." They walked into the entrance with the veranda ahead and the ocean beyond. "Oh boy, what a view." Tom went right out the back door, leaving Sandra and Pam alone.

"He knows about the HIV and is fine with it," she said. "I'm not so sure I even know what's happening. It is all coming at me so quickly."

"You didn't tell him about me?" Pam asked, concern written all over her face.

"No." Sandra said, but thought, *He'll figure it out because he knows we were both sleeping with Jack.*

"Let's go walk out to the water," Tom suggested.

"We just came in from a walk. Go ahead," Pam replied. "We'll fix lunch together." Marie walked out of her bedroom just as the happy couple left for the water's edge. Pam thought, *What a happy group, considering the news we have just all gotten. How fake can you get?*

"I didn't know he was coming," Marie said, a frown on her face. "The last thing I want right now is a strange cop knowing all my business." She thought, *Sandra gets the hunky cop, while I get the aging homosexual.* "Maybe if I keep this damn smile on my face long enough, it will become real."

"My thoughts exactly," Pam said. "Hopefully, his presence will keep things light. I mean, Jeff is coming, too. How much of your business do you want him to know?" Pam asked, standing at the counter tossing a salad.

"Only the facts. He doesn't need to know much. I told him what he needs to have an honest friendship with me and nothing more. My fear is that someone will connect the dots. Why did she have to bring him?" Marie whined. "We should be alone today, not entertaining a room full of strangers."

Pam could see that Marie's craziness was beginning to escalate, and to diffuse it, she went to her and put her arms around her sister as she used to when they were kids. "You'll be fine. Just relax, okay? We don't want to start anything today." Pam patted her back and could hear Marie's breathing slow down. "There you go."

Sandra chose that second to walk in. She had a smirk on her face and tried to make eye contact with Pam, but Pam diverted her eyes. She was not ganging up on her sister today to bond with anyone, let alone Sandra. Marie saw Sandra standing there alone. Tom must have stayed on the beach.

"Group hug!" Marie commanded.

Sandra laughed and walked over to join them.

"We will have fun today! I am going to make it an act of my will! Fun!" Marie said.

They moved apart, laughing.

"So what's on the agenda?" Sandra asked.

Marie wanted to say, *Nothing, now that lover boy is here*, but kept her mouth shut.

They looked to Pam.

"Simply relaxation. We can't talk about anything deep because of Tom and Jeff. I definitely don't want neighbors trying to put the puzzle together. It's just too lurid." Pam thought, *This is my house, my life. Those two can do whatever they want in the city. But Babylon is my jurisdiction.*

"So what is going on with Andy?" Sandra asked. "He seems like such a nice guy. He was very concerned when you were in the hospital."

Pam remembered her anger when she woke up with him standing over her sickbed.

"I sort of hoped he would be here tonight," Sandra said.

"I had to ask him to give me some space. I want to grieve my husband in peace." She said it with the thought in mind, *That's right, ladies, he was* my *husband.*

"You deserve to be happy, Pam. He seemed like such a nice, considerate guy," Marie said. "I hope you'll be able to let him in someday."

"Well, if it's meant to be, he'll be around when I am ready. But for now, I have too much to process, and I don't want my thinking to be cluttered up with worrying about another human being. I still have my kids to think of. Try to remember that if you think I am being dramatic." Assertiveness was not new to Pam, but doing so at the expense of someone else's happiness was not easy for her. She was fighting guilt and trying to explain her reasoning for ditching Andy Andrews at the same time.

"I don't think you're being dramatic at all," Marie said. "You probably know what's best for yourself. Hey, did I tell you about my new stalker at work?"

They got their drinks and went out to the veranda as Marie told them about Steve Marks. Tom was back and listening.

"He sounds like a troublemaker. If you have any issues with him again, call me." Tom pulled out a business card.

Marie thanked him and said she would definitely take him up on it.

"I always said everyone needs a dentist, a lawyer, and a cop in the family, and now we do!" Pam said.

They sat down, all facing toward the water. It was a great beach day, prime spaces occupied by chairs and towels, the whistle of the lifeguard warning bathers not to go too far out clearly heard over the call of the seagulls. The surf was wild, crashing waves on the shore, an indication of a storm out to sea. The sun was bright, but it was slightly cooler than usual because of the wind. Pam shivered, and seeing it, Marie got up to go to Jack's office to get a shawl for her. Once again, Pam was reminded of the approaching fall and her thoughts about moving to the city.

"So may I tell you about my plan?" Pam asked Sandra. Marie came in and put the shawl around her sister's shoulders.

"Okay," Sandra said. "Go ahead."

"I'm thinking about moving into the mansion for the winter. Bernice is defaulting on the loan, so I can let her stay there to live while I pay the taxes and the upkeep and call it a loss, or move in there myself."

Sandra didn't say anything. *Pam in the city? What's bringing this on?*

"Would you be able to leave this house?" Marie asked. "You have loved it so much. I don't remember you liking the mansion, either." She took a big drink of her wine, noticing Sandra glaring at her. She willed her to say something about AIDS and drinking, but Sandra was wisely keeping her mouth shut.

"I think I might like being in the city when the bad weather comes. I can always come back here anytime. It would just be for the winter. Somehow I have to decide what to do about that house. Mother would probably love it, too." Pam didn't think her mother would handle an oceanfront winter. "I can't see my mother liking the nor'easters we get."

"Mother. I keep forgetting about her," Marie said.

Sandra thought about the apartment but decided not to bring it up. And then, surprisingly, because it was so unlike her to bring up personal stuff in front of a stranger, Pam asked Sandra about the business.

"I thought I would have gotten the quarterly statement by now." She looked directly at Sandra. "With the expenses now for all of these Manhattan properties, I would like to make sure Peter isn't driving the business into the ground." She made light of it, her pleasant laugh making everyone smile, but Sandra knew that she was serious.

"I'll look into it on Monday. To tell you the truth, I don't think I saw one, either. Peter Romney has never said a word to me until yesterday, when I told him he was being a dick," Sandra confessed.

Everyone started laughing, although only Pam knew how true the name fit Peter.

"How appalling! It was when I was giving him the file you so graciously brought downtown for me. Thank you, Marie," Sandra said.

"How long are you going to work?" Marie asked her. "I mean, you hear that women stay at work until their due dates, but isn't that pushing it?" She realized how uninformed she was. *How could I have lived a woman's life, helped my sisters through their pregnancies, and not know?*

Sandra didn't seem fazed by it. "I'll work as long as I can. Something in my health insurance policy says I have to work until the doctor says I can't any longer. So they have all the control. I may be canceled once they find out the horrible truth. Anyway, I would like to tell you all about my lovely experience as a kidnap victim of Bill Smith yesterday."

The women gasped, disbelieving that Sandra could be relating something so awful so calmly.

The sun slowly moved over the house, and one by one, the sunbathers packed up their towels and left the beach, and the day-trippers went back to their homes west as Sandra related the scary details of her encounter with a madman. She left out the story of Jack and Bill being lovers. That would be a tale that she would tell when she was alone with Pam. She understood how something like that could happen—the father forcing it and then the two brothers finding solace in each other. But she had to admit to herself that something of what she felt for Jack shifted when Bill repeated the story. It could have been a lie, for all she knew, but something told her it was the truth. Another layer of the man Jack had been was exposed.

She caught herself staring at Tom, wondering if his childhood had anything tainted in it, anything that could compare to the depravity of the Smith family. She hoped not. What happened in secret would always be revealed.

People thought that their sexual sins didn't harm them as long they weren't exposed. But look at what had happened to Jack. The fruit of his father's sin had grown until they couldn't fathom its boundaries. More and more would be exposed over time. Sandra thought of Bill and Anne. *Did Jack infect Bill? How did Jack manage to die in a big city emergency room without his HIV status being revealed?* She wanted to dig deeper into it, but wondered at the wisdom of it. *Would it generate scandal?* She imagined the children being hurt. She didn't want her child to have that stigma. He may have his own health issues to battle. And what about Anne? If Bill had it, she most likely did as well.

Tom excused himself and left the veranda to go make a call.

Sandra grasped the opportunity to talk to Pam alone. "We have to talk about something Bill said about Jack, but I don't want to do it with Tom here, okay? May I call you later, when I'm alone?"

Pam nodded her head yes.

Then they heard a call from the beach, out of sight because of the dunes. It was Jeff.

"Oh shit," Marie said. Sandra looked at her questioningly, but Marie ignored it.

"Hello, my favorite diners! I'm here to rescue you from starvation!" Jeff was loaded down with boxes; Tom was helping him by carrying what appeared to be a huge chafing dish. Jeff was behaving in a most flamboyant manner, too, completely infuriating her.

Why'd he wait until now to reveal this side of himself? Even though it was over, she discovered that she was more than a little disappointed. He had lied to her. Her heart had started to reach out to him, and now there was nothing there for her. She was longing for intimacy. She wanted to lie next to a naked man again, have him lust after her body, react to her sexuality by getting an erection, and saying he wanted her. And she remembered that, even before she knew Jeff was gay, there was zero chemistry between them. He didn't appeal to her. But someone did, someone who was interested in her, who had frightened her with his willingness to lose his job, or at least put it in jeopardy in his pursuit of her. She would think about him for the rest of the evening.

41

Dinner was nice, the food very good and company interesting. Jeff refused all offers of help cleaning up. By 10 p.m., Pam had had it. She didn't even put up a fuss when Marie announced she was leaving, too. She had too much to do in the city to stay; she would be right behind Tom and Sandra. Jeff lingered until Pam told him she was exhausted and asked him if he would excuse her if she went to bed.

"Heavens no! You go. I am going to clean up here and will let myself out. Is that okay with you? I am driving up to Rhinebeck in the morning and like to have all loose ends tied up when I go."

They hugged, and she retreated to her bedroom, not caring that she was leaving a relative stranger in her house while she slept. Just able to get her makeup off and her pj's on, she fell into bed and was fast asleep by 10:30.

Marie drove like a maniac and was back in the city, in her own neighborhood, before midnight. She left her car on the street and went into the same bar where she saw Steve Marks the day before, threatening him with the police if he bothered her again. He was sitting at the bar. Not seeing her until she was seated in the back again, at the same table where she drank her wine, it took a few seconds for him to recognize her. She had on a halter top and shorts, her body lean and fit for a woman her age. She had no makeup on, and you could tell she had been out in the sun; there was the slightest red on her cheeks, and white shown where her sunglasses had rested on her face. He slid off his bar stool and made his way in the back to her, smiling as he approached her table. Marie slid farther over in the booth, making room for him to slide in next to her so they could be seated together, both looking out.

He came close and put his arm across the back of the bench. "I thought you didn't want to see me again," he said. But he was smiling at her. His aftershave was a light, herbal scent of something expensive. His clothes were impeccable for a summer weekend night. He leaned in to kiss her, and she smelled peppermint candy on his breath. His lips were soft, and she could feel a slight picker from his beard. The tension on her mouth from his traveled down her neck, through her shoulders, erecting her nipples, and then straight to her crotch. He didn't open his mouth; it was a friendly kiss, a respectful kiss, one that was asking if there would be more if he played his cards right.

"You know where I live. Meet me there in twenty minutes." She slid out the other side of the booth, and when she stood up and turned to look at him, he was smiling up at her. She found herself wondering if he had an erection already or if he would pop a Viagra in his mouth on the way to her apartment. *What difference did it make?* She desperately wanted him to fuck her. She stood up straight as she walked out of the bar, knowing he was looking at her.

After she put her car in the garage, she went up to her apartment to take a quick shower and straighten her bedroom up a little bit. Her sheets hadn't been changed since she spent the weekend in Rhinebeck, but that was barely a week ago. She used soap that smelled like roses; Jack used to buy it for her and then make her wash with it before they made love. Pam used it, too, so she wouldn't get suspicious if he came home smelling of roses. Tonight, it would make no difference what she smelled of. *Is Steve Marks married?* She didn't know if she cared yet. This was nothing more than a one-night stand; if it evolved into more, then she would ask those important questions.

Putting on Jack's favorite robe, she thought maybe Steve would like it, too. It was a royal-blue silk kimono, short and secured loosely with a tie belt. She was naked under it. Examining her body in the mirror, she still looked young, her stomach as flat as a board and her breasts high and firm. She didn't look forty-five. She would flaunt it tonight.

The buzzer went off. She unlocked the door without speaking into the intercom. A minute later, there was a soft tap at the door. She looked through the peephole and unlocked the door to let him in. She had a moment of fear. *What if he's a murderer?* No one knew she was with him.

He walked in and, without a word, closed the door and gently pulled her to him. If he was a killer, she would soon find out. It was a risk she was willing to take because, tonight, she needed to be loved.

42

Sunday in Manhattan. Sunday brunch was a tradition on the Upper West Side. There were at least twenty restaurants that served brunch uptown. Sandra's favorite was Chantal's, not just because it was the last place that she and Jack went together, but because they had fabulous pancakes. And she was ravenous for pancakes.

Tom spent the night, once again sleeping on the couch downstairs. Sandra was a little disappointed that he didn't stay upstairs with her, but he seemed reluctant. She was more than willing to make love to him, even making a suggestive move toward his crotch, but he backed off without saying anything. The temptation to read more into it than she should loomed large. *Is he not interested in sex with me? Or does he want to take more time before we make love?* It had only been a week! So she kissed him goodnight and allowed him to tuck her in.

She woke up shortly after 8:00, and not hearing any noise coming from the lower level, she tiptoed down the stairs to see if he was still sleeping. She was shocked to see that he wasn't there, and it didn't look like the couch had been slept on. The sheets were neatly made up. If he had slept there, he would have unmade the couch and folded the sheets up. She looked around, checking the bathroom. Nothing. She went back upstairs and found the note he had left her on the dining table. She sat down and, with

314

trembling hands, unfolded the Dear Jane letter that Tom Adams had left for her:

Dear Sandra,

I'm sorry I didn't discuss my intentions with you last night. The timing just wasn't right. I wanted you to get some sleep, and what I had to say could wait until the morning. I knew while we were at your friend's house that I had made rash decisions about our future without knowing all the facts.

First of all, I can hardly expect you to relinquish your past to be in a relationship with me. In order for me to adopt your baby and raise him as my own child, I would want to do just that. The life I had envisioned for us isn't realistic. That guy you were involved with seems to have drawn you and those sisters together pretty tightly. There seems to be bond between the three of you that I don't have the energy or the desire to circumvent.

Secondly, although you were honest with me about your relationship with your lover's wife, it doesn't change the fact that she was still married to him when you were sleeping with him. I guess the impact of the deception didn't hit me until I saw you with his wife today.

I must have been awfully naive to think I could come in and make you forget your past completely. Your future will be tied up in the lives of your lover's family, and I don't have any desire to be involved with them myself.

What I am trying to say is that I don't think we should see each other anymore. I am sorry that I pushed so much on you so quickly. And I swear it doesn't have anything to do with your health concerns.

Good luck! You're a fabulous woman!
Tom Adams

"Huh?" Sandra said out loud. She looked out the window at the birdfeeders. They needed filling before she went for her own breakfast. Restraining herself from tearing the letter up into little pieces, she folded it back up and stuffed it into her purse. Then she went to her closet to get the white sundress she had worn the last time she was with Jack. She was taking herself out to brunch.

43

Bernice Smith was still in bed on Sunday morning when she heard a knock at her bedroom door. She struggled to get up, yelling out, "Come in."

It was Mildred. She had morning coffee and a light breakfast.

"What's this all about, Millie?" she asked.

"Miss Pam called this morning, madam. She said to tell you she was on her way to take you to brunch. She said she won't take no for an answer."

Bernice frowned. "Oh, what does she want to do that for?" she asked petulantly. "I don't want to see Pam!"

Mildred ignored her, pulling a small table up to the bedside and placing the tray there. She helped Bernice swing her legs over the side of the bed so she could eat something. Pam wouldn't be there until 11:00. Bernice had lost so much weight that the staff was alarmed. They made it a point now to cook and serve her something to eat at least four times a day, whether she asked for it or not.

"The coffee smells so good this morning, doesn't it? I'm tempted to have a cup with you," Mildred said. "Here's a nice muffin Alice made just for you."

Since Bill had been taken back to prison last week, Bernice had deteriorated further. Mildred called Pam in the morning to warn her; she was concerned that the doctor should be called on Monday morning. Bernice sipped the coffee and took the piece of muffin Mildred had buttered for her. She slowly came around, the friendly Bernice replacing the whiney, crabby Bernice. They would juxtapose throughout the day.

"When you are done eating, you need to have your shower and get dressed for the day. Where do you think Pam is taking you?"

"How should I know? I've haven't been to brunch with Pam since Lisa was a baby and they moved out to the island." She chewed the muffin slowly, closing her eyes and savoring it. "This is so good. What is that flavor?"

"I think she used nutmeg in this batch. The whole kitchen smelled fragrant this morning. There is nothing like fresh muffins for breakfast." Mildred went to the closet and got out clean clothing for her employer, who could no longer be trusted to notice when what she was wearing was dirty. The phone began ringing. Mildred walked over to the night table and picked up Bernice's phone. "Smith residence," she said. "Yes, she's awake. Who's speaking, please? One moment." Mildred stretched the phone cord to reach Bernice. "It's Miss Sandra, madam."

Bernice's countenance completely changed. She almost bounced up and down on the edge of the bed. She had forgotten that it was because of Sandra that her only surviving son was in prison for twenty years. "Sandra, my dear! How are you? I am so glad you called," Bernice gushed. Then, "Well, actually, Pam is on her way over to take me to brunch. Would you like to join us? Oh, I'm sure it would be okay with Pam!" Bernice looked at Mildred with lowered eyebrows and mouthed, *Goddamned Pam*. She listened some more and then said, "Well, okay, Sandra, I'll tell her to call you as soon as she gets here. I miss you! Good-bye." She gave the phone to Mildred. "She's going to brunch alone, but needs to talk to Pam. Humph! I would have thought she would attempt to come and see me! Oh well, I can't expect everything to go my way, now can I?" She pushed the table away and stood up on unsteady feet. "I want a shower now. I think I can manage alone this morning, Mildred."

Mildred, however, was not going anywhere. History had proven that the old lady might forget what she was doing and never make it to the shower. No, Mildred would stay close by. Ben would get the door if Miss Pam showed up early.

Bernice struggled to get bathed and dressed without help, but she accomplished it and looked a little like her old, self-assured self. But it would not be enough to fool Pam, who was stunned at the transformation of her mother-in-law from a formidable, dignified woman to an old, stooped hag. The years of alcohol, of denial and pain, were clearly written all over Bernice's face. It had finally caught up with her. *Is it inevitable that our sins will be revealed?* Pam thought. A person may not admit them out loud, or even to themselves privately, but they will not be denied. The life you live will show on your face and body eventually. Here was a woman who had, if the stories her son told were true, been drunk every night of her children's youth to escape the acts of depravity being committed right under her nose. She had turned the other cheek when her husband chose the bed of her sons rather than her own and then allowed him back when the boys were old enough to repel their father's advances.

But were Bernice's sins any different than Pam's? Pam had looked the other way, too. She had allowed the worst kind of abuse in her own house, under her own nose. *Jack wasn't as brutal as Harold had been, or was he?* Jack having given her AIDS was proof that there was something else in his life yet to be uncovered. Pam was suddenly cold in the August heat. *What more was there to be discovered?*

Ben had let Pam in when she knocked on the door, and showed her to the den. She inquired after Bernice's well-being, and he would only say, "Madam is well." Mildred came in next with the offer of coffee, but Pam wanted to take Bernice out as soon as she came down, so she refused. Her purpose in showing up today was to let Bernice know she had decided to spend some time that winter living in the mansion. It was hers, after all. She held a mortgage on it, and although the house had been paid for many years ago, the money Jack had given his family in return for the lien had been frittered away on who knew what. She would lay hands on the title to the property and sell it without hesitation if there was any resistance to her request. For some reason, Pam felt empowered by this for the first time in many years. Not normally a bully, this vindictiveness allowed Pam to be assertive. She would only play those cards if she were forced. This was her children's legacy, this giant old place in the most prime area of the city. What had been stolen from them by their father's perversity would be restored in brick and mortar. They would never want for anything, those two.

Bernice came into the den on unsteady feet. Even though she saw her mother-in-law just a short week ago, the change was dramatic. Pam hid her surprise and went to her, putting her arms around her with a cheerful hello.

Before they completed their hug, Bernice said, "Sandra wants you to call her before you go home. She is going to brunch alone and can't join us."

Pam thought Bernice was pouting and let it slide. *My mother-in-law likes Sandra better than me, but so what?* "All righty! Let's you and I go to Tavern on the Green, shall we? I haven't been there since Bill's wedding!"

Pam had pushed the right buttons as she lead Bernice out to the hall and the front door. Bernice cheered right up. "Oh that was a beautiful wedding, wasn't it?" she asked. "I'll never forget the music and dancing into the night. The Tavern on the Green was a monument to grace and civility, don't you think? I heard it was in bankruptcy. How can that be?"

Ben brought the car around front, and the women got into the backseat while he waited, holding the door, a servant from an earlier time when people had expendable wealth as they never would again. Bernice still acted like a rock star. But that would be coming to an end. She was having a time of lucidity and sharp memory. She spoke of the changes the city was going through, the grittiness of some parts of Manhattan that made places like Columbus Circle stand out. It made her sad, she said.

"I used to love going to Anne and Bill's in the Village. I knew Anne wasn't thrilled with me being there, but the change from the mansion, the vibrancy of those little boys, it just revived me. What is going on with Anne and Bill, anyway? No one will tell me anything." She looked directly at Pam, with clarity and not her usual derision.

"Anne is in jail. I thought about dropping the charges and still might. Bill is back at Rikers for holding Sandra against her will." Pam saw no reason to hide the truth from Bernice. "You and I can go to visit both of them—Anne tomorrow and Bill on Wednesday. Would you like that?"

"I suppose. How do you survive visiting your only son in jail?" Bernice stopped there, knowing that if she voiced her opinion of her son's innocence that Pam might argue with her. It was easier just to keep one's mouth shut. She would be able to act the lady for a few hours in her daughter-in-law's presence.

Pam thought it was time to change the subject. "I am going to stay with you for a few days, Mother Smith. It's lonely at the beach right now. The children will be home Thursday, but I thought it might do both of us some good to have company. What do you think?"

Bernice had turned to look at Pam, mouth agape. "You are kidding, correct? Why would you stay with me when you have that lovely apartment?" Bernice did *not* want Pam staying with her, no matter what the circumstances. "I think it would be somewhat of an inconvenience to my staff," she said, with her chin in the air. "Really, Pam, have you lost all sense of propriety? Ha-ha, aren't you supposed to ask before you swoop in to invade someone's home?" Bernice snickered out loud. *Really, my daughter-in-law is a hick.*

"Well, Mother Smith, be that the case, I am staying at the mansion. Also, I intend on moving in for the winter. I don't relish the idea of being alone at the beach in the snow and wind." She rearranged her purse on her lap, and her posture said, *No more need be spoken of this.*

However, Bernice was far from finished. She threw her body forward and pounded on the glass partition. "Ben! Stop the car!" Her driver pulled over to the curb. "Pam Smith, you will not tell me what you are going to do in my own house. That's preposterous. I can't imagine where you got your manners! I don't want you to stay with me. Is that clear enough?" Bernice was trying for an intimidating glare at her daughter-in-law, but she wasn't able to pull it off. She reminded Pam of a cartoon character. Pam didn't want to hurt the old lady, so she stifled her laughter. But she was going to pull the "foreclosure card," after all, not wanting to be a brute, but having to have the upper hand.

"Bernice, I don't want to rub this in, but I own the mansion now. You haven't paid a dime on the mortgage for more than a year. Do we really want to go into that? Wouldn't it just be easier to allow me access to what is legally my home, too? After all, I pay the bills here and the staff salaries. I'm lonely, and my mother and you could keep each other company."

Bernice exploded then. "Your mother? I will not have that lowlife of a woman in my lovely home, not for a minute or a day! What in God's name has come over you?" She fell back onto the seat, out of breath.

Pam tapped on the window and told Ben to return home.

"I never thought this would happen to me. My own home, taken over by scum." And then she started crying, childish boohooing. "I don't want you to move in! I want to be alone with my memories! It's my house!" she whined.

Pam had to turn her head to prevent from laughing out loud. The woman was a lunatic.

"My mother is great, and you and she have enjoyed each other's company in the past. You'll be fine, I promise you." And then to herself, Pam said, *I will tell you that if you don't allow me to come, I am going to fire your staff, and you, my friend, are moving to assisted living. There will be nowhere else for you to go.*

44

Pam and Bernice returned to Columbus Circle without having had brunch. Mildred was waiting for them with a questioning look on her face, but Bernice was not finished with her tirade. Bernice didn't notice that Pam had her arm and was helping her up the steps to the entryway.

Pam asked Ben to bring her bags in and put them upstairs.

"Mildred," Pam said as they were helping a sobbing Bernice into the house, "I'll be staying with you for a few days. What room do you suggest I use? I'd like to be as close to Madam as possible."

That brought a fresh torrent of cries from Bernice.

Mildred and Pam were trying not to smile, although Mildred did think it was appalling for Mrs. Smith to be acting so ungrateful.

"Yes, Miss Pam, I have a room for you" was all Mildred said.

"I don't want her too close to me, for God's sake," Bernice cried out. "What ever happened to privacy? Oh! I wish I were dead!" she moaned over and over. "I want to go to bed!"

Pam shook her head no to Mildred. "We need to get something to eat. Let's call Sandra and ask her to come.

That will brighten your day!" Pam led her to the den while Mildred went to tell Alice to fix something for lunch.

Bernice visibly brightened up. "Sandra! Yes, let's call her!" Bernice slumped into a high-backed leather wing chair, once her throne, now her prison. It would take two of them to pull her out of it later in the day. "Sandra always has something cheerful to say!"

Pam dug her cell phone out of her purse and keyed in Sandra's number. She answered on the first ring, saying she would be over in a half hour. She was done eating and only had to get a cab to Bernice's.

There was an immediate change in Bernice after the call

"I'm going to go upstairs and change my clothes since we aren't going to brunch," Pam said.

Bernice ignored her. She rang for Mildred, who came through the door wiping her hands on a towel.

"Yes, madam?" she said, successfully hiding her frustration. She was trying to help Alice prepare lunch. "Luncheon will be served shortly."

"Thank you, Millie. Sandra is coming, and she has already eaten, but I would like something available for her."

Mildred nodded her head and left the room. *One day at a time*, she thought to herself. *I can take one more day of this*. And then Bernice rang for her again. Mildred took a deep breath before she went through the door.

"Oh, Millie, I forgot to tell you that you are not to take orders from Pam. Do you understand me? You are not her personal servant!"

Mildred waited for a few moments, hoping that Bernice would get it all out before she went back to the kitchen. "Anything else, madam?" she asked, grinding her teeth.

"No, that will be all, for now." Bernice leaned forward, struggling to reach a magazine to read while she was waiting for Sandra to appear. It was just out of her reach, and as she was going for the call button again, Pam walked in and saved Mildred from having to make another trip.

As soon as Sandra arrived, Bernice had a turnaround in attitude, was gracious and kind, spoke to Pam with respect, and tried to be more independent. But the weeks of inactivity had taken a toll. Mildred served lunch, Bernice falling asleep with her chin on her chest shortly after the last bite was taken.

"She really failed in a week," Sandra whispered, nodding toward Bernice. "What brought you into town? I'm happy you're here!"

"After we talked last night about me moving into the city for the winter, I decided to spend a few days here with her to ease into it. She's not happy about it!" Pam giggled. "Saying she is annoyed would be putting it mildly. We were in the car to go out to eat, and she had a temper tantrum."

"Poor Pam. Poor Bernice! She looks awful! What the hell happened?"

"I'll have to dig around and see. It is Bill and Jack and Harold, I think. Too much for one person." Pam avoided repeating her theory about Bernice facing her sins. "By the way, I like your young man very much!"

"Well, it's already over," Sandra replied. "He left me a Dear Jane letter when he left last night. Didn't even have the balls to tell me to my face. I mean, it's not like there was any great love between us yet. I'm disappointed, but jeez, get over yourself, buddy! It'd only been a week!"

"Oh, well, I'm sorry, for whatever it's worth," Pam said. "He seemed like a nice guy. I'm almost afraid to ask what happened."

"He could handle another man's baby and the fact that I was HIV positive, but not my relationship with you and Marie. Here's the letter," she said while she dug in her purse for the folded-up paper.

Pam took it from her and began reading it. Then she read out loud, "*Your future will be tied up in the lives of your lover's family, and I don't have any desire to be involved with them myself.* Well, I suppose he has a point. I don't think most men would be able to be so enmeshed in the life of the former boyfriend. As strange as it seems, I understand him. Do you think you could give up your friendships with us to sustain a relationship?" Pam asked.

"He didn't even give me the option!" Sandra replied. "He made up his mind, and that was that. I think he was looking for an excuse to leave, that he had made a rash decision and was regretful and didn't know how to get out of it. I was grateful that I had someone kind and hot looking who was willing to overlook so much, but the truth is that I won't be shedding any tears over him. I have to grieve, too. I want to be alone for now. The loneliness will get worse once the baby is here."

Pam didn't say anything, remembering her own postpartum loneliness that her sister Marie had rescued her from.

"If I begin now to accept that I may be alone for the rest of my life, it might be easier for me than to have some trumped up idea that prince charming will rescue me. I really should be pissed at Tom for doing that!" Sandra could feel the tiniest bit of self-pity creeping in. She knew it was best to squelch it immediately, because its companion, depression, often followed it close by.

"I'm going to tell you a story, Sandra. May I?" Pam asked. "It's about our beloved Jack. I have never told a soul about this, but since you know all my secrets, one more exposure is not going to hurt me, and it might help you. Shall I?"

Sandra was blowing her nose, trying to cover up the tears that were right on the surface. She shook her head yes.

Pam looked at Bernice to make sure she was still sleeping; she was out cold. It was safe to go on.

"When Lisa was a newborn and Brent was about two, I had what I guess you would call an affair of the mind. Yes, I know! Radical! Silly Pam, perfect Pam! With another man!" She smiled at no one and took a sip of her coffee, which had grown cold. "Jack was never home. I mean, he was often out all night in addition to being gone during the day working. I questioned him, and he told me some lie, which I eagerly accepted because I was afraid he would walk out on me. Subconsciously, I knew he was probably cheating on me, but I would never admit it to myself. He was a smooth liar, that man! Where would I go if he left? Nelda's? Not on your life.

"Anyway, we had a neighbor back then, a man who lived at the Ansonia, right there on Broadway. One day, Lisa must have been about six weeks old, I was walking in the neighborhood with both kids in the stroller, and we stood in front of the pet store on Seventy-sixth—do you know which one I mean? It's still there, I'm sure. I see their ads in the *Times*. I had Brent out of the stroller and his little shoes on the window ledge looking at the puppies, and someone who worked there came out and started yelling at me to get him down from the window. She scared Brent, and he started crying, which woke Lisa up. So I was on the street with two crying children and really not handling it well.

"Mr. Hill happened to be taking a walk that morning and saw me struggling. I recognized him from shopping in the neighborhood and a poetry reading I had attended in his building. He took Brent so I could give Lisa a bottle right there on the street, and we stood talking for at least a half hour.

"'Let me help you get home,' he said. I didn't give it a second thought. The man could have been an ax murderer, and I was taking him home with me. But I was so starved for adult conversation that I would have been a willing victim. So we walked back to my apartment together. He was so helpful with the stroller and the children. Then he told me about a project he was working on—a screenplay adaptation of a novel that he really hated, but it was how he paid his bills. He asked if I would be interested in reading parts for him, and I agreed.

"Every afternoon during the week, I would take the children to his apartment in the Ansonia and read the female dialogue for him. He said it helped him. Who knows if it really did? He had a housekeeper who would serve us tea, the kind Alice used to fix here, with all the trimmings.

She would tend to the children, and I would read for Mr. Hill. I saw him almost every afternoon for years.

"Finally, when Brent was in first or second grade, I was just getting ready to leave for the Ansonia when a messenger came with a note from Mr. Hill's housekeeper. He had died. The day before he was fine; we took turns reading aloud from a book of plays written by women, and we were screaming with laughter it was so much fun!

"So that was that. He was gone. We never, ever touched each other. I don't even know if I ever addressed his sexuality; he could have been gay, for all I know. But I don't think so. Oh, I don't know. What difference does it make now? All I know is that he fed my soul for five years. I had my sister Friday through Sunday, and Mr. Hill Monday through Friday. Jack was sort of superfluous."

Sandra sat quietly listening, but tears were streaming down her cheeks.

"I guess I am telling you this because I want you to know that you will find people who will fill the void in your life. It won't be ideal, but it will stave off loneliness. Mr. Hill was wonderful because he stimulated my mind. I had something to look forward to every day. Because of him, it didn't make any difference if Jack didn't come home at night; I even stopped looking for him. When Brent started kindergarten, I would leave Mr. Hill's and pick up Brent at school on my way home. It was a joy to prepare dinner for my children. We would eat together, and by the time I got them ready for bed, we were all exhausted. Some nights I would hear Jack sneaking in after midnight. Rarely, he was home by eight. I would fight sleep, and he would get angry with me. 'What do you do all day that you are too tired to talk to me?' he'd ask. Oh, Jack, if you only knew.

"Not long after Mr. Hill died, we moved to Long Island. It was the final disconnection from people for me. It's truly amazing how you adapt to your situation. Taking care of the family filled my life with meaning. I loved it when the children were teenagers. My house would be filled with kids playing video games all weekend. We'd order pizza from Shore Pizza, and I would take a carload of teenagers to pick it up. They would be laughing and horsing around in the car, and I enjoyed every second of it. My sister would call me whining that she had six eight- year-olds in her house for a birthday party; I would counter with having eight sixteen-year-olds!

"When Brent left for college, both Lisa and I were miserable. It was so lonely without him. She continued having her friends in every weekend, but we missed the boys. One day in October, she saw a couple of Brent's friends in town, boys who were going to school locally, and she invited them over. After that, they returned each Saturday night. Brent didn't mind, he claimed. He said he was jealous. Of course, eventually they found other things to do, and then Lisa went away to school last year.

"Poor Jack, all of my focus was on him. He and Marie. You'd think I'd have noticed something awry, but I didn't. I went through life happy and content, living vicariously through everyone else." Pam stopped. "So that's the story of my life. One mistake after another. Forgive me for rambling?" she asked. She took a deep breath. "What a sorry excuse for a woman." In a rare display of self-pity,

Pam allowed Sandra to see the complete woman as no one else had.

"Can you take some advice from someone without your life experience?" Sandra asked, smiling at Pam through her tears. She reached out her hand to take Pam's.

Pam had nodded her head yes in answer to her.

"Forgive yourself for whatever you perceived to have done wrong. You're not responsible for Jack, or for Marie. The fruit of your life are those kids of yours. Look at how wonderful they are, how they worship you," Sandra said. "There is something else I need to talk to you about. I don't want to hurt you or shock you."

"Let's go out in the garden," Pam said.

Sandra got up and followed her outside.

They sat at the glass table in the center of the slate terrace, water features splashing and bubbling so that the sounds of the street were muffled.

Once they were situated, Pam said, "I believe I have heard everything, but you might surprise me. Go on."

"When Bill was in my apartment Friday night, he told me that he and Jack had been lovers." Sandra stopped for a moment to compose herself, tears continuing to stream down her face. "He said Harold forced them to have sex while he watched, but I had the impression that it continued after that. His exact words were, 'It's okay between brothers.' Personally, I don't care anymore. Jack was not the man I thought he was, obviously. It doesn't change anything. But it got me thinking about the source of the HIV. Bill could've given it to Jack, or the other way around, in which case he might not know. He would literally rot in prison. There is always Anne, too."

Pam was sitting, ramrod straight, with her hands folded on the glass table. There was a large vase of flowers on the table in front of her—summer flowers like peonies, roses, and daisies, many of them drooping over the vase—so that Pam looked as though she were holding a large, gaudy bouquet. *What the hell am I supposed to say to this?* She didn't respond. There didn't seem to be anything to say. She thought for a while, looking at Sandra, then at the flowers.

"Visiting hours are on Wednesday at Rikers. I'm taking Bernice then and will speak to Bill. There is nothing else we can do but inform him. He may know already. Don't they test prisoners?" She didn't know. Suddenly tired of the any discussion regarding Jack, she asked Sandra if she was going to get in touch with Tom.

"No," Sandra said. "I don't think so. If he doesn't want to make the effort to be in my life, what can I say to him? Would you call him if you were me?"

"Well, do you like him?" Pam asked. "What do you have to lose?"

Sandra smiled to herself. *So like Pam not to answer the question directly.* "Yes, I like him. But I like you, too! I hate it that he is making me think about not having you in my life." Sandra realized that she may be at a crossroads here. Tom hadn't asked her to break ties with Jack's family. He knew it was unreasonable to do so. But it was also unreasonable of him to think that he could pretend to be the baby's father. Someday, the child would have to know the truth. Expecting to wipe out someone's history wasn't realistic. Maybe he was embarrassed of her after all, and it was his way of making her acceptable to his family and the world. Now she wondered if she really did like him. It was slightly easier than she imagined wiping him out of her life. She hadn't gotten attached yet.

"No, I guess I *don't* really like him! He can accept me for who I am. It was decent of him to leave because he knew it was asking too much, if we can believe his letter." *Tom Adams could go to hell.*

"I think you should try to reason with him," Pam said. "He doesn't like either one of us, Marie or me, that's obvious, but it's okay. We probably represent stupidity personified to him. Why not call him?" *Why am I pushing this?* Pam thought. *Do I want her occupied with something else? It would certainly help me if we had to lie about the paternity of the child.*

Sandra listened to the sound of the water bubbling in the fountain. "I don't care if I ever see him again," she said with finality.

Bernice was still sleeping peacefully, and Pam was staring at the sky up over the wall of the garden. The odd trio of women would come together in this way again and again, enjoying the beauty of the mansion in the middle of New York and the luxury of living a charmed life without lifting a finger, thanks to Jack Smith.

45

Carolyn Fitzsimmons worked on Jack's file like a person possessed. It was full of interesting folklore about the area with historical anecdotes. Each section she completed brought more satisfaction than she'd had at work in a very long time. She felt somewhat vindicated; she was older than any of the other women in the office, yet was trusted with an important project the very first day on the job. It had proved to be a Godsend. Life at home with her unhappy husband and aging parents was tolerable now that she was getting some relief at work.

On Monday morning, she arrived at her office before anyone else. A long, narrow table had been set up for her along one wall, and on the surface were ten piles of charts and monographs that related to the individual files. She looked at the organized display with pride. Today she would ask Marie to come in and would make an informal presentation for her. She, in turn, could take the project back to the client, knowing exactly what it contained.

She sat at her desk and opened the main file box. There were a few stray pieces of paper and one eight-by-eleven manila envelope that she had missed earlier. It wasn't sealed, so she didn't think twice about removing the document within. It was composed of several sheets of paper, ranging from yellowed typing paper and ending with newer printer paper. Thumbing through the papers,

338

Carolyn realized it was simply a list of women's names, hundreds of them, the earlier ones with addresses and some with phone numbers, and the last sheet with email addresses. The area codes read like a history of Manhattan phone numbers. She had no idea what the purpose of the list was or if it was related to the file in some way, so she would hand it over to Marie when she came in that day. Marie would know what the significance of the list was. *After all, didn't this file once belong to her late brother-in-law? What was his name? Oh right! His name was Jack.*

Made in the USA
Charleston, SC
03 January 2012